This was the mo
herself. Instinctively,
fired a round into the a... ... ...
slowly toward Mae. The look on his face would have
urged most men to full retreat.

"I said let her go, and I meant it. I don't want to
have to shoot you, mister."

The man let out a bark of laughter. "You think you
can hit me, little lady, before I can take your gun away
from you?"

Mae stood her ground. Her heart was racing and
her insides quivering, but her voice was firm. "You can
try, but I warn you, I will not hesitate."

The man had let go of Emma and now turned fully
to face Mae. "You're the reason I'm here, ain't ya?
You're the one who put some crazy notion in her head,
like she can just up and leave and get away with it.
She's got a home, and I'm takin' her back to it."

As the man reached out to grab Emma again, Mae
fired. The man's arm jerked in reaction to the white-hot
pain. He wheeled sharply and took a step toward Mae,
then stopped. He could see she had gone pale, but her
grip on the pistol was firm, and her arm was rock
steady.

A Heart
Made for Love

by

Linda Tillis

A Heart Made for Love

Cover Art by *Debbie Taylor*

The Wild Rose Press, Inc.
PO Box 708
Adams Basin, NY 14410-0708
Visit us at www.thewildrosepress.com

Publishing History
First Vintage Rose Edition, 2016
Print ISBN 978-1-5092-0797-8
Digital ISBN 978-1-5092-0798-5

Published in the United States of America

Dedication

This book is dedicated to
the South Georgia House of Hope,
where good folks do the real work of helping women—
women who need a place to
recover, reset, and renew their faith.
www.sogahouseofhope@gmail.com

~

And to my loving husband, my Beau,
who had faith in me when no one else did.

Chapter One

The cold rain on Mae's face brought her to the edge of consciousness, but it was the pain running through her battered body that pulled her into a world she didn't want to face.

She could still hear the men's voices, feel their rough hands, and smell their whiskey-drenched breath, even though they'd been gone for what must have been hours. She'd been beating the rag rugs hanging on the rail fence when they came upon her. Papa must have told her a thousand times, "Never go out without the rifle." Now she understood one of the dangers he feared.

Papa...oh, dear Lord, he and the boys would be coming home from the sawmill soon. That realization cut through the pain and brought her to her knees. She swayed there for a while, taking note of each ache as she tried to remember which offense may have caused it. There was at least one loose tooth, and she well remembered the fist that loosened it. She could feel the blood and pain between her legs, but the blessed fist had made the memory of that horror dark and vague.

Mae managed to crawl over to the rail fence and pull herself to her feet. As she leaned there, catching her breath at the fiery pain in her ribs, she saw she was resting on the quilt she and her mama had made together when she was but ten. And so came the tears.

Mae raised her head and saw the Florida sun sinking low in the west. She was startled by how much time had passed as she'd leaned on the fence. She needed to make it to the water bucket, to try and clean some of the blood and dirt from her face and hands, even if she was never able to wash the stain of this event from her soul.

She managed to strip off her dress and do a meager washing before crawling into bed and drifting off in pain. She was pulled from her semi-conscious state by the sound of her Papa's voice yelling her name.

"Mae, girl, where are you?" Papa never shouted, and she could hear the panic in his voice.

Oh, Lord, she'd left her bloody clothes on the porch. "I'm here, Papa, in the bedroom."

Garth Hinton came roaring into the room, wild eyed and pale. When he saw Mae struggling to rise, he dropped to his knees beside the bed. Her two younger brothers stopped at the doorway, showing round eyes and frightened faces.

She rolled away, saying, "Papa send them outside. I don't want them to see me like this."

Garth did as she asked. "Boys, run fetch water and put it on to boil." As they continued to stand frozen in the doorway, he shouted, "Now!" The boys jumped to life at the sound of their father's command and turned to run out of the house.

Garth Hinton was a strong man. He'd survived the Civil War as a young child. He'd lived through carpetbaggers stripping his family's farm. He'd even managed, with the Lord's help, to move on after the death of his beautiful wife, Ruth. But he was damn near broken by the sight of his daughter, lying there covered in bruises and cuts, he weakness apparent in her attempt to sit up.

"I'm so sorry, Papa. I forgot the rifle," was all Mae could manage to sob.

Her father held her hand and tried to soothe her. He was afraid to touch her anywhere else, as he couldn't tell the extent of her injuries. "Mae, honey, listen to me. The rifle is not important now. Just tell me what happened."

"There were men, Papa, and they hurt me," she whispered, not able to make eye contact with her papa, that gentle man who had always been her tower of strength.

"Oh, God," he moaned, as tears filled his eyes.

Garth heard the boys coming back. He stepped to the door and looked at Samuel. Samuel, at fifteen, was six feet tall and as muscular as a grown man. Now his eyes were dark and hard, and his jaw was clenched, as he returned his papa's look. Cyrus, just twelve, was right behind him, with eyes still round and filled with worry.

Cyrus turned to his papa. "What happened to Mae, Papa?"

While Garth was trying to find a suitable explanation, Samuel spoke up. "Mae fell out of that big water oak down the hill. She was trying to see if the bees had made honey yet." Garth blinked. He'd never known Samuel to lie.

"Well, why'd she do that? She's a-scared of high places."

"Never mind that now, son. Just jump back up on my horse and hie yourself to town and get Doc Walters out here as fast as you can. Now, go."

3

"Yes, sir," Cyrus yelled as he took off for the horse.

"Papa, do you know who hurt Mae? Do I need to load the rifles? Just tell me who did this, and I'll find 'em." Samuel's voice vibrated with his anger.

Garth put his arm around the boy's broad shoulders. "Son, you're a good brother. I don't know who did this, but until I have a chance to really talk with Mae, we're going to keep this to ourselves. Right now, the best thing you can do for your sister is to drag that tub in here and fill it with the hot water from the stove. Doc will need it to clean her cuts."

Garth went back to Mae's bedside and pulled up a stool. "Mae, honey, I've sent Cyrus for the doctor. We need to know what injuries you have."

"Oh, Papa," she cried. "I don't want anyone to know."

Garth gently wiped the tears from her face. "Honey, Doc has to see you. You might have injuries that need attention, and Doc's not going to be talkin' about it. While we're waiting, can you tell me any more about what happened?"

Mae took a deep, shuddering breath, closed her eyes, and began to speak so softly that Garth had to lean in to hear her. "I was beating the rugs on the fence. I heard a step, and then there were hands on me. Somebody threw something over my head and I couldn't see. I started kicking and fighting. I know I hit some of them, 'cause they yelled."

She paused so long Garth was afraid she might have fainted. He waited, not wanting to force her.

When she continued, her voice was just above a whisper. "I was thrown to the ground and hands were holding me down. I started kicking and heard one of them screaming and calling me a she-cat. That was when something hit me real hard. I think it was a fist 'cause I don't remember much more till the rain woke me." By the end of this she was sobbing again.

Garth gathered her into his arms and held her while she wept, until there were just little mewling sounds now and then. He laid her back onto the bed, and she rolled to her side to drift off once more.

He'd never missed his wife more than now, nor had he ever felt so inadequate with one of the children before; but then, few men were required to face something so horrible as this, thanks be to the good Lord. What do you say to your baby girl when her whole life has been altered? How do you tell her everything will be all right when you're not sure that it will be? Ruth had always known just what to say or do, whether it was a piece of motherly wisdom or a fix for some ailment; she'd always risen to the occasion. But Ruth was gone, and Garth was treading unknown territory.

Mae had fallen into a restless sleep, just moaning now and then. Garth was wondering what horrors she must be reliving when he heard Doc Walters' buggy squeaking into the yard. He stepped out onto the porch just as Cyrus bounded up the steps. Not wanting the boy to hear any more than necessary, he said, "Son, take my horse to the barn, wipe him down, and give him some oats." Cyrus reluctantly did as he was told.

Doc Walters waited until the boy was out of earshot before asking, "What's going on, Garth? Cyrus was babbling about finding Mae's torn and bloody clothes on the front porch."

Garth hadn't thought beyond getting help for Mae.

Now he just stood, searching for the right words. Doc gave him a moment, and then said, "Well, how hard can it be, man? Out with it."

Garth looked at Doc and, as tears ran down his cheeks, answered. "I think she's been raped."

Martin Walters had been a medical assistant, as a half grown kid, during the last two years of the war. He'd seen some pretty gruesome things, but he paled as Garth's words sank in. "Oh, hell, where is she?" he barked. Garth raised an arm, indicating inside.

"Do you know who did this? Did she give you a name?"

Garth's jaw clenched, and he swiped a shaking hand across his face. "There was more than one."

Doc muttered a curse, picked up his bag, and stepped inside the neat, wood-frame home.

He noted, and was grateful for, the pot of water simmering on the wood stove. When he pushed open the door, his heart broke at the sight of Mae, curled in a ball in the middle of the bed. He was immediately struck by the bruising on the slender arm that had worked its way from under the quilt. When he saw the swelling and purple blotches on her pale, heart-shaped face, it hit him like a fist in the gut.

Doc moved to the bedside but did not touch her. "Mae," he called. She winced and made a soft moaning sound. "Mae, honey, it's Doc. Can you open your eyes for me?"

Those blue-veined lids fluttered, then slowly opened. As recognition and remembrance came, her dark eyes began to fill with tears, and she whimpered as she drew her arm back under the quilt, as if hiding under the covers could make the whole thing not have happened.

Doc had witnessed the strength in this girl when her mother died. He'd watched her grow into a strong young woman who was given to curiosity and a joy for life. How she handled the next few hours would determine whether she survived as a whole person or just a piece of her former self.

"Mae, listen to me now. Your pa told me some men had hurt you. I need you to tell me all you can remember, and Mae, I'm not your pa. You can tell me anything and not be embarrassed. I need to know what happened so that I know how to treat your injuries. But before you start, I want you to pretend you're telling me a story about someone else. I want you to look at the event in your mind, not in your heart. Tell me about this thing that happened today."

Mae pulled herself up a little, took a deep, shuddering breath, and closed her eyes. This was the moment she'd dreaded since she had wakened. Mama had shared some womanly things with her before going to be with the Lord, but Mae wished there was a woman to guide her through this now.

She knew enough to understand that this event was not what the Lord intended when a man "took" a woman. Her time of the month was not for another three weeks, and she should not be bleeding the way she was. The pain and bleeding were brought on by what the men had done to her. She was grateful to have very little memory of those actions.

Mae looked over Doc's shoulder and started to speak. "The girl was airing quilts and beatin' rugs on the fence. She was supposed to have the rifle with her, but she'd forgotten it. But it wouldn't have mattered 'cause she never heard them until they were on her. Someone threw something over her head; it might have been a shirt. Then they grabbed her arms and dragged her down to the ground. She fought. She fought as hard as she could."

Mae started to sweat and didn't even realize she was wringing her hands. Her eyes were open wide as if she was seeing all that she described. "And she got one of them in the face, 'cause he started screaming that she had blinded him. Someone was holding her shoulders to the ground. She couldn't use her arms anymore, but she kept fighting. She kicked out and must have got a good shot at one of them, 'cause she heard a scream. Then something hit her in the face. It must have been a fist. After that the girl didn't hear or feel anything for a long time."

Doc thanked the merciful Lord that she must have lost consciousness at that point, so perhaps she didn't know that probably she was repeatedly abused.

"Think, Mae. Did the girl recognize any of the voices? Can she remember anything else? Just think a minute."

Mae closed her eyes. After a minute or so, she started to tremble; it began deep inside her. Hands were holding her down. A button pressed into her face. Something was dancing around the edges of her memory. Something that was new to her and she could not recognize…Wait! It was a smell, no, a fragrance. It was sort of like the lemongrass Mama used to grow, only different. Her heart was racing. Even as Doc reached out to her, she began to scream.

"Mae, open your eyes! Mae, look at me, honey. You're okay. The men are gone, Mae. Do you hear me?"

Mae was pale, and her eyes were almost glazed over when she opened them. When she began panting, Doc knew what was coming. He grabbed the bucket beside the bed just as Mae started heaving. Doc held her sweat-matted hair aside while she emptied her stomach into the bucket. Afterwards he bathed her face with the damp cloth Samuel had placed by the bucket. She lay back on the bed with her eyes closed, and in time her tremors eased off.

"Did you remember something, Mae? Can you tell me any more?"

She said, "It was a shirt. A shirt they put over her head. She...I could feel the buttons cuttin' into my face, and the shirt smelled. Not like, you know, not dirty or sweaty, but clean like flowers. No, not like Mama's roses, but like the lemongrass in the garden."

Her eyes flew open, round and fixed on Doc. "There was one man," she started. "He was different from the rest. I heard them all, and the others all sounded just like anyone from town. But this man sounded different. His voice was smooth and deep, and he spoke like you do sometimes. Like a schoolteacher."

"What did he say, honey, that sounded like a teacher?"

She lay there gazing across the room, wanting to remember but afraid to remember too much, lest she remember everything. "He said, 'Perhaps this is not such a good idea after all.' "

Mae looked into Doc's eyes and whispered, "Is the girl going to be all right?"

Doc took Mae's hand, gently stroking it as he spoke. "You tell me, Mae. Is the girl going to be all right? Does she realize she did not do anything wrong? Does she know the Lord loves her, weeps for her pain, and will always be there for her?" He paused, searching her eyes for any signs of guilt or remorse. "Mae, does the girl understand not all men are good? That some are driven by their own weaknesses and therefore try to control anyone they can? Does she know life is not always fair; sometimes the innocent have to pay for the sins of others?"

Doc swept a lock of dark hair away from Mae's face. "Mae, the girl will be all right if she can accept that while she will never be the same, she can be stronger, and let this event show her how to gauge other men in the future. She can accept that life is not always perfect, but it can be rewarding for those who learn to move past the times that are painful, and not let them taint their outlook. The girl will be okay, Mae, because she has folks who love her, because she has so much to bring to this life she is making, and because the future holds great things for her. She wants those things, doesn't she, Mae?"

Mae withdrew her hand from Doc's. She pulled the quilt more tightly around her shoulders and looked at him for a while. "I'm alive. I hurt, but I don't think anything is broken. The bleeding seems to have stopped." She reddened somewhat at this confession. "I do wish Mama was here, but Papa means well and will do what he can to help me."

The tremor had left her voice when she answered, "Yes, sir, I think the girl will be okay. In time."

Chapter Two

Garth was sitting on the porch with Samuel when Doc came outside. Cyrus, tired of waiting, had gone to the creek to catch crawfish. Papa looked older and very tired, and to see him this way made Samuel's insides seethe; it was like a murder waiting to happen. Doc set his bag down and dropped onto Mama's favorite bench.

"Well," he sighed, "she is going to be all right. I gave her a sedative to help her sleep through the night. I left a small jar of powder on the chest of drawers. If she has pain tomorrow, you can give her a half-teaspoon in a glass of water twice a day. It will be a while until she heals. We'll have to wait until next month to know if there will be any lasting effects."

Samuel heard his papa's suddenly indrawn breath and realized the real consequences of this assault. The two men fell quiet, and Samuel guessed they thought he was too young to understand what effect this could all have on Mae's life.

Samuel was known to have a temper. His mother had worked hard at helping him learn to control his impulsive side, but she had been gone almost five years now. Try as he might, sometimes his quick temper got the better of him. If Mae could have put names to these men, Samuel would be stalking them right now. Heck, he was grown enough to understand what had happened here today, but just the bruises on Mae alone were enough to tell him somebody needed a whippin', or worse.

He would be tall one day. He was already two inches taller than Mae. Being a tad younger didn't mean he couldn't hold a deep sense of responsibility to his family. He worked hard at the mill with Papa, and at fifteen years he was already as strong as most of the men. He no longer thought of himself as a boy. The good Lord knew his temper was that of a grown man. Mama had schooled all her children in responsibility, dedication to family, and love of the Lord. Sometimes Samuel's mind would stray during the Bible reading, but he would always remember her saying that family was everything; you needed to support each other in all things. Losing Mama at an early age had only strengthened her lessons for Samuel.

At times, when no one was around, he would sit by the family Bible, and if he listened real hard, he could almost hear her sweet voice reading her favorite passages. Mama would understand how he felt right now, how the sound of Mae's cries seared his heart. She would know how much he wanted to make someone pay for Mae's bruises. Mama would have helped Samuel reckon with his anger, would have calmed him down, but Mama was gone.

****

Garth sliced some ham from the smokehouse and paired it with beans to feed the boys. The boys cleaned the kitchen and brought out the books for the evening lessons. Garth would have let the lessons pass, but none of them were ready for sleep yet. After an hour of having to reread pages and refigure calculations, Garth gave it up.

"All right, boys, that's enough for tonight. Let's try to get some sleep," he said as he banked the coals in the cast iron stove. Ruth had insisted that the children be as well educated as possible. She'd saved all her schoolbooks and borrowed from Doc Walters' collection to keep her up to date. He placed tonight's efforts back in the chest reserved for schoolwork and stepped outside for some fresh air.

Garth sat on the porch for a while, talking to his Ruth in his mind, before finally going inside to stretch out on the bed. He was just beginning to drift away when a bloodcurdling scream startled him awake. Mae! It was Mae! He grabbed the rifle on his way to her room, where he found her sitting upright, her hands clasping her throat. Her eyes were like saucers, and she kept screaming, "It's gone! It's gone!"

He was afraid to touch her, as she was all but covered in blue or purple bruises, but he gently tried to pry her hands away from her poor throat. "Mae, it's Papa. Honey, look at me. Mae, stop screaming, girl. Papa's here, and you're okay. Baby, you're scaring Cyrus."

True enough, both boys were standing at the foot of her bed, eyes wide.

As her father's voice finally got through to her, she focused her eyes on his face and began to weep, her chest heaving. Garth sat on her bedside and folded her gently into his arms as he tried to think of something soothing to say.

"Mae, honey, what's gone? Whatever it is, me and the boys will find it for you."

She raised swollen eyes to his face. "Mama's locket! It's gone. I never took it off, Papa. From the day you gave it to me, I've never taken it off, and it's gone. They must have it."

Garth and Samuel exchanged a look of horror. That locket had meant so much to Mae. Garth had always thought of it as the cord that tied them all to their memories of Ruth.

Cyrus, on the other hand, was just curious. "Who, Mae? Who has the locket?"

Samuel punched him in the arm, and Cyrus squealed, "What'd you do that for?"

Mae looked at the boys. "Oh, boys, you're in your nightshirts! I'm so sorry to cause a ruckus in the middle of the night." She slid back down in her bed, pulled the covers over her head, and continued to cry.

Garth stood. "Back to bed, boys. We gotta be up early in the morning."

Samuel took Cyrus by the shoulder and turned him toward the door

Garth sat back down. He slowly pulled the covers down from Mae's face. "Honey, that locket meant almost as much to me as it did to you. I've spent the last few hours grateful to the good Lord that I still have you. I can learn to live without the sight of that locket, but I'm not sure I could have gone on if someone had taken you from me. You are the dearest reminder I have of your mother." His voice broke, and he paused before continuing. "You have her looks and her loving ways, and her memory is still alive for the boys through you." Garth softly wiped her tear-streaked face. "Honey, I promise you, we'll get through this, just like we've handled every trial that's come our way. We will be strong in our faith, we will work and live, and in a while we will smile and laugh again." The sedative was working again and Mae was dozing off, even as he tucked the covers in under her chin.

Garth walked to the barn, plunked down on a bale of hay, and dropped his head into his hands. Unable to hold in his sorrow any longer, he cried, a deep feeling of helplessness washing over him.

****

The locket was gone. Garth could still see the joy on Ruth's face when she first held that locket in her slender fingers. It was not the conventional gold heart-shaped thing most women would call a locket. No, it was truly an original work of art.

Garth had gone on a business trip to Virginia to bring back a small steam engine for the sawmill. When he arrived at the docks in Richmond, he went straight to the offices of Harris and Bolton, the shipping company that had brought his engine down from New York.

When Fred Harris saw Garth, he grinned, with a hint of mischief. Garth wondered why he had such a "this is going to be fun" look on his face, but being a patient man he figured he'd find out soon enough.

"Mr. Hinton, it's good to see you," Fred welcomed. "I have your new engine right here in the back storage room. Follow me."

At the rear of the warehouse, a wooden crate sat against the wall. Next to the crate was a small, wizened Chinaman. His legs were crossed, and he appeared to be asleep. When they stopped, the little man raised his head and looked up at Garth.

"You new boss-man?" he asked softly. Confused, Garth looked at Fred Harris, who was grinning like an idiot.

Fred explained, "He says his name is Hansu. He

came with the crate. Came all the way from New York. Said he was the only one who could make the engine sing." Fred grinned again.

Garth looked down at the little man. He looked to be somewhere between seventy and long dead. Hansu smiled at Garth. "I goin' work hard for you. You not have problem with engine. It always sing for me."

"Do you have a family, sir?"

The old man smiled and said softly, "I have family now with you."

Garth looked at Fred, who shrugged his shoulders. "We tried to run him off three times, but he just kept coming back. We couldn't figure out how he kept getting into the warehouse, but every morning we would find him asleep on the floor beside the crate. Said he was waiting for his new master. We reckoned that must be you."

Garth gave up trying to reason with Hansu. He finally told him to climb up on the wagon so they could start the trip back to Trenton, Florida. During the long trip, Garth watched Hansu meticulously carve a piece of ivory. It appeared to be a small box with intricate designs.

Two days before they got home, Hansu said to Garth, "Your wife will be happy with this gift, yes?"

Garth, taken aback, answered, "Well, yes, I guess so."

Hansu smiled. "She is curious woman, yes?"

"Oh, yes, but how did you know?"

Hansu just smiled. He held up the little box, used a finger to stroke a petal on one flower, and the little box opened to show a hidden recess.

Garth laughed out loud. "Oh, yes," he proclaimed,

"she will love the box!"

Ruth had indeed loved the box. She'd worn it hanging from a rawhide cord. In the box, she'd placed a small curl from the head of each of her children. When Ruth died, Garth had removed the treasured box from around her neck.

On Mae's thirteenth birthday, Hansu had given Garth a yard of beautifully painted silk to present to Mae. Garth had wrapped the little box in the silk and given it to her. Like Ruth, Mae would have worn it until her death, but now it was gone.

Chapter Three

Mae stood at the edge of the porch, watching the fox squirrels jump from tree to tree. The morning air was still cool and filled with the sound of singing birds. It was springtime again. She was glad. Mama's roses would be blooming soon. She always felt closer to Mama when she could fill the house with their fragrance.

She looked across the yard and was moved by the sight of Samuel cutting firewood. She was going to have to speak to Papa. It was time to free the boys from watching over her. She'd been physically healed almost a year now. She seldom woke with cold sweats at night. Her woman parts had healed, with her menses settling in to a regular pattern again. Thankfully this had occurred within a couple of months of "the event," as she called it in her mind. Still, Papa had insisted one of the boys always be near.

At first she'd been glad to have one of them hover around. She hadn't been able to lift more than a ten-pound bag of flour for a couple of weeks. Thanks to Papa and the good Lord, there was now a pitcher pump in the kitchen. There was no reason now for the boys to miss work at the mill. Papa needed them more than she did. Besides, she had the pistol Doc had brought her. She had gotten so good with it the boys were calling her Sergeant Mae. She'd sewn a hidden pocket in each of her skirts and dresses, and Doc's little beauty had become her constant companion.

Yes, it was time to talk to Papa. She'd turned eighteen a few weeks ago; she had now pulled all the schooling she could give herself from Mama's books. It was time for her to find a school she could attend. Mae had given much thought to her future, over the last year, and finally determined what she wanted to do with the life the Lord had allowed her to keep. How to make it happen was another story, but a good education was the first step.

****

Garth could feel his stomach drop as he listened to Mae. He had always known this day would come, but he was not ready for it. Not yet. He sat on the porch, looking at his remarkable daughter in wonder.

"Now, Papa, I won't be that far away. Tallahassee is where I need to be if I'm goin' to get the education I need to build a home for young women. You know as well as I do it was only by the grace of God I didn't find myself in a much worse condition than just bruised and a little scared. All right," she said as her Papa raised his eyebrows, "a whole lot of scared, but you know I'm right."

Garth tried again. "Mae, it's not just the going so far away. It's the whole idea of you someday dealing with the kind of women who might find themselves in such a position."

She gazed at him in amazement. "Papa, I do go to town once in a while, and I do have eyes. I may not spend a lot of time with other people, but I know enough to be sure there are a lot of women who had little or nothing to do with how they arrived in the place in life they find themselves. Women, Papa, who were not fortunate enough to have families who loved them, like me, to give the help they needed. Didn't Jesus forgive Mary Magdalene?"

"All right, young lady, there's no call to beat me with your Mama's Bible," he answered with a weak smile. "So tell me all the plans you and Doc Walters have cooked up behind my back."

Mae had the grace to blush. "It wasn't so much behind your back, Papa, as it was trying to spare you all the little details. I wrote up all the negatives, like who would care for you and the boys. You know, like keep you fed, and the house reasonably clean, and your clothes washed and cared for. Well, Irene Peters is a very nice lady, Papa. She was never able to have children, and Mr. Peters passed on from a heart attack last year. Doc says she is alone, with no family, and could use a little financial help. She would be happy to ride over in the mornings, take care of the house cleaning and laundry, and do lunch and supper for you and the boys. She's a much better cook than me. I've tasted her pies at church suppers, and I can tell you Samuel will love her straight away.

"She was tickled to death when I told her about the hand pump you put in the washhouse for Mama. The idea of being able to pump water straight into the washtub or bathtub seemed like a dream come true to her. She said she'd heard you spoiled Mama something fierce, what with always bringing in the newfangled conveniences from up north. But she did say she would be doing all your clothing repairs by hand." Mae laughed. "The ladies from church told her you bought Mama one of those foot-pedaled sewing machines, too, but she was very clear she would be afraid of it."

Garth's eyes clouded a little at that remark. Ruth had never asked for a thing. She had always been content with whatever she had to hand. The sawmill had been bringing in good money by the second year, and Garth had always wanted Ruth to have the best he could give her. Oh, she'd always insisted the Lord's share came right off the top of any profits. Then came the savings to set aside for those times when things might slow down at the mill. If there was a little left over, then she might allow Garth to spoil her, like when he built the washhouse and installed the hand pump. Folks talked about places in New York and Philadelphia that had indoor toilet facilities, but Ruth was adamant about having no odors in her house. She said outdoor privies had to be cleaner than indoor ones. She had loved the sewing machine, though she had still taught Mae to quilt by hand. Garth missed being able to spoil Ruth. Seeing her fascination with new things had always warmed his heart.

"Mae, I'm sure Mrs. Peters is a wonderful, competent woman, but the boys and I are not exactly helpless. That doesn't tell me what you and Doc have planned for you. Just what makes you think I would agree to you going off to Tallahassee without being darn sure you'd be well taken care of, not to mention safe?" Garth's fears were there in his voice.

Mae was almost moved to tears at the sound of it. Her papa had been through so much, from losing a daughter and his beloved wife to having his remaining daughter abused so ruthlessly by strangers. It was a miracle he would allow any of his children out of his sight.

"All right, Papa. I have spent just as much effort on making sure I'm well cared for as I did for you and the boys," Mae answered. "I knew good and well you would not agree to this if there was the slightest doubt about my wellbeing, but I think you'll have to concede all will be fine. Doc Walters' sister, Mrs. Finch, is a very kind woman to even consider taking me on as a project. Her husband is a lawyer in Tallahassee. They had three children, but they lost both their daughters to yellow fever in 1880. Their son, the youngest, was spared. He was so affected by his sisters' deaths that he was determined to become a doctor. He's in England now, learning from a man Doc Walters worked with years ago. That leaves Mrs. Finch with an almost empty house. Doc has spoken with her about my coming to stay, and she is very excited. She assured Doc that if the local schools didn't provide me with what she considered a good education, she would personally set out to find me the best tutors." Mae paused, as she could see the wheels turning in Papa's head.

When she spoke again, it was to tackle the question of money. "Now, Papa, I'm not expecting you to pay for all this yourself. I will only agree to all this if I can find a job. I have a very legible hand and could do well as some sort of companion for a suitable lady. I can also work the fancy sewing machine you gave Mama, and I learned to make good use of those new paper patterns in the ladies' journals. So I will be providing a good portion of the monies I will need."

Garth could feel a large lump growing in his throat and a burning in his eyes. He looked at Mae in wonder again. *When did this happen? When did my little dark-haired elf become a self-assured young woman who is now ready to step away from her family?*

Garth was proud that she wanted to become educated and polished, and that she wanted to help women who were not assured, or educated, or emotionally prepared for the circumstances life may have dropped them into. She wanted to be a tower of strength for others. Much like her mother, she never wanted anything for herself. *Ruth, if you could see this child now you would be so proud. You'd say, 'Garth, if she's ready, let her fly!' That's the problem, Ruth, I'm not sure I'm ready for her to fly. She has suffered so much. Losing you. Having to grow up so quickly without you to lean on. As if that wasn't bad enough, to be violently attacked by strangers. Sometimes I think your soul has come back and taken up residence in her body, Ruth. She has become a woman, practically overnight, and there's nothing I can do to change that.*

Garth became aware that Mae was speaking to him. "Yes, honey, I'm all right. You just have to slow down a little and let this old man catch up to you. You're going ninety to nothing, and I'm still stuck back there on the idea that my little girl is growing up and there's nothing I can do to stop it!"

Chapter Four

Today was going to be a beautiful but hot June day. The cool of the night was long gone, and the sun had been up for only a few hours. By noontime they would all feel drained by the humidity. However, Mae did not intend to let the discomfort of the onset of summer in Florida steal her joy in this day. She was moving. She was moving forward to what she felt in her heart was part of the Lord's plan for her. He would not have given her such a depth of curiosity if He had not intended for her to go to school where she could fill her need for knowledge of all things. Well, maybe not all things, and for certain not all at once. She smiled at her own foolishness. She had the rest of her life to travel on this journey of learning.

What she needed to learn right now was how to be patient, and try not to swallow up the whole of knowledge in one big bite. She almost laughed aloud. She could remember when Mama would tell her, "Slow down, baby girl; one small bite at a time is the way to enjoy pie. If you gobble it all up in a rush, you'll miss how good it tastes, and you won't be happy with the bellyache it gives you." Well, Mae would slow down, take all this newness in, one bite at a time, and savor each day—starting with this one.

Mae stepped into the dining room where Mrs. Peters had set their lunch basket on the table. The very efficient little lady had already cleared the table from breakfast and was placing the last of the cookies in the basket. Mae had been right in her choice for a housekeeper for Papa and the boys. Even Papa admitted that Mrs. Peters was a cheerful soul and an above-average cook. Of course, Samuel had put on at least ten pounds in the two weeks she had been with them. That was a good thing. At sixteen, the boy was already over six feet. It had happened so suddenly that he looked like a scarecrow, all arms and long legs.

She would miss Papa and both the boys, but Samuel was dear to her heart. He had been so worried about her after the event. He never said much, but he was always near, always watching for a break in Mae's armor, or a sign that she was frightened or in pain. She had awakened in the night, many times, to find Samuel asleep on the floor just inside her bedroom door. When she would rise in the morning, her faithful guardian would be gone. Now she was leaving him.

He had come to her one evening, several weeks ago, and just stood, looking at her.

"All right, Samuel," she'd said. "Out with it."

Samuel had given her that slow almost-smile of his. "Are you sure about this? You're not just trying to run from somethin' here, are you? I mean, are you all better now? You're ready to be on your own?"

As her eyes had filled with loving tears, she put her arms around his neck to hold him close. Suddenly she realized just how much he had grown. "Good heavens!" Mae exclaimed. "Just when did you gain three inches on me?" She held him close, smelled the scent of pine, and felt a deep sense of love and loss. Neither of them were children anymore. The event had forced both of them to an awakening of the world around them, forced them to acknowledge that life was not a pre-written book, that unforeseen, often painful happenings could alter perceptions, needs, and beliefs.

She had set a goal for herself and was moving toward it.

Samuel had also chosen a path. He had adopted Hansu as a mentor. The old gentleman had been with them since Mae was a baby. Papa used to tell them the story of how Hansu entered their lives with the "singing" steam engine for the sawmill. Hansu had tutored Samuel in woodworking and a type of fighting, something called martial arts, as soon as Samuel learned to slip away from Mama. Mae had been amazed one day when she came upon them behind the washhouse. She had watched the eight-year-old Samuel close his eyes, take a slow, deep breath, then give a scream and kick a bare foot toward a board that Hansu was holding. She was not sure who was more surprised when the board broke, she or Samuel. Samuel had always been an intense child. Mama tried to teach him to talk things out. It was her way of helping Samuel cope with a short fuse and bad temper. With Mama gone, Samuel drew further into himself.

From the start Hansu had been quick to see the potential in him. The woodworking gave Samuel a creative outlet. He was producing some beautiful pieces of furniture, while his physical training gave him a means of burning up any anger or frustrations he held inside. The combination of both was producing a young man with a quiet but self-confident manner, and a loving brother who recognized her need to move on.

Garth came in from the barn and stopped short

when he caught sight of Mae. There she stood, tall for a woman, at least five foot ten inches. Her long, dark-brown tresses had been twisted up into one of those newfangled styles. He could blame Doc Walters for that. Doc was the one always bringing her those darn ladies' magazines with the new patterns and pictures of women in New York or wherever those ideas came from. She was standing there now in a dress she'd made using her Mama's sewing machine. It was a soft green thing with tucks that accentuated her shapeliness and ruffles around the bottom that sashayed when she moved. She was holding a large white hat with green flowers and a large green bow. She looked sweet and innocent, and it scared the daylights out of him.

He had to remind himself that she was, through no fault of her own, not as innocent of the world as he would have wished. It pained him to know she had gained this composure she presented to the world through pain, humiliation, and months of recovery. He knew she had every right to stand there before the world and declare herself ready. She was ready to learn, to grow, and to conquer any who would try to prevent her from doing so. He was so damn proud of her he could hardly swallow past the knot in his throat. *Ah, Ruth, I hope you can see this beautiful creature you gave birth to.*

Mae turned to her Papa and saw the mistiness in his eyes. She smiled and took a moment to soak up the sight of him. This man who had loved her mother so dearly that he still talked to her on occasion, who had raised his children with a firm hand backed by relentless love. This man who did not want to but would let her go, because it was time. She tried to lighten the moment. "So how do I look, Papa?" she asked.

"Like a piece of key lime pie, girl," he replied.

Mae laughed with delight. "Well, I'll probably be melted by the time we get on the train. My bags are on the wagon, and Mama's sewing machine is safe in the crate Samuel built for it, so…" She trailed off, looking around her. Her gaze made a pass around the house, resting a moment on Mama's Bible in the corner. She gave a deep sigh and returned her gaze to her Papa. "It's time." Mae turned and headed for the door.

Mae, Papa, and Samuel were taking a wagon to Lake City, where they would get on the train to Tallahassee. Papa and Samuel both had business in Tallahassee. Papa wanted to talk to some builders about a project. Samuel had an appointment to meet with a friend of Doc's who owned a dry goods store and was interested in the furniture Samuel had been making.

Cyrus would be staying at home with Hansu and Mrs. Peters. The youngest of Ruth's children had been gifted with her affinity for animals. Now fourteen, he had decided years ago he would be a veterinarian. He was constantly trying to pump Doc Walters for healing ideas for his menagerie of animals.

He had been six years old when his mama died. He'd been raising goats and cows and chickens ever since. Ruth had always felt it was better to raise your own food. That way you knew what you were eating.

From the time Cyrus could walk, he'd toddled after Ruth, gathering eggs, throwing corn into the hog pen, and running from the goats. Ruth had stressed the point that the animals were not our friends or companions but food given to us by the good Lord. If you wanted a pet, it would have to be a dog or cat, or maybe a bird, but not something you would have to help slaughter. Ruth's wisdom had saved the family a lot of grief over the years.

Cyrus was now standing, straight and solemn, by the wagon. Hansu was standing behind him, as if to support him if need be. Mae walked to her little brother and looked him up and down. He was the spitting image of Papa, with that black hair and chiseled jaw. He'd gotten those blue eyes from his grandpa and his sweet smile from his mama.

"Cyrus, how sweet of you to stay clean long enough to hug me goodbye," she whispered in his ear as she enveloped him in a hug. Golly Moses, he was growing; he was up to her shoulders now, and he was four years her junior.

She looked to Hansu and said, "Now, you take care of our boy, Hansu. I wouldn't leave him with just anyone, you know." Hansu gave a wide smile, deepening the wrinkles across his leathered face.

"You no worry, Missy. Young master be fine with Hansu." The old man had been standing in the background for years, taking care of each of them in his own way. He had been right about the steam engine singing for him—and it was still singing

Mae took her Papa's hand, climbed up into the wagon, and adjusted her beautiful hat on her curls. She had no way of knowing this journey would start a chain of events that would turn all their lives upside down.

Chapter Five

Mae was so excited she was sure she would not sleep a wink. It had been six months since she'd seen her family, and tomorrow they were coming for a week-long Christmas visit. The Finches had graciously invited them to stay for the holidays.

Mae recalled the first day they had met Mrs. Finch. They had taken the wagon to Lake City, and then climbed aboard the Pensacola & Georgia Railroad to make the last leg of the trip to Tallahassee. It was near dusk when the hired buggy from the station pulled up in front of a sprawling, two-story Victorian home.

Mae was struck dumb by the size of the house. Not so Samuel.

"Good golly Moses!" he exclaimed. "Are you sure only two people live here? There're enough rooms here for half of Trenton!"

"That's enough, Samuel. You don't want anyone to think we're uncivilized. You'll embarrass your sister, and remember, she's the one who'll be living here," Garth said in a firm voice, just as a footman opened the gate.

The tall footman was dressed all in black and had a deep, gruff voice. "Young sir, I'll take your bags up to your rooms. You may take the buggy down the side alley to the back, and we'll unload the trunks, and that crate there," he said with a sideways look at the crated sewing machine.

Papa helped Mae down from the buggy, and she stood looking up at the house that held such dreams for her future. She could see the lace curtains hanging in the lower windows. The lamps shone through like veiled eyes, beckoning her. A pair of matching rocking chairs sat to each side of a dainty little table on the front porch. It looked like the perfect place to sip lemonade and watch the world go by. As they were ushered up the stairs, Mae noticed the hand-stitched pillows on each chair and was given over to a moment of sadness.

Her mama would have loved those pillows and the chairs, and oh, just the whole peacefulness of this place would have pleased Mama so much. Mae swallowed the lump in her throat as the front door opened and a woman stepped out. She was of average height, around sixty years old, and might have gone unnoticed on the street—that is, if she had worn a bonnet.

She had the purest white hair Mae had ever seen. It looked soft and thick, styled high on her head. Mae was sure she remembered seeing the same fashion in the last batch of magazines Doc brought her.

"Oh, you're here! I'm so excited to meet you, dear. My brother speaks very highly of you, and of your family. It will be wonderful having a young lady in this house for a while, someone I can talk with about sewing, fashions, and socials—all the things my poor husband has had to listen to for a long time." As Mrs. Finch paused to catch her breath, Papa stepped forward and took her hand.

"Ma'am, it is a pleasure to meet you. I can't tell you how much we all appreciate you, and Mr. Finch, for allowing Mae this opportunity to spread her wings a little."

Louise Finch seemed taken aback at Papa's gallantry. Mae smiled to herself. Mama had always insisted on good manners in her home. It was obvious Mrs. Finch had expected a man who owned and operated a sawmill to be less than genteel. Mae was never more proud of her papa than at this moment. It was the first time she had looked at him as a man and not just her father. He was handsome, personable, and still a young man.

Before Mae could continue that thread of thought, Mrs. Finch swept them into the parlor and offered them cool drinks. A young maid came to the door and ushered Samuel inside. Mae was pleased when he turned to the young lady and smiled.

"Thank you, ma'am. I would have lost my way without you." He then turned to Mrs. Finch and said, "It's a pleasure to meet you. Any sister of Doc Walters must be a remarkable lady."

Mrs. Finch burst out laughing and exclaimed, "Young man, just the fact that I lived through being Martin Walters' sister is remarkable!"

Mr. Finch was not home yet. He was meeting a client for dinner. After a light supper, the rest of the evening was something of a blur to Mae. For the past ten hours, she'd been soaking up new sights and sounds. She was starting to feel a little overwhelmed by the time Mrs. Finch took them all up to their rooms.

Color was the first thing Mae became aware of when she entered her room. There were soft pink walls, cool white furniture, and a beautiful rose print bedspread. Mae heard a light tap on the door, a pause, and then a smiling woman wearing a crisp apron entered. "Miss, is there anything I can do to help you get ready for bed? Would you like a bath before retiring?"

Mae was unprepared for this kind of luxury. "Oh, thank you, ma'am, but I couldn't ask someone to carry water this late in the evening."

The woman looked at the floor and tried to contain her smile. "It's no trouble, miss. We have a water closet and bathing room on this end of the house. The water is piped in from the cistern out back."

"Oh," Mae whispered, "I see."

Mae blushed now, remembering how naive she had been just six months ago.

It had taken time for her to adjust to living in the city. The few days Papa and Samuel were there with her had flown by, and then she was alone.

Oh, never alone. Mrs. Finch had allowed her to rest for a day or so and settle into the household, and then began a whirlwind of activity.

She and Mrs. Finch took a carriage to the shopping area in town. Mae was wearing one of the three "town" dresses she'd sewn herself. It was of a pale blue lawn, with little hand-embroidered violets strewn over the close-fitting bodice. Mae had altered the original pattern, as she was not fond of its "pigeon chest" look. She kept the neckline modest and used only her meticulous embroidery as trim. The skirt was full, with a slight bustle. The underskirt was a darker blue that showed about two inches below the sheer lawn overskirt. Altogether, it was feminine and age-appropriate for a young woman. She had fashioned a small white hat out of a piece of satin that Hansu had given her.

Mae never asked the little man where he got the little bits of lace and trims he would present to her. Yet it always seemed that, as soon as she decided it would be nice to have something, Hansu would show up with something even better suited.

The carriage stopped in front of a building standing alone. "Mae, the lady who owns and operates this shop is a widow. Her husband was coming home from a business trip when he was shot, robbed, and left for dead only two years ago. She had to start a business to support herself and her young son. She has a wonderful eye for what best suits each woman. Our church ladies supported her for a short while, until she was able to stand on her own. It didn't take long for the word to get out that if you wanted the most stylish, newest fashions, you had to come to Taylor's."

Mae was assailed by color as they stepped inside. There were bolts of vibrantly hued fabric arrayed on several tables on one side of the room. It was like the Lord had splashed a rainbow across one whole side. The other side of the room held a settee and three brocade side chairs, each separated from the next by a small table covered in beautiful silk. On the tables were platters of cookies, steaming teapots, and pitchers of lemonade.

The woman who walked toward them was stunning. Her red hair was the color of aged copper, and not a strand was out of place. When she smiled at them, Mae felt a warm glow. The woman's smile radiated her kindness, which pulled at Mae's heart.

"Hello, Mrs. Finch, how are you today?" Eleanor Taylor enquired as she approached her visitors.

"I'm wonderful, dear," Mrs. Finch replied. "I

would like for you to meet Miss Mae Hinton. She has been kind enough to agree to stay with Mr. Finch and me while she studies at the university."

"How lovely for you and Mr. Finch. It is a pleasure to meet you, Miss Hinton. And if it wouldn't be too forward, might I ask where you purchased that fine dress?"

Mae blushed and answered, "Please, ma'am, just call me Mae. I made this dress myself."

Eleanor raised one eyebrow, cocked her head to the side, and smiled. "Are you about to give me some competition, young lady?"

Mae was shocked. "Oh, no, ma'am," she stammered. "I've never sewn for anyone except myself and my family. I wouldn't begin to know what to do with all this wondrous material you have here."

"It's all right, dear, I was just teasing you. However, don't sell yourself short. That is a very stylish dress, and from the looks of it, a very well made one. Come sit down and you can tell me how you did that."

They spent a couple of hours over cookies and tea. This was the height of joy for Mae. She'd had no female companionship for much too long. And to sit and listen to these two wise and beautiful women converse about things like church socials and education and even politics was pure joy to Mae.

Occasionally a well-dressed lady or a lady's maid would pop in to see what new fabrics had arrived or to pick up a finished order. Mae was in heaven. At last she worked up her nerve for the task at hand.

"Mrs. Taylor, I will be needing a job while I am at school. I cannot expect my papa to keep me in spending money while I am here. If there is ever a time that you may need some help with anything here in the shop, I would be humbled to work for you."

Eleanor's face softened as she looked at Mae. "Are you saying you would be willing to come here for a few hours a week and help with the shop?"

"Oh, yes, ma'am. As long as it does not interfere with my studies, I would be thrilled," Mae exclaimed.

Eleanor and Mrs. Finch laughed in unison. "Mae, honey, we have been having a little joke on you," Mrs. Finch said, as she caught her breath. "When Martin wrote me about you, he said you might need a tutor for some classes, as you had not had any formal schooling. He also told me you did all the sewing for your family. I was delighted beyond belief. Eleanor was a schoolteacher before she married. She was the first person who came to mind when I considered finding you a tutor. She can prepare you for university tests while you work for her. She had spoken of needing someone part time, and *voilà*, there you were!"

Mae looked to Eleanor. The soft smile on her face was all the agreement Mae needed. Hallelujah! She had a beautiful tutor and a job she was going to love. She would remember all this in her prayers tonight, because surely the Lord had blessed her.

The remembrance of that meeting brought a smile to Mae's face as she drifted off to sleep. Papa would be here tomorrow, and Mae couldn't wait for him to meet Eleanor.

Chapter Six

Garth glanced across the seat of his new truck. Samuel was looking through a catalogue of furniture Doc had brought him last month. The boy was becoming the talk of the north end of the state. Samuel had created some stunning pieces of woodwork, with Hansu's guidance. Each piece held a little secret as a tribute to Mae's lost locket. Samuel had included a hiding place in each one, a small hidden drawer or recess behind a carved flourish.

Cyrus had his own little enterprise going. He was breeding chickens. He was keeping a detailed ledger on which varieties laid the most, and the size of their eggs. He had narrowed his preferences down to three. He said the Rhode Island Reds laid the most eggs, at about two hundred and sixty a year. They lived longer than most breeds. However, so far, the Dominicker was his favorite. They weighed in at six to eight pounds at maturity. When he butchered one for meat, Cyrus used the feathers for stuffing pillows. The trait that made them his favorite was their calm disposition and the fact they were meticulous mothers. At the first sign of trouble, they would spread their wings and herd the little chicks up under them. He told Garth he remembered Mama had always been partial to them for that very reason.

Garth considered it a testament to Ruth that both

her boys still remembered their mother. They often spoke the little sayings Ruth had scattered throughout her speech, like Samuel's "good golly Moses," or Cyrus's "God bless a milk cow with green and yellow spots on it." Ruth hadn't been a woman to curse, but her peppered speech had let you know what she meant.

As the truck rattled down the road, Garth realized he did not speak to Ruth quite as often as he used to. While Ruth had colored every part of his life long after her passing, Garth recognized he was moving on now. He was beginning to see life through his own eyes. He imagined Ruth would be happy about that. She was the kind of woman who would want each of them to remember her with kindness but not hold back anything from the life the Lord had given them. He decided this was the day he would begin to move forward and make the most of the rest of his life.

****

Mae was so happy. Papa and the boys had been here for two days now. They had spent hours catching up: laughing at Cyrus's stories about his "babies," Mae oohing and aahing over Samuel's jewelry boxes, and just enjoying being together.

Today, though, they each had separate plans. Mae was taking Papa to meet Eleanor so he could see where she was spending so much of her time. Samuel was going to deliver several of his furniture pieces to Mr. Nordstrom's store, and Cyrus was spending the day with Mr. McDougal, who took care of the Finches' horses and the house garden. Cyrus wanted to pick his brain about the differences in the liniment and the herbal rub the horseman had been using for a swollen hind hock on one of the carriage horses.

As Mae and Papa made their way across town, she said, "Oh, Papa, I can't wait for you to meet Eleanor. She has helped me so much these last few months. It took me a while to get over being so impressed with her, but I soon came to realize she is a lot like me. She also had an event in her life, one that set her on a course of action. The murder of her husband left her with two choices. She could retire to a small cabin and try to make ends meet while raising her son, or take what little she had and just barge into the world to make a life for her and the boy. It is true, the ladies of the church supported her quite a bit the first few months by using her services, but it was no time at all till the word got out. Now she is busier than a bee, which has been great for me. I have learned so much from Eleanor, and not just about being a dressmaker. Once I was comfortable enough with her, I explained what I wanted to do with my life."

This took Garth by surprise. He wouldn't have believed Mae would be able to discuss her event with anyone outside the family. This woman must be someone special, to work her way into Mae's heart so soon.

"So what other things have you learned from this paragon?" Papa teased.

Mae laughed and said, "All right, maybe I do go on a bit, but it has been wonderful to talk with a woman who knows what it's like to have a dream."

Garth's heart contracted with regret. Mae had lost the most of all with her mother's early death. She had been forced to grow up, almost overnight, without the support of another woman to lean on. If for nothing else, he owed this Eleanor a debt of gratitude for helping ease Mae into self-awareness. It was plain to see the confidence Mae had gained over these past six months. "So," he said, "what else have you learned?"

"Oh, I've learned a lot about bookkeeping. You know a store has to run on a profit. You have to keep up with the prices of things and always be on the lookout for new resources that might have better prices. You also have to know your competition. You have to keep up with what others are doing and see if you can beat their prices while still making a profit. But you don't want to lower the quality of your work or you'll soon lose business."

Mae was positively glowing as all this business savvy spilled out of her. It never occurred to her these were all principles to be applied to any business, including a sawmill. Garth was not going to burst her bubble of happiness. He was just glad to see her enjoying this new experience.

Garth was impressed with Taylor's. He eyed the place as the carriage pulled to the front curb. The building was modest, the exterior neat and clean, with the windows giving a suggestion of what might be hidden inside this female fortress. A small bell tinkled above the door as they entered. When the door closed behind them, Garth was aware of the smell of roses. He could see small vases of lush blooms scattered about the room. A quick look at the interior told him the owner was indeed a sharp businesswoman. This room was designed to draw a woman in. From the lavish, upholstered furnishings to the dainty teacups and colorful assortment of hats on display, this room was designed to grab and hold a woman's attention.

"Good morning, Mae. How are you this morning?"

Garth turned his attention toward that soft voice. He was stunned. He was not sure what he'd expected, but he was sure it wasn't this vision in front of him. He was standing there gawking at a petite redhead. She had the clearest gray-green eyes he had ever seen, and her complexion was like a peach warmed by the summer sun. It took a moment before he became aware that Mae was speaking to him.

"Papa, I said, this is Eleanor Taylor, my employer and mentor."

Garth found himself holding a small, soft hand. Those magnetic eyes were filled with humor as they looked up at him.

"How lovely to meet Mae's papa. From all the wonderful things she's said about you, I had begun to think you must be just a dream, not a real flesh-and-blood man. Thankfully, I see I was mistaken." Eleanor smiled as she gently removed her hand from Garth's grasp.

Garth found himself blushing, something he couldn't remember ever doing before.

Eleanor said, "Won't you please have a seat? Then we will talk about this amazing daughter of yours."

Garth found himself seated, with a cup of tea in hand, as he watched Eleanor move among the hats on display.

"I cannot tell you how surprised and delighted I was," she said, "to find a young woman of Mae's age with the talent to create something as well made and sophisticated as these hats. With just a few lessons on construction, she was off and running, putting her special touch on every creation. My customers have been delighted."

He looked at Mae as he spoke. "My daughter is a constant joy and surprise to me. I have yet to see her take on a task she did not put her whole heart into."

"Thank you, Papa." Mae smiled, her face glowing with a sweet pride.

"I commend you, sir. A man who will love and encourage a daughter is a man who recognizes the importance of women in this world. I have found that to be a rare quality in men." Eleanor turned to give Garth her warmest smile. "When Mae told me about her dream, I was at first skeptical, to say the least. After these months of watching Mae put her whole self into learning, I can see it's not a case of *if* she will able to pull this off, but *when* she will be able to open her house. After accepting she is going to do this, we took another look at the direction her education would need to take to make it happen. After all, ancient history and French lessons would be of little help in trying to train young women to find their place in this world. I would, of course, want your input in this conversation. Mae very much respects your opinion, and I, too, would want to be sure you feel I'm giving Mae the proper preparation for the task she is going to undertake." Eleanor set her cup on a side table. With one graceful movement, she dropped onto a stool and gave Garth an expectant look.

Garth looked out across the room, taking in all the displays of fabrics, hats, and laces. The dresses hanging on the mannequins could have come off the pages of the ladies' magazines lying on the tables. It was clear a shrewd businesswoman ran this place. To do this, she would have to know how to make her way in a man's world. To do this effectively, and still retain her grace and femininity, a woman would have to be very confident and strong; it was obvious to Garth that Eleanor was all this and more.

He turned his attention back to Eleanor. "Ma'am, from what I've seen so far, I can't imagine a person more capable than you to prepare my Mae to meet the world head on."

Somehow, the lowering of her eyes and the blush on her cheeks made Garth feel warm inside, and as he glanced at Mae he observed an ear-to-ear grin.

****

Across town, Mr. Nordstrom was speaking with Samuel about future business. He'd been very pleased with the items Samuel had brought him this morning. His customers were the well-to-do of Tallahassee. They liked the idea of owning something that couldn't be found elsewhere, such as the one-of-a-kind items this young man was producing. Just as Mr. Nordstrom handed over the check for the current shipment, a young clerk stuck his head in the door.

"Excuse me, sir, there is a gentleman here looking for something special as a gift. I thought you might want to show him one of the new items."

"Very good, Nelson. Tell him I'll be right out."

As they stepped out of the office, Samuel observed a gentleman standing by one of his pieces. It was a two-drawer standing chest made of burled pecan wood. He had used the burl of the wood as the focal point and then enhanced this with his carvings.

The man turned as Mr. Nordstrom approached him. "I'm looking for something as a gift for an elderly relative. This is a beautiful piece, but too large. Perhaps you have something smaller, like a jewelry or trinket

43

box?"

Mr. Nordstrom smiled. "Well, sir, this is your lucky day. I have just accepted a shipment of items from this young man. I'm sure there is something there that will fit your needs." Nordstrom motioned to Nelson, the clerk. "Nelson, bring one of those jewelry boxes in from the back. Perhaps the one with the magnolias carved on it."

As Nelson took off to fetch the box in question, the gentleman turned to Samuel. He observed the boy to be dressed like a farmer, complete with callused hands. He smiled in a condescending manner. "Never say you built this cabinet, young man."

Samuel considered a moment before answering, "Well, sir, I guess I can say it, seein' as how I did build it."

Nelson had returned with a jewelry chest. It was made of black walnut and had been oiled and polished to a beautiful sheen. Mr. Nordstrom took the chest and turned to the gentleman. "Not only does he do beautiful work, sir, but all are originals, no duplicates, and they all have little secrets. Each one comes with a sealed envelope holding the instructions to locate a secret compartment."

Mr. Nordstrom now had the gentleman's full attention. He handed the small chest to the man. The gentleman turned to Samuel and looked him up and down before he spoke. "This carving is superb, young man. The flowers appear too delicate to touch. Where did you learn such a trade?"

Samuel had always been a little slow to warm to folks, but there was something about this man that made him a little more cautious than usual. "I learned this technique from an old Chinese gentleman, sir."

"Have you ever done anything in ivory? I recall once seeing a much smaller box, similar to this, but in ivory."

The hair on the back of Samuel's neck bristled. He looked the man in the eye and said, "And where might that have been, sir?"

There had been a thread of steel in Samuel's voice. Both Mr. Nordstrom and Nelson turned to look at him. The gentleman managed a cold smile and gave Samuel a long stare before answering, "I'm sure I couldn't say. I travel a lot."

After a long moment, Samuel turned to Mr. Nordstrom and said, "Thank you, sir, for the order. I'll be in touch." He turned and left the store.

Mr. Nordstrom, thinking Samuel may have offended the customer with his curtness, said, "Nice young man, but not used to the city."

The gentleman replied, "Really? Where is he from?"

"I believe his family runs a sawmill in Trenton, south of Lake City."

It would have taken a very observant person to see the tightening of the gentleman's jaw.

****

Garth and Mae were at the shop door. Mae said, "Now remember, Eleanor, Mrs. Finch is expecting you tomorrow evening. It will be a wonderful dinner, and I can wear my new dress for Papa."

Eleanor smiled at the young woman and said, "Well, I won't want to miss the premier of this gown, dear. So I will see you both then, and thank you again, Mr. Hinton, for meeting with me today. I am relieved to know your thoughts on Mae's curriculum."

"Please, ma'am, call me Garth." He smiled.

"Only, sir, if you will call me Eleanor."

Garth took her hand. "Till tomorrow, then, Eleanor."

Samuel and Cyrus were on the porch when Garth and Mae got home. Cyrus was excited about all he had learned that day. His mind was full of oil of clove, iodine, and herbs like arnica to be used for bruising and swelling. He was sharing all this with his brother Samuel, who had not heard a word. Samuel was carving a small piece of maple, but his mind was on a tall, well-spoken man who said he'd seen a small intricately carved ivory box.

Chapter Seven

It was the second week of March, and Easter was five weeks away. Mae had six hat orders to complete. Keeping up with her schoolwork would be a challenge, but you would hear no complaints from her. She loved the excitement of showing a finished hat to a customer and seeing her eyes light up when she put it on.

Eleanor had sent up a prayer of thanks many nights since Mae had arrived. The young woman was not just a hard-working, talented, and valuable employee; she had become a good friend, as well.

Both women were busy when the bell tinkled over the front door. Mae looked up from the confection of butter-yellow chiffon she was working with to see that Eleanor was almost buried in yards of rose-colored lawn. Mae laughed and volunteered, "I'll get this one."

As Mae entered the showroom she observed a tall, thin woman in elegant attire. She was leaning on an ebony cane covered in elaborate carving. The lady gasped when she looked at Mae.

Mae smiled as she stepped closer. "I'm so sorry, ma'am. I didn't mean to startle you." She could see the poor soul had paled and was trembling. "Please, ma'am, have a seat, and I'll get you a glass of water."

Eleanor listened to this exchange and moved to check on the customer. She was surprised to see Lady Wellington sitting in a chair with her eyes glued to Mae as she poured a glass of water for the frail woman.

"Good morning, Lady Wellington. What a nice surprise. How kind of you to visit us." Eleanor smiled as she approached the old lady.

The lady tore her eyes away from Mae and turned to Eleanor. "Good morning, Mrs. Taylor. I hope I haven't interfered with your work, dear, but I find I have need of a new hat."

"Well, then, you have come to the right place." Eleanor gestured to Mae. "Mae, this is Lady Wellington, one of my first and certainly one of my dearest customers."

"It is a pleasure to meet you, ma'am. Again, I apologize for startling you," Mae said as she handed the glass to the lady.

"Mae is my assistant, Lady Wellington, and she will make you a hat you will love to wear."

Regaining her color, the woman was able to control her trembling, so the ladies visited for a few minutes. Mae showed the lady some swatches of beautiful pastel silks, along with some of the newest patterns. After some debate, she selected a soft dove gray, trimmed with pale blue and dark purple flowers.

As the frail woman made her way to the door, she turned to Mae and asked, "My dear, perhaps when you have completed my hat, you could deliver it to my home? I don't get out often, and it would be a pleasant change to have a young visitor."

Mae turned to Eleanor with a question on her face.

Eleanor smiled and said, "That would be a wonderful outing for Mae, Lady Wellington. Thank you for the opportunity. We will see your hat is finished and to you by the Thursday before Easter."

****

Mae was excited. She was sitting in the back seat of the luxurious motorcar the lady had sent for her. The smell of fine leather filled the air. The beautiful wood-trimmed interior would have made Samuel smile. The hat was secured in its box on the seat next to her.

Mae had taken extra care with her appearance this morning. After all, she was a representative of Taylor's today and had an esteemed reputation to uphold. She had chosen a medium blue, lightweight woolen suit with an attractive light blue blouse ruffled at the neck. She had twisted her dark hair into a French knot at the base of her long neck. To top off her ensemble, Mae had chosen a matching straw bonnet.

Eleanor had assured her it was all right for her to be away from the store today. They'd finished every single Easter order by noon yesterday, so Eleanor declared she was staying closed today and Good Friday. She wanted to rest up before the holiday weekend. She told Mae the trip to Lady Wellington's estate would be very enjoyable and prepared her assistant for the visit with the information that the lady and her husband were originally from England and had lived previously in New Orleans, where Lord Wellington had numerous shipping interests.

Some sort of tragic event had occurred causing Lord Wellington to put all his business connections in the hands of overseers and retire the two of them to Tallahassee. This had been many years ago, and the poor lady had lost her husband to illness only a few years later. She was considered something of a recluse now, attending only the rare charity or musical event.

Mae sat a little straighter as the motorcar left the

main road and turned down a serene, tree-lined lane. The crepe myrtles had just begun to bloom in soft pinks and lavenders. They were a good quarter of a mile down the lane when the trees opened up to a sunlit meadow, showcasing a large, two-story limestone home, with a one-story wing on each side. They approached it and pulled up in a circular drive lined with deep pink azaleas smiling at the morning sun. Mae gazed around the meadow, soaking up a sense of calming warmth. This was a place to rest, to think on life, and to renew one's goals. This was what Mae wanted women to feel when they first gazed upon the home she would one day build, the home that would open its doors to women of all ages, women who needed comfort and assistance to heal themselves.

A middle-aged woman with a cheerful face met Mae at the front door. "Good morning, miss. I'm Mrs. Patrick. Let me take that pretty hatbox for you. You just come along with me to the back parlor. Lady Wellington will be down soon."

Martha Patrick was a whirlwind. She had scooped up the hatbox and had Mae halfway to the back of the house before she could catch her breath. She barely had time to notice the incredible high ceilings and the wide doorways as she was herded along.

They entered a large room warmed by the morning sun. French doors opened outward to a terrace lined with large clay pots full of red amaryllis. The room was set up for the obvious enjoyment of music. A large piano stood regally in a back corner. Inviting upholstered chairs and settees were scattered around. Tall floor lamps with beaded fringe brightened the room. Mrs. Patrick placed the hatbox on one of the chairs and turned to Mae.

"I'll just pop out to the kitchen and get the two of you some tea and cakes, dear. Please make yourself comfortable. Milady will be right down."

Mae set down her gloves and reticule and strolled around the room. The view from the terrace doors was serene. The house was on a slight rise, allowing the back lawn to slope gently down to a small lake. Mae could see several white birds floating along the calm water. She turned back to the parlor and observed a large artist's rendering of a portrait atop the piano. As Mae approached the piano she began to feel odd. What was that old saying? A rabbit ran across my grave? A closer inspection of the painting caused her eyes to widen in dismay. If she had not known better, she would have sworn the painting was of her. The young woman's style of dress was from a period at least forty years earlier, but the face, the hair, the dark eyes and long neck—all were Mae.

Just as she was reaching to lift the painting from the piano, a soft voice spoke behind her. Mae gasped as she turned to the hall door.

Lady Wellington stood in the doorway. She was staring at Mae with an odd half smile.

Mae blushed. She was embarrassed at having been caught about to lift the painting for closer examination.

The lady spoke as she entered the room. "She is lovely, isn't she? Of course, you can't answer such a question without seeming to be filled with conceit, can you, dear? You are the spitting image of her, aren't you?"

Again, Mae had that odd feeling, as if she was in a play and did not know what it was about. "Who is she?"

Lady Wellington had seated herself and now gazed out the terrace doors. After a long pause, she began to speak. "Her name was Lavinia. She was my daughter and my only child. She was nineteen when she sat for the portrait. It was a gift from her for my birthday. Lavinia was a kind child. She was always thinking of ways to please someone. She was engaged to a young lawyer. They were planning to be married at Christmas—much cooler, you see, for the reception."

The lady stopped speaking, dabbed at the trail of tears on her lined face, and then continued in a voice just above a whisper. "She insisted on riding to her childhood friend's home to show her the swatches of fabric for the wedding dress. She was supposed to take Shelton, our head groom with her. He asked her to wait a few moments while he attended to a horse with a bad sprain. Lavinia was so excited she told him he could catch up to her when he was finished tending the horse. The poor man rode all the way but did not find her. He was in a panic, heading back to the plantation, when he spotted her horse in the nearby woods."

"He found Lavinia, as well. She had been attacked, beaten, and left for dead. Poor Shelton was near hysterical by the time he got her home. He had the field hands send for the doctor as he rode by them." Lady Wellington paused, shivered, and wiped the tears away.

"Lavinia broke her engagement. She wouldn't believe a man could still love her. Oh, Richard tried to make the effort, but she locked herself away from everyone."

As the lady spoke, Mae could feel the blood leave her face. Her heart pounded and her skin was clammy. She wanted to scream for Lady Wellington to stop, but she couldn't make her voice work.

The lady continued, "Poor Shelton. It was his misfortune to be the one to find Lavinia hanging in the barn." Lady Wellington heard a gasp and turned just as Mae collapsed.

Mae became aware of soft voices and a bitter, acrid smell. She forced her eyes open, only to see a white-faced Lady Wellington, a red-faced Martha Patrick, and a butler who had the look of a condemned prisoner. Mae blinked a few times as Mrs. Patrick began to pray out loud, "Oh, we thank you, dear Lord, for bringing this child back to us, in the name of the Holy Father, Amen."

When she became aware she was stretched out on the settee, she tried to sit up. "No, no, dear, just stay there until you have recovered!" Martha Patrick scolded.

Mae gave a weak smile. "Please, I'm fine. Just let me sit up." She took Martha's hand and pulled herself up. "Now, please, all of you go about your day. I am fine. I'll just have a sip of tea and be right as rain in no time."

The butler made a beeline for the door, but Martha tried to linger. It took a sharp word from Lady Wellington to get her attention. "Mrs. Patrick, please go see if the cook has a broth going. A bowl of broth may be good for lunch." Martha understood that tone. She closed the door behind her as she left the parlor.

Lady Wellington sat beside Mae and took her hand. "My dear, I cannot tell you how sorry I am. I should have known you were much too young and inexperienced to hear such a story."

If Mae had not been so touched by the concern in

the dear woman's voice, she would have laughed out loud at the irony of that statement. To relieve the guilt she could see in those kind eyes, she would have to open a wound she thought had healed. She took a shuddering breath and said, "Ma'am, now I have a story to tell you. I don't want to upset you, and you should know that no one outside my family, with the exception of Eleanor, is privy to what I am about to say."

As Mae spoke, she was aware of the tears wetting both their faces. She was detached from the telling, as if she sat across the room and observed the two ladies holding hands and consoling each other. When she had finished, she turned to Lady Wellington with a weak smile and said, "Do not fear for me, dear lady; I have a purpose in life. My mama was a big believer in the power of prayer, and so I prayed—sometimes while I did my chores, sometimes at night, when I would wake screaming and covered in sweat. And somewhere, during all the prayers, the Lord spoke to my heart and gave me a mission." Mae looked down at her tightly clenched hands and willed herself to relax before continuing.

"I will someday, somehow, build a home for women who don't have the support of a loving family as I had. And for women who find themselves with a child, or those who cannot see past the horror of their particular event. They'll learn a trade so they can care for themselves and any children they may have. And they'll learn they are never alone, for the Lord is always with them. I will teach them to live the lives they have been given, without fear and without guilt."

Lady Wellington, the dear lady, said, "Your father must be so proud of you. Your mother must have been a gift from the Lord. You are a magnificent young woman, and I am proud to know you."

Mae was overwhelmed and embarrassed. She patted Lady Wellington's hand and said, "Well, you may want to save some of that praise until after you've seen your new hat."

****

Lady Wellington was deep in thought as the motorcar faded in the distance. Mae had been self-conscious after her disclosure. Even though she would have loved to keep her, the lady sent Mae home with a hug and high praise for the stylish creation she would wear to Easter services on Sunday.

Her mind was rushing ahead as she moved back to the parlor. The doctors had told her it was just a matter of time before her heart gave out. She had no relatives other than one several-times-removed cousin, who visited once a year just to make sure she had not passed on and he had not missed out on what he believed was his. He was a young man, but a possible reprobate and gambler. She had never cared for him even though she had paid for his education and provided him a quarterly allowance. While she would never leave him high and dry, she now knew where the bulk of her estate would go upon her passing. She smiled at the thought of the surprise young Mae would get when she found out just what that bulk entailed.

Chapter Eight

It was the first week of June, and Eleanor and Mae were each working on little dresses. The president of the Mainstreet Bank had commissioned them to do a summer wardrobe for his granddaughter.

They were both enjoying the change from women's wear to little ruffles and bows, and sweet little embroidered butterflies. Mae was going on about how excited she was to be going home for a visit. Eleanor always closed the shop during the month of July and made a point of spending the whole month with her son, Patrick. Both women were excited at the prospect of the time away from the shop, but for different reasons. Eleanor's inner voice told her it was time to share something with Mae.

"Mae, I have something to tell you, and I hope you will be as pleased about this as I am. Do you remember when your father and brothers visited at Christmas? You may not be aware, but your father and I were quite taken with each other. I have a confession to make, Mae. We have been exchanging letters since then, almost weekly. It started with me keeping him informed of your studies but soon progressed to personal notes. Mae, your father has invited Patrick and me to visit with you in your home for a few days. I hope this is not uncomfortable for you."

Mae was smiling a sly little smile. "I knew it," she

squealed with joy. "I could tell he liked you, and how could you not like Papa? He is the kindest, most sincere man in the world, and being handsome doesn't hurt. Oh, Eleanor, I am so happy I could dance!" But then Mae's face fell. "Oh, dear, our house is smaller than you are used to, and I'm not sure how we'll all fit in."

"Well," Eleanor drawled, "your father did mention a few months back he may be making some changes to the house." She did not want to spoil Garth's surprise, but she couldn't let Mae worry for no reason.

"Oh, he didn't mention it in any of his letters, so maybe he wants to surprise me." Mae's smile grew again. "Oh, what fun we will have! The boys will love showing Patrick around the farm, and you'll get to meet Hansu. You will love him. He is so kind and wise."

Eleanor appreciated Mae's excitement at having her in their home, if even for a short while, but she was not going to allow herself to make more of this than what it was: just a visit. She would not set herself up for pain, in case this friendship did not mature into a relationship. But if ever there was another man she could let herself fall in love with, it would be Garth Hinton.

****

It was the first of July, and Mae was on her way home. She stared out the train window. She was going home after a year away, and she was taking Eleanor and Patrick with her. With the train line now running all the way to Bell, it would be just a short truck ride to the farm.

She turned to look at Patrick. He had his nose pressed against the window of the train car. Mae was glad to see his excitement. He was a tall boy for his seven years. This was a gift from his father, along with the sandy blond hair and the sprinkling of freckles across his nose. He had been very close to his father, and the murder had taken the joy from his childhood. He was much too quiet, by Mae's measure. She was used to her younger brothers being boisterous and curious about everything. She was glad to see Patrick show some enthusiasm.

Mae turned her gaze to Eleanor. She was thumbing through the pages of the latest pattern book from New York. Eleanor could have stepped off one of those pages. Her copper hair was styled in a twist with a tortoiseshell comb holding her curls in place. She had worn a crisp traveling suit of lightweight linen. The color looked like ripe cantaloupe and complemented her beautiful hair. Mae was filled with a deep sense of peace when she looked at Eleanor. She believed this visit home was a beginning for Eleanor and Garth. Mae was happy for them both. They were good people, each of whom had been forced to deal with one of life's greatest trials: the loss of a mate.

They deserved to have a second chance at happiness. If Mae's wishes had anything to do with it, they would find happiness with each other.

****

Garth yelled across the yard. "Cyrus, those chickens can wait till you get back home! We can't leave the ladies standing on the platform."

Garth had taken great care to clean his truck inside and out. He looked back at the house. He hoped Mae would approve of all the changes. Garth had built onto the kitchen, combining it with the dining room. He'd put large windows on three walls to allow airflow to cool the rooms. The back of the house now had two additional bedrooms. It was time the boys had their own rooms. A bathing room was added as an extension to the washhouse. There was a woodstove to warm water, and the hand pump eliminated all the carrying of buckets to and from. If there was ever going to be another woman in the house... Garth couldn't think beyond this point. He did not want to dream of something that might not come to pass. He would just let these next few days flow naturally. If they grew to be something wonderful, then so be it.

As Mae and Eleanor stepped out on the platform, the afternoon sun reminded them it was July. Mae spotted her father walking toward them. In that moment, she was no longer the mature and sedate young businesswoman. She was the little girl who hadn't realized how much she missed her papa. She threw herself at her father, locking her arms around his neck. "Oh, Papa," she cried. "It's so good to see you! I have missed you so!"

Garth struggled to keep from falling. "Girl, you've grown a good inch, and who would have believed you could get any prettier," he said with pride.

Mae laughed and turned to Cyrus. "Mrs. Peters' cooking must be great, little brother, 'cause I'm not going to be able to call you my 'little' brother much longer! You're as tall as me now. Come and say hello to Patrick."

Before Cyrus could answer her, Patrick had grabbed him by the hand and said, "Mae claimed you would show me all the animals and take me fishin' and teach me to swim and we could pick berries and..."

"Whoa, there, partner!" Cyrus interrupted. "You've

gotta breathe, little buddy." They all laughed as Patrick jumped from one foot to the other.

"Well," Garth said, "let's get these bags loaded and get back to the farm. I'm guessing this young man has a big list of to do's and needs to get started on them."

Mae was surprised by the wave of sadness washing over her as they pulled into the yard. Mama's roses made a splash of color as they wove themselves through the split rail fence. She swallowed a lump in her throat, reminding herself no one would want the family to grow beyond their loss more than her dear Mama. She smiled to herself, and then Samuel strolled out through the front door. She squealed and jumped from the truck and ran to hug her brother.

"Good golly Moses!" he exclaimed. "What happened to the well-mannered seamstress we sent off to Tallahassee?"

Mae laughed. "She remembered she was from the country, and all her proper upbringing just flew out the door."

"Well, Mrs. Peters won't allow hooligans at her table, so you better straighten up, or you're gonna miss out on a fine supper." He laughed.

All the bags had been placed in their rooms. Mae was delighted by the changes Papa had made in the house. She and Eleanor were sharing a room, as were Patrick and Cyrus, seeing as how Patrick had practically glued himself to Cyrus all evening. Eleanor had insisted on helping Mrs. Peters clean up after a delicious dinner. Now they were all sitting on the front porch listening to the frogs down by the stream. Papa fired up the citronella cans on each end of the porch to run off the pesky mosquitoes.

Patrick was firing questions at Cyrus. "Can we go fishing in the morning? I don't have a fishing pole. Are we gonna pick berries? 'Cause I love berry cobbler. Do we have to dig worms to fish with?"

Cyrus just looked at him in amazement. "Okay, peanut, this is how it's going to be. First, we have to do our work."

Garth smiled at this. He could remember the times he'd said those very words to the boys. Work always came before play. Then you could play even harder.

Cyrus continued, "Which means we feed and water the animals, milk the cows, gather the eggs, and then we talk about fishing." If Cyrus believed this was going to put a damper on Patrick, he was mistaken.

"Oh, boy, did you hear, Mama? I get to milk the cows and gather the eggs!" They all laughed.

Chapter Nine

Eleanor was just wakening when Patrick's voice broke through her slumber.

"Oh, yes," he said, "I'm ready, and I have a hat, too."

Cyrus tried not to laugh as he said, "Well, peanut, let's get going, then. The cows are ready for us."

"I'm going to have to tell Cyrus he is not expected to put up with Patrick for our entire visit." Eleanor shook her head.

Mae smiled at her. "It's his first chance to be a big brother. He's always been the baby, and I think he is enjoying being the older one for a change."

Mae slipped into a split skirt of dark blue denim and a red-and-white checked blouse. She twisted her hair into a bun, wrapping a red kerchief around her head. She looked at Eleanor and smiled. "Take your time. I just want to help Mrs. Peters in the kitchen. It's been so long since I've had a chance to cook, and I find I miss it."

Eleanor sat on a stool at the end of the bed and brushed her hair. She had slept well last night and was anticipating a beautiful day. She smiled to herself, like a schoolgirl with a silly crush. It had been much too long since she had known this feeling. She almost laughed out loud as she finished braiding her hair.

She was going to wear a blue-and-white gingham

dress, tie on a white apron, and pretend she was a young woman again. She was going to laugh, flirt, and just enjoy this interlude. If the good Lord meant for it to be more, He would make it happen.

****

Garth was returning from his early morning ride to the mill. He had slipped out before daylight and met with Hansu, who had become his right-hand man years ago. Some of his men had balked at first, not sure they wanted to take orders from a little Chinaman. However, after a couple of weeks of Hansu working circles around them, they soon warmed up to the little man.

Garth's mind slipped back to the time before he and Ruth had married. He'd purchased the four hundred acres of good timberland located between Bell and Trenton. There had been money from a small inheritance, and he had worked hard to pay off the rest. The crosstie and sawmill business had been booming for the last six or seven years.

Even though it would probably last another couple of years, Garth was a prudent man, testing ideas that might secure the future. With the railroad running from Bell to Tallahassee, and south to Deland, he could easily ship any crops he might grow. He would have to explore the possibilities.

Right now, though, he had other, more interesting, possibilities to explore. He wondered how he was going to get Eleanor alone so they could get to know each other better. Their personal correspondence had been very enlightening. She was a shrewd businesswoman. She was well educated, and there was a definite spark between them.

Eleanor was strolling behind the house when Garth

found her. She was wearing a blue-and-white dress and had her hair braided and coiled around her head. She looked about twenty years old and deep in thought. She would pause at one of the flowerbeds Cyrus had designed, reach down, and pluck a bloom to place in her basket.

As Garth got closer, he could hear her singing softly. He gazed at her, and just then the sun broke through the trees, and for a moment she was lit from above. It was as if the Lord had sent forth a beam of light from heaven to guide him to Eleanor. His heart told him this was the woman the Lord had sent to him; this was the woman he hoped would travel with him into the latter years of his life. And he was filled with peace and joy. The only thing left to do was convince her.

Eleanor paused, stopping here and there to pick flowers for the breakfast table, a relaxing activity, and her song changed to, "I come to the garden alone, while the dew is still on the roses…" Becoming aware she was not alone, she turned and found herself looking up into Garth's smiling face. She blushed a soft rosy hue as she returned his smile.

Before she could speak, he took her hand, brought her close, and whispered in her ear. "The Lord just spoke to my heart. He told me I was being given a treasure more rare than rubies and gold, and to cherish and care for it the rest of my life. Would you be my treasure, Eleanor?"

Eleanor looked into his eyes, knowing he meant every whispered word. With great tenderness, she took his face in both hands and asked, "Who are we to argue with the Lord?" Then she pulled his mouth to hers and kissed him with a passion that shook each of them to the core.

****

Mae placed the biscuits on the table. When Garth and Eleanor walked into the kitchen, she glanced up at them, started to turn to the stove, and then stopped. She looked at them again, and a slow smile warmed her face. She clasped her hands in front of her and said, "Isn't this a beautiful day? Eleanor, I see you were able to find some flowers. Papa, why don't you find a couple of jars from the pantry while I call the boys in to breakfast and see what's keeping Mrs. Peters at the icehouse?" Mae stepped out to the back porch, leaving Garth and Eleanor alone in the kitchen.

Eleanor was the first to speak. "Mae is nothing if not diplomatic."

Garth was reaching to the top shelf of the pantry, where Mae kept the jars used for flowers. He turned to Eleanor. "The fact she holds you in such high esteem is going to make the idea of the two of us becoming one much easier for her."

Eleanor felt a thrilling shiver run through her. Just hearing Garth say those words excited her. She was going to have to compose herself. She was not a giddy young virgin, for heaven's sake! She was a forty-year-old widow. She knew about marriage.

Maybe it was the knowing that caused her to feel so giddy. She was well aware of what occurred between a man and woman, and that when it was the right two people it was breathtaking.

Eleanor smiled when she heard Mae say, "Hold on, little man. Swing yourself by the hand pump and let Cyrus get you some water to wash with before you set yourself at my table."

Breakfast was a boisterous affair. Patrick was so full of everything he had seen and done this morning he had trouble staying in his chair. Between mouthfuls, he was keeping them entertained with his funny observations about farm life.

"And Mama, I helped get the milk you're puttin' in your coffee!" he announced with a proud grin.

"Oh, did you, now?" Eleanor teased. "I didn't know the milkman delivered out this far."

Patrick exclaimed, "No, no, Mama. I got the milk from the cow. You just squeeze and tug on her, and she squirts it out!"

Eleanor almost choked on the coffee as she tried so hard to hold in her laughter. Cyrus and Samuel both whooped so hard they had to slap their hands over their mouths to keep from spitting out their eggs.

Garth sat at the head of the table and observed all this with a smile. He was filled with a sense of rightness, a bone-deep happiness he had not experienced in years.

For the most part, Garth was a contented man. While he had been through his share of pain and heartache, he never let them become the focus of his life. He was aware the Lord had blessed him many times over. He tried to live a life worthy of all those blessings.

Something had been missing since Ruth passed on—that warm spark within, that which made a man want to run out and meet the day, the spark that made him feel like he could take on the world. He could feel it now, growing inside him. Oh, he didn't try to fool himself into thinking there wouldn't be any rocks in the road ahead. He and his little family were facing many hard choices in the next several months; how would Eleanor feel about moving her business to Trenton? Or what would the boys say about relocating to Tallahassee? Or how would Patrick accept having to share the woman he'd had to himself for most of his little life?

None of these issues were going to be strong enough to stop the forward motion of all their lives. This little family was on a path to a great life. While they might have to steer around some big rocks, Garth was going to see to it the journey was good for all of them, with the help of the Lord. Garth was wise enough to know he'd not come this far in his life without the Lord at his back. Prayer had given him the right answers to so many of life's questions. He wasn't about to try a different formula now.

Mae sat at the opposite end of the table. She could see the inner peace reflected on his face. It was obvious her Papa had forged a plan in his mind. He had always been a man who looked at all sides of an issue, waited for a word from the Lord, then did his best to fulfill whatever mission he was given.

It was one of the many things she loved about him. He was humble, giving credit for all his successes to his Lord. He understood being humble did not make him weak. Papa was a man given to strong opinions, and while he would not force his ideas on anyone, he did not hesitate to speak up when he witnessed a wrong being committed. Mae thanked the Lord each night she had been blessed with such a man for a father. She was aware of other fathers who would not have been so wise if they had been faced with the type of decisions Garth had been forced to make. For instance, he had been ready to storm into town and hunt down the men who had attacked Mae, but to do so would have let the whole town know what had happened.

Mae's life would have been very different. There were always those people who'd have believed she'd caused the attack herself. They would've said she'd lured those men into behaving like animals. Papa may have wanted to find and kill them, but he put Mae first. By swallowing the hurt and anger, he did what was best for his little girl, and she would always honor and love him for that.

Garth rose from the sturdy pine chair Samuel had made and spoke to his little family. "I'm going to take Eleanor into town so she can see we are not completely cut off from civilization. Does anyone need anything while we're there?"

"Are you going to ride horses?" Patrick chirped.

Mae read his mind and was one step ahead of him.

"No, they'll be taking the buggy or the truck. You, my little friend, will be berry picking with Cyrus and me. Mrs. Peters promised a cobbler if we find enough berries. I don't know about you, but I would love a warm cobbler after supper!"

Eleanor smiled her thanks to Mae for her cleverness.

"Patrick," she said, "you be sure to do everything Cyrus and Mae tell you. Mind your manners, and watch for snakes."

"Don't worry, ma'am." Cyrus beamed. "I'll keep a good eye on the little fellow. Besides, Mae always has her 'little beauty' with her if we need it."

Mae was glad this last remark seemed to fly right

over Patrick's head. She didn't want to have to come up with a reason why she kept a pistol with her all the time. Explaining it to Eleanor had been painful enough.

Chapter Ten

Eleanor had been stunned the first time she saw the pistol. They were working on a dress for the mayor's wife. Mae had to put on the skirt so Eleanor could check the drape. Mae took off her skirt and placed it on a chair. Eleanor was startled when it slid off and hit the floor with a thud. "What in the world was that?" Eleanor said.

Mae froze in embarrassment. This kind woman had every right to an explanation. If she learned the truth, would she look at Mae differently? Mae's breathing quickened. Eleanor could see she had paled and looked as if she might faint.

"Mae, come sit down. Take a deep breath. Whatever it is, I'm sure it can't be that awful." Eleanor picked up the skirt and pulled out the pistol. She turned to Mae. "Dear, is there something you need to tell me?"

Eleanor's kindness had sent Mae over the edge, and she burst into sobs. "I'm so sorry! I didn't want you to know. It was not my fault!" she cried as she tried to get her breathing under control.

Eleanor had no idea what Mae was talking about but believed it must be awful. She took Mae in her arms and held her close. "Honey, whatever it is, if you want to talk about it, I'll be glad to listen."

Mae's sobs became softer, and she hiccupped her way to an awkward silence. After taking a shuddering breath, she started to talk. By the time she finished her story, there were tears in Eleanor's eyes, as well as fire.

"Did they find the animals? Did they hang all of them?" Eleanor snapped.

"No, ma'am. Papa and I talked about it. I couldn't remember enough to be able to say who may have been responsible. And there was no way to search for them without the whole county knowing what had happened. Papa wanted to go after someone, but he said he would let me decide how to handle it.

"I chose to let it go. I felt dirty enough as it was. I don't think I could have faced everyone in town, knowing they would all be watching me to see if there were 'consequences.' Of course, some would have blamed me. Folks are just that way." She smiled sadly. "So when Doc Walters rode out to check on me again a couple of days later, I was more than happy to take the gift of the pistol. It was small enough to conceal in hidden pockets I sewed in my skirts, and it gave me a sense of security. I'm not sure I could kill another human being, but I could sure scare the daylights out of someone. Actually"—Mae blushed—"I'm very good with it and could hit a man's heart at thirty paces. Samuel spent weeks working with me, until he could declare me a crack shot.

"I could never say I was happy about what happened, but I can say one good thing rose from it. The Lord showed me what I should be doing with the rest of my life. That's how I came to be here. That's why I needed a broader education. The Lord has helped me deal with the past. What I need from you is to learn how to deal with the future. I am going to build and operate a safe place for women who need help, where they can heal from life's wounds, where they can learn to be strong, independent, and never feel guilty about the circumstances that may bring them to me."

Eleanor sat looking at Mae. She had a feeling this young woman was not as strong as she wanted the world to believe. She was sure Mae's pain and shame had been covered very well by this outward show of strength, but the wounds had not yet healed. It would be some time before Mae was as strong as her words implied.

For Eleanor, one thing had been certain: Mae was one of the bravest young women she'd ever met. She would do everything she could to help this remarkable young woman reach her goal.

****

Garth and Eleanor took the truck into town. Eleanor was glad to see there were several stores, a gas pumping station, and even a hotel. Garth explained that the hotel had been built to accommodate the men who built the railroad. When they stopped in at Doc Walters' office, he had just seen his last patient. He invited them into his office.

"Doc, I want you to meet Eleanor Taylor from Tallahassee. She is Mae's tutor and employer. Eleanor, this is our local doctor, Martin Walters."

Doc looked at the petite redhead and smiled. "I think we may have met at an event of some kind, possibly something my sister was hosting?"

"Yes, Dr. Walters, I think you may be right. I'm sure it was a few years ago," Eleanor replied.

"Well, ma'am, how is our girl doing?" Doc asked.

"Sir, I can tell you that Mae is like a sponge. She soaks up knowledge like it was water and she was lost in the desert. She has been a blessing to me, for sure."

After a nice visit with Doc, Garth and Eleanor took their leave. As he helped Eleanor into the truck, Garth announced, "I have a surprise for you."

"Oh, and just what might that be?"

"I had Mrs. Peters pack a picnic for us. We are going to a favorite place of mine to have lunch."

Eleanor gave Garth a long look and then smiled. "I like a man with initiative, one who isn't afraid to make a decision."

Forty-five minutes later, Garth's truck left the roadway to cross a meadow. He stopped the truck under a large oak tree, and Eleanor could see a stream several yards away.

Garth took Eleanor's hand as she stepped down. Still holding onto her, he reached behind the seat and pulled out a blanket, which he spread in the shade of the tree.

"Have a seat, sweetheart, while I get lunch."

Eleanor found herself blushing. It had been a long time since a man had called her "sweetheart." She was aware she had missed these spoken endearments. It was nice to feel special again. She was amazed as Garth opened a basket and produced sliced ham, a small block of cheese, a jar of pickles, and two pieces of chocolate cake from its depths.

Garth caught her surprised face and laughed. "Nothing is too good for my girl," he teased. Eleanor laughed out loud.

In reply, Garth smiled and gave her a long look before saying, "You don't know how good the sound of your laughter makes me feel, as if I could conquer the world. There has been too little laughter these last few years, but I intend to make up for that."

They ate in a comfortable silence that allowed them to soak up their surroundings. It was the kind of quiet that seeped into your bones, leaving them feeling at peace with the world.

Eleanor was the first to speak. "Garth, we have a lot of things to talk about."

"I know, dear." He smiled. "There are a lot of details to be worked out, but that's all they are, minor details. The important thing is we have found each other and have many years to be together. Now, tell me, what details are worrying you?"

Eleanor looked up into his eyes as he stroked her hand. "Well, Trenton is a nice little town, but I'm not sure there would be enough business to support Taylor's. And what would you do in Tallahassee? And how would Samuel and Cyrus feel about all this? Would they be willing to relocate, or would they blame me if they were uprooted?"

Garth heard the tremble in her voice, and guessed it was caused by fear of the unknown. "All right, the first thing to do is stop throwing rocks in the road. We have the rest of our lives to work these things out. We'll talk with each of our families. We'll get a feel for what they want and would be happy with. Then you and I will sit down and sort it all out. I will be looking at the wisdom of keeping the sawmill going. I'll take a look at what I would need if I were to farm in the Tallahassee area. There's a good market for cattle right now, and that could be very big in the near future. I would like to make you my wife this coming Christmas."

Garth smiled at the sharp intake of Eleanor's breath. "Well, you do know that was what I had in mind, right? I mean, you do know that just being here with you now is wonderful, but not enough for me? I want to be with you every day and every night."

Garth slowly lowered his mouth to Eleanor's. Her lips parted in anticipation as he stroked her face. "Eleanor, I love you. I want to make you mine forever."

Garth leaned against the old oak, pulled Eleanor across his lap, and held her soft body against his hard chest. He could feel her quickened heartbeat. They were not imprudent young lovers who could be ruled by lust, but Garth was glad Christmas was only six months away.

****

Two weeks had flown by, and now Mae watched as Samuel loaded Eleanor and Patrick's bags onto the train. They'd enjoyed wonderful days filled with fishing and swimming, berry picking and pickling. Evenings were filled with games, and laughter, and lightning bugs in jars. Stories were told, and new dreams spoken of with excitement.

Papa stood looking down at Eleanor, loving possession in his eyes. "We'll write each week. I'll be in touch with some folks I know up your way. I'll be doing some checking into the dress shops in Gainesville. You will, of course, be missing me, right?"

Eleanor burst out laughing. "Yes, I will be missing you very much, along with all the other things I have to do."

Mae turned to give them a bit of privacy, in time to see Patrick throw his arms around Cyrus's waist. "I'll miss you too, little buddy." Cyrus looked up with a sheepish grin. He'd obviously gotten quite used to being a big brother.

Samuel knocked Cyrus's hat askew as he walked by him. "You're a pretty good teacher, little brother. Patrick even caught some fish yesterday."

Jumping from one foot to the other, Patrick chirped, "And I'm gonna catch more at Christmas, too. Mama said I could come visit again, and I'm bringing my marbles this time, and I bet I can beat you both!"

They all laughed at his ear-to-ear grin. He had a few more freckles across his nose that had turned a nice golden brown in the sun, and this pleased Mae. He was much more outgoing and boisterous than he'd been before, just like she remembered Samuel and Cyrus being at his age.

Mae was also happy that they were all comfortable with each other now, like a real family. She was proud of her brothers. Papa had made no secret of his feelings for Eleanor. Mae had seen Samuel smile when Papa held Eleanor's hand as they strolled through the back yard. Cyrus had blushed like a girl when Eleanor told him he was going to be as handsome as his father.

Yes, Mae imagined all their lives had been improved by her deciding on moving to Tallahassee. She had to remind herself to take no pride in that decision. The Lord had dictated it, and she was happy to accept the blessings of His wisdom.

She hugged Eleanor and Patrick and said, "I'll see you both in two weeks. Patrick, take good care of your mama."

He stood very straight and looked solemn as he said, "I will make sure she doesn't work too hard."

Garth looked down at that freckled nose, laid a hand on the little shoulder, and said, "I have complete trust in you, son, so take good care of her."

Patrick straightened his back. "Yes, sir," he snapped.

Mae took Papa's hand as the train pulled away. "Papa, are you happy?"

"Mae, girl, you know I loved your mama, and always will, but Eleanor has opened my heart again. I want to make her happy, as well. Can you accept that?" he asked.

"Papa, it will make me almost as happy as you!" she replied, hugging him.

Chapter Eleven

Labor Day morning dawned clear and hot, but a fast moving shower cooled the afternoon air. There was to be a ball held at the Leon Hotel on East Park Avenue. There would be speeches, fireworks at dusk, and then an orchestra would play for the ball.

Mae and Eleanor had made many of the gowns that would be seen there. She'd finished her own modest gown a few nights ago and could not wait to show it off. It was a deep rose taffeta with an almost off-the-shoulder neckline. Mae had tried it on so Eleanor could pin for the last fitting, and it had rustled like dry leaves when she moved. She'd also fashioned a smart hat with a single silk rose and a small piece of pale Chantilly lace. The same lace adorned the neckline and cap sleeves. It made Mae feel quite the lady. She laughed at herself. While the dress would be fun to wear for an evening, it would hardly be appropriate attire for a modern woman running a household for troubled girls. It would be relegated to the back of a closet later, but for one evening, Mae would shine.

She was now sitting patiently while Maggie Sullivan wove her shiny, dark-chocolate curls into an elaborate hairstyle. Mae blushed as she remembered her first day in this wonderful house. No doubt Maggie had believed her to be a backwoods hick when she'd shown her surprise over the indoor plumbing.

Maggie was a true Irishwoman, with a loving, kind nature, and had taken Mae under her care at their first meeting. She'd been discreet in steering Mae through those first days of new sights and mannerisms. Maggie had helped Mae to adjust to city life with as little discomfort as possible.

Mae looked at her now and smiled. "I'm not the same country bumpkin I was a year ago, am I, Maggie?" she asked.

Maggie met the smile in the mirror and raised an eyebrow. "Begging for compliments are we, little missy, and you not even at the dance yet? You just remember who you are and don't let all those fancy young men sweep you off your feet. Your head will be swelling enough from all their foolishness, without old Maggie addin' to your conceit."

Maggie always kept the family grounded. She had been with the Finches since before they lost their daughters to yellow fever. She'd grieved as if the two little ones had been her own. She was glad to have Mae in the house, for herself and for Louise Finch. It was bittersweet to see this beautiful young woman blossom and wonder how the lost little ones would have looked now. As a rule, Maggie was never one to dwell on the past. She felt there was always living ahead of you and only a fool would not enjoy every moment of it. When life was over, well, it was over, and until the end arrived, Maggie believed she had an obligation to the Lord to savor every moment He gave her.

Her face softened as she looked at young Mae. Maggie knew how nervous she was about this big social outing. There was no need for Mae's concern. Maggie had seen her bloom this past year. Mae was quick to learn all about the societal expectations put on a young woman, but still managed to hold onto those qualities given her by a loving mother. Mae managed to put the needs of others first without giving up her inner soul in the process. As Maggie slipped the last hairpin into place, she patted the daydreaming girl's shoulder. "All right, little missy, will this hold up through all your wild dancing?" she asked with a slight smile.

Mae tore herself away from her daydream and looked in the mirror. She observed a tall young woman, dark brown eyes staring back at her. There were slight waves in the lustrous hair pulled up and placed in a crown of lofty curls at the back of her head.

The small pink hat was pinned to one side, leaving a lone ringlet of hair spiraling down past a long, slender neck, to rest just below her collarbone. "Oh, Maggie, you are wonderful! It is more than I expected even from your gifted hands."

"All right, now off you go to the parlor, little missy. Mrs. Finch asked for the cabbie to be here at six o'clock on the dot, so you've got about ten minutes to spare," Maggie said as she gathered Mae's small reticule and soft pink shawl. Mae gave Maggie a quick kiss on the cheek, took her things, and appeared to float down the stairs.

Myron Finch was discussing one of his clients with Louise when Mae swept through the double doors. They both turned at the sound of her slippers. "Good heavens!" moaned Mr. Finch. "Surely no one expects me to be responsible for the stir this young beauty is going to cause tonight."

Mae laughed as she blushed a pale shade of rose. "You, sir, are surely teasing. There will be a bevy of beautiful women there tonight, not to mention your lovely wife. It will be a thing of wonder if anyone even notices me."

Louise's eyes sparkled with unshed tears as she took Mae's hands. She admired the gift her brother had sent her. She allowed just a moment of sadness to pass, in memory of her own lost daughters, before her face took on a motherly smile. She tucked her arm through Mae's and said, "I cannot tell you how wonderful it is to look at you tonight. I'm proud of how much you have grown, in so many ways, this past year. Thank you, dear, for allowing us old folks to be a part of your transformation..." And before any of them could become even more maudlin, Louise said, "Ah, I hear the cabbie. Come, let's get this show on the road."

****

When she was younger, Mae had attended church suppers and even a birthday party or two, but nothing had prepared her for the sights and sounds that met them when they stepped out of the cab. It seemed like every window in the Leon Hotel held a glittering light. The sun was just below the horizon, and there was a soft breeze wafting through the opened windows and doors. Riding on the breeze was the sound of music, laughter, and clinking glassware.

Mae's senses were overwhelmed by color, sound, and fragrance as they walked up the stairs to the open double doors leading into the ballroom at the north end of the hotel. There were men in light linen suits and women in every color of gown imaginable.

Mae recognized many of Eleanor's creations, and some hats she herself had labored over.

It gave her a wonderful sense of accomplishment to

know these ladies had enough pride in her creations to put them on display at such an important event. Everyone was smiling. Couples were moving through the massive ballroom, greeting friends, business associates, and even strangers.

Mr. Finch took each of his ladies by the arm and said, "We have a table reserved for us near the back balcony doors, ladies, so come this way and let me get you seated."

As he led them across the room, his wife told him softly, "How thoughtful of you, dear, to obtain seating near an open door where we can catch the breeze."

Once they were seated, he said, "I'll just see if I can get you ladies some lemonade. Try to keep all the admirers at bay while I'm gone. Oh, and keep an eye out for Mrs. Taylor. I sent her a note inviting her to sit with us."

"Oh, how sweet of your husband." Mae smiled at Mrs. Finch.

"Yes, he is a dear, and I think I'll keep him, now I've smoothed out all his wrinkles."

Mae laughed. It had been apparent to her from the first time she met these two that they completed each other. They were able to read each other's minds with just a sidewise glance, after thirty years together.

The two women spent the next few minutes admiring the table settings, the floral arrangements, and the groupings of small palm trees scattered around the room. The City Council and Business Association had outdone themselves this year. The Leon Hotel was transformed into a place to make memories. Tallahassee had become the state capital in 1884, and there was no looking back. It was a growing cultural center, a booming college town, and a growing business area attracting entrepreneurs from all around the country.

Mae was reflecting on how her father might take advantage of all this growth when she spotted Mr. Finch on his way back with two glasses of lemonade. Eleanor was at his side, wearing her own royal blue creation. It was an off-the-shoulder gown with a diaphanous overskirt that swirled around her trim ankles. True, hemlines had started to creep up, showing the anklebones, but for a formal occasion like this Eleanor had chosen to hold to the "dusting the floor" length.

Mae smiled as they progressed across the crowded floor. She knew her father couldn't love Eleanor any more in this beautiful gown than he had loved her in a starched white apron in the kitchen, serving biscuits right out of the oven. It gave Mae such peace of heart and mind to know the two of them felt as they did about each other.

As they neared the table, Mr. Finch said with a smile, "Look what I found while getting the lemonade. I was afraid I was going to have to fight a couple of strapping men when I stole her away from the counter. Apparently they each had thoughts of entertaining her with their presence."

"Well, you can't blame them." Mrs. Finch laughed. "What man in his right mind wouldn't want to be seen with her on his arm?"

Eleanor chuckled as she blushed. "It wouldn't have taken either of them long to become bored with my conversation about hats and silks and the newest patterns!"

Patrick stepped out from behind his mother and smiled at Mae. His face was flushed with excitement.

He was having a difficult time keeping both feet on the ground. It was clear he wanted to bounce around but was doing his best to maintain the proper behavior for a young man allowed to participate in this wonderful party.

"Hello, Mae. Isn't this grand?" he exclaimed. "I fetched you a lemonade 'cause Mr. Finch only has two hands, so he borrowed mine, and I didn't spill a single drop!" Mae was quick to take the two cups from him before he was overcome with excitement. She didn't want him to spill lemonade on the little linen suit his mother had sewn for him.

"Mama said I could go to the upper balcony later and watch the fireworks. I can't wait to see them, can you?"

Mae laughed. "I'll be glad to take you up after dark and watch them with you."

It was about a quarter before nine, and the sky was darkening. The mayor had given a rousing speech about the growth prospects, the ever-growing work force, and the numerous opportunities to be found in Tallahassee, and the crowd had cheered with enthusiasm. Afterwards, folks once again started to mill around and seek out familiar faces or business prospects to chat with.

Mae turned to Patrick and announced, "All right, young man, I think it's time you and I move upstairs and see if we can find a seat for the fireworks show."

Eleanor smiled at Mae and asked, "Are you sure you don't mind, dear? Would you rather stay down here and listen to the music? Perhaps some young man would ask you to dance, if given the chance."

"Oh, no." Mae laughed. "I'd much rather see the

display than become a display. My dancing skills leave much to be desired. You just sit here and relax. Peanut and I will come back later and tell you all about what we've seen."

Patrick was a complete chatterbox as they climbed the stairway at the end of the veranda. They found a bench just outside a pair of open French doors on the upper balcony. Once Mae was seated, she watched Patrick cling to the rail, bouncing up and down on his toes, in anticipation of the wonders to come.

He was chatting like a magpie to another little boy, who'd also been given the wonderful opportunity to have his eardrums strained from the explosions and his vision blurred by the brightness of all the colors. As Mae sat on the bench, she was aware of people moving behind the grouping of small palms at her back, but she was too wrapped up in thoughts of Eleanor and Papa to focus on the conversations behind her.

A faint breeze drifted across the balcony, bringing a whiff of something that brought Mae out of her daydream and began a growing sense of unease.

As her nose caught the elusive scent again, her stomach tightened, and she began to tremble. The fragrance, wafting in and out of the reach of her memory, was lemongrass. Mae understood it was unreasonable to be this frightened by the hint of lemongrass on the breeze, and she'd almost calmed her foolish nerves when she became aware of male voices. Right behind the palm trees at her shoulders, one of the men said something she could not understand, and then the second one said, "Perhaps this is not such a good idea after all."

Mae wanted to stand, to run, to scream, but she

found herself frozen to the bench. Time stood still. She could no longer hear anything. There was just the roaring in her head. She could see Patrick clapping his hands and jumping up and down as the fireworks display illuminated the evening sky. Everyone on the balcony was staring off to the north, where the beautiful colored lights made intricate patterns in the air.

Mae could only hear her inner roar—the sound of the culmination of a fear so strong she was almost paralyzed by it. The only sound she made was the soft rustling of her satin dress as she first stood, then collapsed as if her bones had melted. It was a good minute or two before anyone became aware that the young woman lying on the balcony floor had fainted dead away.

Chapter Twelve

Mae could hear frightened voices. She could feel the coolness of a damp cloth on her face. These things seemed to be coming to her as she lay in the bottom of a deep, dark hole. She was comfortable at the bottom of the hole. Deep in the recesses of her mind she was aware that if she climbed out of the hole she would have to acknowledge something evil, dark, and dangerous. Suddenly her nose and mouth were filled with an acrid smell, and she coughed. Even as her eyes began to flutter, she was screaming, "NO!"

Mae became aware of two things as her mind cleared. Eleanor was bathing her face with a cool cloth, and someone was watching her from across the balcony. He was tall and dark-haired, and immaculate in black evening clothes. Even in her confused state she understood he was a stranger to her. Mae blinked her eyes, tried to sit up, and as she refocused her eyes on the man, he was gone.

Eleanor called her name several times before she got through. "Honey, can you hear me? Do you hurt somewhere? Take your time. You're still white as a sheet."

Mae could see Patrick behind his mother. His face was streaked where he'd swiped at tears. It was clear she had frightened the poor boy.

Mae stretched out a hand to him and said,

"Sweetie, don't cry. I'm all right, I promise." To Eleanor, "Just help me up and let me sit a moment. I'll be fine."

She was, however, not so sure. As her mind cleared, she remembered the voice. Mae stiffened in Eleanor's arms and began to look frantically around the balcony.

"What is it, Mae? What are you looking for?"

Mae closed her eyes, gave a deep shudder, and whispered, "Eleanor, I must get away from here. Now. Please just get me to a cab. Now!"

Eleanor was alarmed by the urgency, bordering on hysteria, in Mae's voice. "It's all right, dear. Mr. Finch has one waiting for us behind the hotel."

At that moment, Mr. Finch appeared, bounding up the stairs two at a time. "Can you stand?" he asked Mae. "Just hold on to me, missy, and we'll get you home in no time."

As they were making their way down the back staircase, Mae's eyes filled with tears. "I am so sorry I have ruined everyone's evening!" she cried.

"Shush such foolishness, child. Your health is more important to all of us than any old party," Mr. Finch crooned. As they reached the ground floor of the hotel, Mae realized Mr. Finch had chosen the rear exit to avoid making a scene. How kind these people were to her, and how secure she felt in their love. Even so, right this moment she wanted nothing more than her papa, and his rifle, by her side.

****

After much discussion about telegrams and doctors, Eleanor was able to calm Mr. and Mrs. Finch. She assured them it was nothing more than the excitement of such a new event in her life that had caused Mae to become overheated and faint. Only after they had seen for themselves, and Mae had recovered her natural color and was tucked neatly into her bed, were they able to leave her alone with Eleanor.

"Now, young lady, do you have enough energy left to tell me what happened? I don't want to upset you again, but I don't believe for one moment your little fainting spell had anything to do with heat or excitement." Eleanor sat very still and waited for Mae to open up.

Mae's eyes filled with tears. She looked so frightened that Eleanor almost gave in, but she understood it would not be good for Mae to keep whatever this was locked inside her.

In a low and halting voice, Mae spoke. "It's been over two years. I believed I had moved past the fear. Then tonight, in just seconds, all my bravery left me." As she leaned toward Eleanor, imploring her to understand, Mae continued, "One moment all was well, and the next moment he was there, somewhere near me."

Eleanor shivered as a chill ran down her spine. "Who was there, sweetie?"

Mae hesitated long seconds before answering. "Him, the only one I could remember from the event, the voice and the scent that used to haunt my dreams. One moment I was daydreaming about you and Papa, and the next I was aware of the scent of lemongrass. Before I could rationalize my fear, I became aware of a voice behind me, and I wanted to run." Mae closed her eyes and tears ran down her cheeks. "But I was paralyzed with fear. All I could think was that he had found me. That he had been searching for me and had found me. Then everything started to fade. I don't even remember hitting the floor." Mae opened her eyes, searching Eleanor's face.

Eleanor gave Mae a sympathetic smile holding all the love and concern she could put into it. "You'll remember well enough in the morning, because you have the makings of a very impressive bruise on your poor forehead."

Mae managed something between a laugh and a sob. As she raised a shaking hand to her forehead, she paused with it in midair and turned startled eyes to her friend. "Eleanor, when I opened my eyes, there was a man standing across the balcony. Did you see him? He was tall, dressed in black, and had dark eyes."

Eleanor pondered for a moment. "One of the gentlemen who was on the balcony when you fainted was the one who scooped you up. He placed you on the bench, and perhaps it was him you saw. That's when poor Patrick ran to get me. I'm sorry, dear, but I don't remember much about the man. I was so concerned about you I didn't notice anyone else. I do know you are safe here.

"Mae, you've been through a terrible ordeal. Perhaps you have not put it all to rest in your mind. Maybe some repressed memories were triggered. I can't explain what happened, dear, but I want to assure you, you are safe, and surrounded by people who love you. Now, you need to close those eyes, get you some much needed sleep, and then tomorrow we will see how you feel." Eleanor kissed Mae lightly on her already discolored forehead and softly closed the door as she left.

Mae lay thinking about all that had passed. She was not a foolish girl, or given to flights of fancy. She had dealt with the event, but she knew, as well as she knew her own name, "he" had been there tonight.

Oh, his intent might not have been to find her, but he'd been there. She rose from the bed, moved to her wardrobe, and took the pistol from the shoebox in the bottom. Now she might be able to sleep. She knelt and prayed.

"Dear Lord, forgive my weakness. Lord, please clear my head of the fear and let me sleep in peace. Amen."

****

It had been a week since the Labor Day ball. The lump on Mae's forehead had gone down, but the fading bruise was still visible. It was not a complimentary green, and Mae would be glad when it had run its course. She had convinced the Finches and Eleanor all was well, there was no need to mention this to Papa, and she was completely recovered. Only Maggie was aware she slept with the pistol each night.

Each morning Maggie applied a cream to the dark circles under Mae's eyes to prevent those probing questions. She was better. She had reached an agreement with the Lord. She would stop worrying. He would keep her safe. She had learned long ago that in order to maintain balance in her life she must trust in the Lord. And she did. He had delivered her through so many trials. There was no reason to think He would abandon her now.

So, she would continue to carry the pistol and continue to study. Exams would be coming up in a couple of months.

Mae stood at her bedroom window and listened to the birds calling to each other. It was hard to believe time was flying so quickly. It would be Thanksgiving before she knew it, leaving only a few short weeks before Christmas and the New Year. She had to get ahead in her studies because this was a very busy season for Eleanor. Mae wanted to be able to help with the many orders coming in. There was also a wedding to put together. My goodness, just thinking about all that had to be done was mind-boggling. Well, one thing at a time. Mama had always said the only way to get through was to finish one thing at a time.

Chapter Thirteen

Elizabeth Wellington was enjoying the view from the back parlor. The slope down to the small lake was dotted with wildflowers—black-eyed susans near the house and beautiful cream-colored turtleheads near the lake's edge.

When she was younger and still able to work the flowers, she had chosen the perennials that would continue to reseed themselves. She smiled to herself. That had been one of her better choices in life, not that she regretted any of the decisions she had been forced to make. The only things she regretted in her life were the losses, first of her beautiful daughter and then, much later, of her wonderful husband. Of course, she'd had no control over either of those life-changing events. As a woman in the 1800s and now into the early 1900s, there were many things she could not control.

But she was about to take care of the one thing that was hers alone to determine, which produced another smile. She was so happy to have found a way to settle the question of what to do with her fortune. She liked the idea of her money going toward bettering the lives of young women; maybe a few could go on to be strong and wise, and raise daughters in the same way. With that thought, there was a light tap on the parlor door. Her bustling housemaid opened the door and ushered in Lady Wellington's guest.

"Please don't get up, ma'am," Myron Finch said with a smile. "I can seat myself."

Lady Wellington waved to a chair near her. "Thank you so much for coming all the way out here to see me. I realize I am cutting into a large part of your work day. I am truly grateful. The doctor has advised my heart is going to give out soon. Since there are a few important things I need to take care of before then, I try not to overdo too often."

"So, dear lady, how can I be of service?" he inquired.

As Elizabeth Wellington ended her explanation, she could see by the look on his face she had caught Mr. Finch completely off guard.

"Well, sir?" She smiled. "Are there any extenuating circumstances to prevent you from handling this piece of business for me?"

"Ma'am, as I am not a legal guardian of the young lady, then there would be no legal complications, but ma'am, have you given this action appropriate consideration? Do you not have any other relatives? We are talking about a great sum of money here." Mr. Finch needed to be sure there was never a question as to the integrity of such a decision.

Lady Wellington looked him right in the eye and said, "Sir, it is a fact. I am an old woman, and sometimes, as I sit here in my parlor and waken from a small nap, I may be a little confused as to what the time of day is. However, when it comes to millions of dollars' worth of property and cash assets, I can assure you no decisions are made without great consideration. I do, in fact, have a very distant vagabond cousin, a Langford Hardwick, who shows up here at least once a year to make sure I am still alive and he has not missed word of my passing. I personally believe he is a scoundrel and womanizer, but it is not my place to judge. So I will leave him two million dollars on my death. As I said before, I want the balance of my estate, including lands, minus the personal gifts to my servants, to go to Mae Hinton, to be used to promote her wish to create a home for young women." This little speech was delivered with all the sharpness one would expect from an aristocrat who had, in fact, been making all her own business decisions for the last twenty years.

Mr. Finch swallowed to cover the grin that might give him away. He was filled with admiration for this dear old lady. He had known her for many years and had so much confidence in her wisdom that he would have been glad to let her handle his own finances.

"My dear Lady Wellington, I shall take care of this for you. I will personally draw up the necessary papers this afternoon and have them back out to you tomorrow for your signature. An assistant from my office will accompany me to witness the signing, and then you can rest in the knowledge things will be handled as you wish. No, dear lady, don't rise. I can see myself out. You just indulge yourself in one of those little naps you spoke of, and I'll take care of everything."

****

The signing was finished. Mr. Finch and his assistant had left Lady Wellington tired but relieved she had taken care of such an important piece of business. Mr. Finch's mind was deeply engaged on the drive back to town. Did young Mae have any idea how her life was going to be affected by this? Just what was this dream of opening a residence for young women? He was glad

Mae's father would be available to help the young woman make sense of all this. The man had good business experience and would be able to guide young Mae, even through such an endeavor as a home for wayward girls. Whoever heard of such a thing?

It was apparent today: Lady Wellington was not long for this world. She had been pale and shaky as she signed the many papers that would distribute her vast fortune to her satisfaction.

She had been very generous to her servants but had also expressed the hope they would be kept on by Mae as she proceeded with her endeavor. She had, in fact, left two million to her wastrel relative. Mr. Finch had met him once, several years ago, when Lady Wellington had set up a quarterly allowance for one Langford Hardwick.

Hardwick had been educated in England, an education paid for by the kind lady. As far as Mr. Finch was aware, he had never taken any steps toward bettering his own place in life. He merely relied on his relative to take care of him. The man was in for a rude awakening at some point in the near future. In fact, Mr. Finch had meant to ask Lady Wellington today if Hardwick was in town. He was sure he had seen him at the ball, but with all the excitement then, he may have been mistaken.

****

The man in Myron Finch's thoughts was sitting in the back corner of one of his favorite establishments. The serving women were almost clean, the whiskey was plentiful, and there was a steady stream of new customers who did not know him and therefore might be willing to play cards with him. The Crossroads Inn sat a few blocks away from the railway, several blocks west of downtown Tallahassee. While he preferred a higher quality of surroundings, he was a little short on cash. He would sit here and watch for a good pigeon to pluck. As he waited, he pondered his dilemma.

He was not mistaken. The young woman who had fainted at the ball last week was definitely known to him. He'd made her acquaintance under circumstances he would not care to divulge to anyone.

The men he had been in the company of during that acquaintance had long since headed west, which was fine with him.

He had only taken up with them because they all had the same destination, Tallahassee. He'd been on one of his annual treks to check in on the old bird and had procured himself a seat on a boat traveling the Suwannee River. He and the others had disembarked somewhere south of a little town called Trenton. They had skirted the town, since a couple of the "gentlemen" had made a prior acquaintance with the local constable. They were all a little under the weather from the past two nights of heavy drinking, and so conversation had been nonexistent. They had been trudging along through the woods when they heard a female singing. It was a voice like a songbird.

As they got closer, they could see a young girl beating rugs over a rail fence. Before he could react, one of the men had snatched a shirt from his valise and thrown it over the girl's head. The others gathered around and were trying to take her to the ground. She fought like a young lioness, catching one of them in the eye and then another in the groin.

He had said, "Perhaps this is not such a good idea

after all," when one of them slammed a fist into her face and ended the discussion.

Once she was out cold, they took the shirt off and he looked upon a truly beautiful face, and the rest was not bad either.

She was tall, with well-formed breasts and full hips tapering into long shapely legs. He was not a man who usually had to knock a woman out to get her favors, and the sight of her bloodied face was not arousing to him; however, the sight of her sprawled there on the ground with her legs open... Well, he wasn't a man to look a gift horse in the mouth, either. Since the others were doing the holding, he was the lucky "first," in more ways than one. He was surprised to see the blood and realize she had been untouched. Ah, well, the state of her virginity would not have lasted much longer, not with those looks. An hour or so later, they had left the area.

That day had not crossed his mind until the night of the ball. My, how she had grown. Not much taller. Maybe "matured" would be the better choice of words. She had still been able to give off an air of innocence. She had never seen his face and so did not recognize him as she lay there on the bench, but prudence demanded he make himself scarce.

He had already had his visit with the old bird and had given her the carved jewel box he had picked up at Nordstrom's, the one with the secret nook...carved by the angry backwoods boy. The old bird had loved it.

Ordinarily, he would have been on his way after the visit, but with the ball only a couple of nights away, and so many affluent pigeons all gathered in one spot, it was tempting.

So he had stayed—and found the little she-cat.

Sometimes he had an uncanny sense of when to stay and when to go. Right now his inner voice was saying, "Run, man, run," but he wasn't so sure. It might be interesting to hang around a while. His next quarterly installment from the old bird would be deposited next week, so he would be flush for a while. Just this once, he thought, he might ignore the voice.

Chapter Fourteen

Myron Finch recognized bad news when confronted with it. He could see it all over the face of Lady Wellington's business manager, Arthur Bennett. Mr. Bennett was somewhere near fifty years of age and had been with Lord Wellington for about ten years before the good gentleman passed away. He had been the right-hand man to Lady Wellington for the past twenty years. As Finch watched Bennett enter and seat himself, he took a moment to consider how Bennett would feel about the new arrangements for Wellington Manor. Once Bennett was seated, with hat in hand, it was clear he was distressed.

Mr. Finch spoke first. "Mr. Bennett, I feel it is safe to assume you are delivering sad news."

"Yes, sir, I am sorry to tell you of the passing of Lady Wellington. The dear woman has been weakening over the past month and passed peacefully in her sleep last night. I had received direction that you were to be notified immediately. So, sir, here I am."

"I appreciate your promptness, sir. I know you have been a devoted assistant to the good lady for many years, and she depended greatly on your loyalty. I am sorry for all of you who served her, for she was a true lady, in every sense of the word. She cared deeply for all of you. I know she discussed her final plans with you, and that you can be relied upon to make all the arrangements. Today is Thursday, and I suggest we hold the services on Saturday, if you are agreeable. Please assure all the servants they have been provided for handsomely. I will attend the services, then on Monday meet with all parties concerned, for the reading of the will." Mr. Finch walked around the desk, and they shook hands.

Mr. Bennett gave a wan smile. "The servants will be relieved to hear they were remembered, sir. That is always a concern when one is in service, but I believe I speak for all of them when I say the loss they feel today goes much deeper than monetary concern. She was like a mother to us all."

The man turned and left the office quickly, but not before Mr. Finch caught the glint of moisture in his eyes.

Mr. Finch sat back at his desk and made a short list of immediate things to do. At the top of the list was a telegram to Garth Hinton. He wanted him present at the reading of the will. Next on the list was to contact the bank, not only to notify them of the impending changes but also to have them locate Mr. Langford Hardwick.

The man had already received his quarterly allowance in September and should have left the bank a forwarding address. It was now near the end of October, but surely the man had enough left for travel arrangements if he had, indeed, left the area.

****

Garth was about to leave the mill for the day when he saw Race Milford's son ride up on his daddy's horse. Garth stepped out to meet him. "Well, hello, Daniel. What brings you out this far?"

"You have a telegram, Mr. Hinton. Dad said what

with Mae bein' up in Tallahassee, I should probably get it right out to you."

Garth's breath froze in his chest. "Please, Lord," he thought, "don't let anything be wrong with my girl."

Garth took the telegram from the boy. "Go on inside and get some water, Daniel, and let your horse rest a little before you start back. Tell your Pa I said thank you." Garth walked over to the bench under the magnolia tree and sat. With shaky hands, he opened the telegram.

"All is well with Mae. Stop. Need you in Tallahassee for important meeting Monday morning. Stop. Reference Mae's future. Stop. Yours, Myron Finch."

What in the world could this be about? Garth considered a moment; the important thing was that Mae was all right. He'd just have to wait until Monday for the rest. He would take the train up Sunday afternoon and stay over with the Finches.

It worked out well, as he needed to go up anyway to meet with a man about some property outside of town. He was looking for some ground to plant cotton.

He'd made the decision to sell the mill to old Frank Bell, who'd been after him to buy it for some time now. Garth had researched the area between Trenton and Gainesville, deciding Eleanor might not be able to maintain the same level of business here that she enjoyed in Tallahassee. He also had spoken with the boys about a possible relocation. Samuel had liked the idea of being closer to a larger town so he could get other sources to buy his furniture. Cyrus, well, Cyrus needed to have his animals and his gardens. He wouldn't care where he was as long as he could be near them. He had been very impressed with the Finches' groomsman, who had a lifetime of knowledge and experience to share. So, all in all, it was going to be a good choice for all of them.

****

The funeral for Lady Wellington was a small, private affair. All of her servants and groundskeepers attended, as well as the Finches, Mr. Bennett, Eleanor and Mae, and Mr. Langford Hardwick. Reverend Simmons of the First Methodist Church of Tallahassee performed the service at graveside. The lady had always been very generous to the church, so Reverend Simmons was glad to be of service to the family.

Lady Wellington had requested only a graveside service. She was being laid to rest beside her beloved husband. They would spend eternity together under a towering magnolia tree about a half mile from the main house. As the minister spoke, each of the attendees was engaged in personal considerations.

The bank had notified Langford Hardwick of the passing of Lady Wellington.

From that moment on, his head had been filled with visions of world travel, high-class women, and any other damn thing he wanted. He had waited long enough for the old bird to kick off. As the minister droned on, his only other thought was, "What the hell is she doing here?" as his gaze landed on the girl who had fainted at the Labor Day ball.

Arthur Bennett only half heard the minister. He assumed Lady Wellington would be as generous in her death as she had been during her life. He wondered where he would go. He didn't think Mr. Hardwick would be interested in keeping him on. He shuddered to

103

think how soon the reprobate might go through the dear lady's fortune. Bennett was not a young man and had never married. His only relative was a younger sister, who lived in New York. Perhaps he would visit her and then decide what to do with the rest of his life.

Martha Patrick, the head housekeeper, was truly saddened to see her beloved lady go. She had been a sharp old girl, running her late husband's business with an iron hand. She had been kind to all who worked for her. With a quick glance at the young rogue who would probably want to move to the big house today, her heart told her she would not be able to work for him.

Mr. Finch had not told Mae her father was coming, as it would be a nice surprise for the young woman. He knew what to expect at Monday's meeting, but he had chosen not to have a sheriff's deputy present. He was sure Garth would be able to handle anything Mr. Hardwick might start.

Eleanor was remembering when she was newly widowed and almost destitute. She remembered Lady Wellington commissioning her to do an entire wardrobe. Her generosity had been the salvation of Eleanor's business. She'd been grateful to the dear lady ever since.

Mae was overcome with sadness. She'd only met this wonderful lady on a few occasions but had developed a true closeness with her. They had shared stories filled with pain, anger, and heartbreak. Each had recognized a survivor in the other. The poor woman should have been mourned by a loving daughter and a horde of grandchildren, Mae thought. *But who are we to question the Lord?* Did not the heartbreak in each of their lives make it so much easier for them to develop a true affection for each other? Mae could only promise to hold tight to the memory of Lady Wellington's strength, her determination to live life to the fullest, and her continued faith in the Lord, no matter what the world threw at her. Mae would use Lady Wellington as a pattern to fashion her life after.

The Reverend Simmons had closed with a solemn prayer and now turned to Mr. Finch. "I believe you had something to share, sir."

Mr. Finch turned to the assembled group and spoke. "As executor of Lady Wellington's estate, I would like to thank all of you for your attendance. There will be a formal reading of her will on Monday morning, to be held in the library of the manor at ten o'clock, at which time the estate will be turned over to the rightful owner."

Hardwick experienced a flash of irritation. What the hell did that mean?

Well, he guessed he could pay another couple of nights' lodging at the hotel, since it would be the last time he'd have to worry about his lodging arrangements. Right now he had something else on his mind.

He turned to Finch and said, "I recognize Bennett and the servants, but who are these two lovely ladies?"

"Allow me to introduce you," Finch replied.

Mae was still deep in memories when she realized Mr. Finch was standing in front of her. She looked up and was caught off guard by a pair of dark eyes in a handsome face.

With a stiff smile, Mr. Finch said, "Eleanor and Mae, allow me to introduce a distant relative of Lady Wellington. Mr. Langford Hardwick, this is Mrs.

Eleanor Taylor and Miss Mae Hinton."

The gentleman nodded to Eleanor, but reached out his hand to Mae, who without thought placed her hand in his.

"Sir, please accept my condolences at the loss of Lady Wellington. She was a dear lady and will be missed by all who knew her." As she was making this polite little speech, Mae became aware the gentleman was holding her hand a little tighter, and longer, than was socially acceptable. She could see in his eyes he was aware of this. She was forced to drag her hand from his. On a second look at the gentleman, she observed his eyes were red and a little puffy. While their condition might have been caused by grief, somehow Mae did not think so. This man made her very uncomfortable, and she was not sure why.

Eleanor, ever her protector, took Mae's elbow and said, "So sorry for your loss. May you find solace in knowing she passed peacefully in her sleep." She then turned Mae around, and they headed for the carriage.

As they were climbing into the carriage, Mr. Finch approached Eleanor and said, "Eleanor, Mrs. Finch asked me to invite you and Patrick to an early supper Sunday afternoon, say about four?"

"Why, thank you, sir, we'd be delighted."

Chapter Fifteen

Mae was curled up on the settee studying for a test when she heard voices in the front of the house. Mr. and Mrs. Finch had gone to visit a sick friend. One of the maids would handle it if they had a visitor, so she continued to read. A few moments later she felt someone's gaze on her, looked up, and squealed in delight.

"Papa! What are you doing here?" She jumped up and threw herself into her father's arms. She squealed again as she spotted Samuel over his shoulder. "Oh! What a wonderful surprise! Does Eleanor know you are here? How long will you be staying? Where is Cyrus?"

Garth Hinton laughed out loud. Lord, it was good to see this girl. "Slow down there, girl. Give me a chance to answer some of those questions before you throw any more out there."

Mae was swept into Samuel's bear hug. She was on her toes when the realization came to her.

"Good golly Moses!" she exclaimed. "What have they been feeding you? You've grown at least four inches." Samuel just picked her up and swung her around, and by then they were both giggling like the children Garth still perceived them to be.

Maggie came to the door, and her face lit with joy as she watched Mae giggling. It was good to see the child happy. "Excuse me, sir, will you and the young man be needing anything? We will be having an early supper around four."

Garth smiled and said, "No, Maggie, we'll be fine until then. Mrs. Peters packed us a good snack for the train ride, but thank you."

"Now, Papa, sit down and tell me what you're doing here," Mae said as she dropped back down on the sofa.

"Well…" Garth smiled. "If I had a clue, I'd be glad to tell you. I received a telegram from Mr. Finch telling me I had to be here Monday morning for an important meeting. I already had some things I had to take care of, so here we are."

"Well, how odd. He never mentioned you were coming. If he meant to surprise me, then he did a wonderful job!"

They spent the next two hours filling each other in on all the day-to-day events of their lives. Mae was laughing over a story about Cyrus and a raccoon when they heard voices in the hallway.

Mr. Finch came to the door, smiling. "So glad you could make it before dinner. There's an extra beautiful young woman tonight. I was afraid I would not be able to entertain them all."

Patrick burst through the door yelling, "Where's Cyrus? Did he bring me anything? Is he out in the stables?" He would have made a beeline for the back door if his mother had not grabbed him by the collar to rein him in.

"Lower your voice, young man. You are a guest in this house, and please remember your manners! And you, sir"—she turned to Garth—"why didn't you tell me you were coming? As glad as I am to see you, a little warning would have been nice."

Garth moved across the room and took her hand in his. "Please forgive me. If I'd had an opportunity, I would have let you know, but maybe Mr. Finch here can shine some light on this business."

They all turned to Mr. Finch. His face was a little flushed, and he had a sheepish look. "Well, truth be told, I cannot explain at this time." He turned to Garth. "You will understand all, after tomorrow morning, and I would be grateful if you would just trust me on this."

Garth smiled. "Well, I'm a patient man. I get to spend the evening with some of my favorite folks, so tomorrow will be just fine."

After dinner and a pleasant hour or so of conversation, Garth used the Finch carriage to take Eleanor and Patrick home.

It was a cool evening, the moon was shining full, and the ride was not long enough. When they stopped in front of the cottage, they realized Patrick had fallen asleep. Garth picked him up and carried him to his room at the back of the cottage. After Eleanor had turned down the covers and taken off his shoes, Garth placed him on the bed and then stepped aside so Eleanor could bend down and kiss her son's forehead as she pulled up the covers. Garth was overcome with a deep sense of pride. This beautiful woman, this accomplished, self-reliant, precious woman, had agreed to marry him. He still could not believe it. They slipped out of the room, closing the door quietly behind them.

Before Eleanor could speak, Garth swept her into his arms and kissed her, slow and deep. "I'm sorry. I have waited all afternoon to kiss you."

She smiled up at him. "Well, be sorry if you must,

but I'm certainly not. I, too, have waited all afternoon for your kiss!" She took his hand and led him to the kitchen table.

"Now," she said, "sit, while I make you a cup of coffee, and tell me why you are here."

He laughed. "Well, I wasn't joking. I have no idea. I received a telegram from Mr. Finch late Thursday afternoon. It said, 'All is well with Mae, need you here for important meeting Monday morning, may affect Mae's future.' So, you tell me. What does it mean?"

Eleanor became still. She turned from the stove with the coffee in her hand. She placed the cup in front of Garth and sat next to him before she spoke. "I can only think of one reason he would have needed you here Monday morning. We attended a funeral for Lady Wellington on Saturday afternoon. Mr. Finch made an announcement at the end of the services, saying there would be an official reading of the will at the manor house at ten o'clock Monday morning, at which time the estate would be turned over to the new owner."

"All right, but what has this to do with Mae's future?" Garth asked as he sipped his tea.

"Well," Eleanor replied, "she was quite taken with Mae. It seems Mae is the spitting image of the lady's only child. Her daughter committed suicide when she was Mae's age. Oh, my!" Eleanor's eyes went wide. "Perhaps she has left Mae some money in her will."

"Well, we'll just have to wait and see. Now," he said as he rose from the chair, "since your housekeeper is not here, you can walk me to the door, kiss me goodnight, and send me on my way."

Eleanor made sure the kiss was pleasant enough to stay in his memory a while, then waved him goodbye.

As she walked through the house checking the windows, she said a prayer of thanks to the Lord. Thanks for this wonderful man, this strong, handsome, God-fearing man, who wanted to marry her.

****

It was eight o'clock Monday morning, and they were all enjoying a pleasant breakfast together. Mrs. Finch turned to Mae and said, "Dear, you are going to be traveling with Mr. Finch to an important meeting this morning. I have asked Maggie to lay out your most grownup outfit, and if you will run upstairs, she will help you get ready."

"What do you mean?" Mae turned to Mr. Finch. "Do you not have an assistant to accompany you? Do you need me to take notes or something?"

Mr. Finch shook his head. "No, dear. You will not be assisting me. We will be attending the reading of Lady Wellington's will. You have been mentioned in the will. It is why I have asked your father to be present. Anything that is bequeathed to you will be under the care of your father until you attain the age of twenty-one."

Garth had a surprised look on his face as he turned to Mae. "Well, sweetie, you may have mentioned this lady to me once, but I don't remember you saying anything about being so close to her."

Mae swallowed around the lump that appeared in her throat. "Lady Wellington had only one child, Lavinia, and she looked just like me. When I visited the manor to deliver a hat, I saw her portrait. Lady Wellington told me the story of how Lavinia died, and we cried together."

Mae looked her father in the eye and said, "Lavinia

had a terrible thing happen to her, Papa. She could not get over it, and she hanged herself."

There was a collective gasp around the breakfast table. Garth never broke his gaze with Mae. "Well, I'm sure it was comforting to the lady to talk about her daughter with someone as understanding as you, sweetie."

Mae stood, kissed her papa's cheek, and said, "Thank you, Papa. Now I had better get myself ready."

Mrs. Finch smiled at Garth. "You, sir, have a remarkable daughter."

Garth smiled sadly. "Thank you, ma'am. No one knows that better than I."

Chapter Sixteen

It was a cool, fall morning, with the smell of harvest in the air. Mae let her mind wander on the drive to the manor. Papa and Mr. Finch were talking about shipping lumber and cotton; Samuel was deep in his own thoughts, so Mae daydreamed at her leisure.

She could not imagine why Lady Wellington might have left her something in her will. Mae had understood the poor woman's loss, and she could sympathize with what the family must have suffered when Lavinia had been attacked, but Mae had assured Lady Wellington she was not in a vulnerable state. She had explained how her faith in God and the support of her family had left her even stronger than before her event.

Perhaps it had made the lady feel like she was helping her own daughter in some way. Obviously they had not been able to reach her in life; maybe gifting someone in her name was the next best thing. In any case, Mae was very touched by, and grateful for, whatever small gift she might receive.

"How much farther?" Samuel asked, as he stared out across the meadow.

Mr. Finch smiled and said, "Well, son, we are now on the Wellington property, but it will be another half mile or so to the house."

Garth looked to the stand of pines, several acres of meadow away, and said, "Well, it seems to be an impressive holding, and well cared for."

Mr. Finch nodded. "Yes, the whole of the property comes to about two thousand acres, with a couple of lakes and one river thrown in."

"Whoa, that's a lot of work for somebody," Samuel exclaimed. By now they could see the manor house in the distance. "Good golly Moses!" Samuel said in awe. "That's a lot of house for one little old lady."

Garth cut him a look, and Samuel sat back in his seat.

Mr. Finch gave the boy a glance. "Well, Samuel, as you said, it's a lot of work for someone. There are servants' quarters above the large garage in the rear, and I believe Mr. Bennett has an apartment above the equipment building."

He turned to Garth and explained, "Mr. Bennett has been Lady Wellington's right-hand man ever since her husband passed on. He has a complete working knowledge of all the Wellington holdings."

Garth nodded. "Well, I could see how such a man would have eased a great burden for the lady."

Mrs. Patrick opened the front door as the motorcar stopped in the drive. Her face was pale above her black mourning dress, and to Mae she looked almost angry.

She bade them all good morning and then turned to Mr. Finch. "Mr. Hardwick has been here this past hour. He is in the library and has had one of the stable hands take his bags upstairs." Mr. Finch arched an eyebrow at her.

He turned to the others and said, "The library is at the end of this hall and on the right. Please make yourselves comfortable. We'll be right along."

As Mae led her papa and Samuel down the hall,

Mr. Finch turned to Mrs. Patrick.

"Martha," he said quietly, "tell the stable hand to use the back stairs, remove Mr. Hardwick's bags, and place them outside the front door." As Martha's face took on a quizzical stare, he added, "Then you come straightaway to the library. Don't worry, all will be explained soon."

It was all Martha could do to keep from skipping into the kitchen. After giving instructions to the stable hand, she made a beeline for the library.

Garth became aware of two men as he held the library door for Mae to enter. One was tall and thin, maybe in his late thirties. He had one leg draped over the arm of a beautiful, high-backed chair as if he owned the place.

The second was older, maybe in his mid fifties, and looked like he wished he were somewhere else. He stood as far away from the first man as possible.

As Mae entered the room and stopped to look first at one man, then the other, Garth noticed two things. The older man seemed glad for the entrance, and the younger man's jaw clenched.

The older man walked forward with an outstretched hand. "Hello. My name is Arthur Bennett. I was Lady Wellington's business manager. Please, have a seat, and I'm sure Mr. Finch will be here shortly."

Garth shook the man's hand and said, "Good morning, sir. I'm Garth Hinton, and this is my daughter Mae and my son Samuel. In fact, we arrived with Mr. Finch, who was speaking with the lady who welcomed us. He said he would be right in."

As his father spoke, Samuel observed the other man. The man now had both feet on the floor. After a moment they made eye contact, and both had instant recognition. Samuel thought, "Ah, the man who has seen a small, carved ivory box somewhere before."

The man thought, "Ah, the nosey backwoods carver." Hardwick couldn't stop his stomach from clenching just a little. "What the hell are they doing here?" he wondered silently. He had yet to make eye contact with the girl when Mr. Finch swept into the library.

Mr. Finch glanced around the room. He could feel the tension. He was glad Garth Hinton was here this morning. He was not sure just how Hardwick was going to respond to what could only be bad news for him.

"Everyone, please be seated. Mrs. Patrick will be here soon. As you all know, we are gathered here for the reading of the last will and testament of Lady Elizabeth Wellington." Mr. Finch turned as Martha entered. "Ah, here we are. Mrs. Patrick, please take a seat." Martha moved to the back of the library and took a seat behind Mr. Bennett.

"Now, as you all know, Lady Wellington was very fond of all her employees. She had known for several months she did not have long to live."

"It was her wish to make proper arrangements for everyone. She wanted anyone who wished to stay with the new owner to be allowed to do so."

Martha and Mr. Bennett both glanced at Mr. Hardwick. Both knew in their hearts this so-called gentleman would not be keeping them on. He had expressed his displeasure with both of them on occasion, when he made his annual visits to their dear lady.

As Mr. Finch was speaking, Garth was observing

those around him. He could sense the disdain of Mr. Hardwick. It appeared there was no love lost between the servants and this man. The man in question already looked bored with the whole process. He did not seem to be mourning his relative. In fact, he appeared to be completely unaware of anyone else in the room. Garth had no way of knowing how far off the mark he was.

Hardwick was not mourning, for sure, but he was very aware of everyone in the room. His mind filled with possible scenarios. Were Mae and her family about to expose him? Did they think they could somehow lay some sort of claim to his estate because of his past sins? And did Finch think he was going to retain the services of Bennett? The last thing he needed was an old bulldog telling him how to spend his money.

Mr. Finch turned to Mr. Bennett and smiled. "Arthur, you have been a true and faithful servant to Lady Wellington for the past thirty years. She often spoke of your astute business sense and was always grateful for any insight you were able to give her when faced with decisions. She left you a lump sum of five hundred thousand dollars, sir."

Mr. Bennett looked surprised. He, better than anyone, was aware of the extent of the lady's wealth, but it was a nice surprise, nonetheless.

Hardwick almost gave a snort. Well, if it would get that watchdog off his back, then he could part with it.

Mr. Finch then turned to Martha. "Martha, you served the good lady with grace and devotion for many years. She held you in deep regard and considered you a family member. She left you three hundred thousand dollars."

Martha gasped, and her eyes filled with tears.

"May the angels make her welcome in her new home." Martha whispered the old Irish blessing as she wiped her eyes.

Again, Hardwick considered it a little overboard for an insolent old Irish housekeeper, but at least no one could say she was turned away with nothing.

Garth had been surprised at the generous amounts given to the lady's caretakers, but then, it was probably an indication of just how much wealth the lady had accumulated over the years. Eleanor had mentioned Lord Wellington had been heavily involved in shipping matters in New Orleans before the couple had lost their only child and moved to Tallahassee.

Mr. Finch turned to Hardwick. "Mr. Hardwick, as the last living relative of Lady Wellington, be it greatly removed, she acknowledged you had been kind in your visits over the past ten years. She has left you two million dollars in a lump sum, which will negate the quarterly allowance you have enjoyed these past five years."

Garth watched as Hardwick changed from detached to very aware to downright stunned. There was a gasp from Mrs. Patrick.

The man slowly stood. "Finch, if this is some kind of joke, I don't appreciate your brand of humor."

"Sir, I do not make light of a matter this serious," Mr. Finch replied.

Hardwick growled, "Are you telling me the bulk of the Wellington estate is only worth two million dollars?"

"On the contrary, sir, the Wellington estate is worth many millions. However, your portion of this estate was decided by Lady Wellington, and it is the aforementioned two million dollars."

Hardwick's face, while pale before, was now turning a bright red. "What the hell are you trying to pull, Finch? Did you think I would fall for some sort of scheme, or did the old bird completely lose her mind at the end?" By now, Hardwick was in a full sweat, and yelling.

Mr. Finch lowered his voice. "Sir, there are ladies present, and I would ask you to control yourself. I assure you, Lady Wellington was in her full senses at the time the will was drawn, and in anticipation of just such an accusation, I hold a statement signed by her physician of many years, to attest to her mental state."

Hardwick shouted, "I don't give a…" At this point, both Garth and Samuel stood, and Hardwick stopped in mid speech.

Garth drawled slowly, "Sir, I realize this is a difficult moment for you, but I would ask you to consider your speech in front of the ladies."

Hardwick was not unaware both Garth and Samuel were strapping men, but his anger had chased any caution from his mind.

He turned to Mr. Finch and yelled, "Well, if I am not the full beneficiary, then who the hell is?" Every head in the room turned to Mr. Finch. He picked up a large, sealed, cream-colored envelope and turned to Mae.

"Miss Mae Hinton is the full beneficiary of the Wellington estate, which is to be held in trust by her father, Garth Hinton, until she reaches her majority at the age of twenty-one years. If she should succumb to death prior to reaching the age of twenty-one, the estate would then go to you, Mr. Hardwick."

Several things happened at once. Both Mr. Bennett and Mrs. Patrick broke out in satisfied grins.

Mae half rose from her chair, then sank back down, as if she felt faint.

The only thing in the room Garth was aware of was the look of complete hatred on Hardwick's face. Garth knew in his heart this was a dangerous man. A man who would not hesitate to cause harm to anyone who stood between him and the money he had anticipated.

Hardwick made eye contact with Garth and said with a hiss, "This is not over."

Garth eyed the man for a several seconds and then replied, "For the sake of your general health, sir, I sincerely hope it is, in fact, over."

As the two men evaluated each other, Mr. Finch spoke. "Mr. Hardwick, I have taken the liberty of having your bags placed out front. You have the use of my coach for your return to town. The bank has been notified of the amount they are to have placed in your account this morning. Garth, if you would be so kind as to escort Mr. Hardwick to the door?"

Everyone in the library could hear Hardwick cursing all the way to the front door.

They all sat in silence until Garth and Samuel returned and took their seats.

Mr. Finch turned to Martha and smiled. "Ma'am, do you think we could have some tea or coffee? We still have several things to discuss, but perhaps this is a good time to pause." As Martha headed to the kitchen, smiling from ear to ear, Mr. Finch turned to Mae.

"Mae, I have here a letter Lady Wellington left for you. I want you to know, regardless of what Mr. Hardwick may have implied, that Lady Wellington was very clear, in her heart and in her mind, as to how she wanted her estate handled."

Mae was pale, and her hand shook a little as she took the large envelope from Mr. Finch. She walked across the large library and curled up in the window seat. For a while she just looked out over the lawns and tried to calm her insides. She took a deep breath and broke the seal on the envelope. There were several pages filled with a distinct penmanship. Mae began to read.

"My dear, if you are reading this, then I am at peace. Please don't be sad. Nor should you feel guilt over decisions I have made on your behalf. You and I have a connection of the heart such as few people would understand.

"When we first met, just for a moment I was shocked and shaken. Seeing my beloved Lavinia before my old eyes was quite a jolt. Once I had pulled myself together, I was able to enjoy you as the person you are, not the one I wanted you to be.

"That day I was greatly impressed with your strength and moral character. I'll never know what my dear Lavinia lacked, causing her to be unable to cope with what happened to her. But I was able to see in you what she might have become, had she been stronger.

"Perhaps it was your love of God and your belief in Him which was your strength. I only came to know the Lord in my latter years, and therefore failed to instill this in Lavinia. Perhaps, if I had been a better mother... Ah, well, I have made my peace with God about my shortcomings. And it is time to look forward, not back.

"As I sit here writing to you, I wish I had more time—time to watch you grow, time to see the development of your dream, time to see all the young women who will thrive because you and your faith will be strong enough to help them. Oh, Mae, you have such a rewarding life ahead of you!

"But, now, allow me for one moment to presume to step into the role of mother. While you will be filled with a deep sense of achievement through your efforts to help others, there will be another side of you, a side that will feel empty if you don't make the time to be a woman. Be careful in your choice of a life companion. Choose a man whose touch takes your breath away, one who makes you laugh, but most importantly, one who shares your beliefs. Your life will be most rewarding if you and your husband share your faith.

"Now, dear, you are young, and so you must make the most of older, more experienced minds for a while. Your father will always have your best interests at heart. You would also be wise to make use of Arthur Bennett, as he knows my businesses inside and out. Martha Patrick is a woman full of love and wisdom, and this house has been her home for many years. I think she would be more than happy to aid you in your endeavors to create a warm, loving atmosphere for your girls.

"Well, this is all the wisdom I have to impart, dear. If, over the next few years, you give me a passing thought, and smile with love or gratitude, then my life here on earth will have been of use. I leave you with much love and admiration, yours most sincerely, Elizabeth Wellington."

Mae placed the pages gently on the window seat. When she raised her head, she realized every eye in the room was on her. She colored faintly, wiped tears from her face, then stood and walked straight into her papa's arms.

"Well, baby girl, you've had quite an eventful mornin'." Garth smiled at the understatement.

Mr. Finch chuckled. "That's certainly one way to put it."

Mae was no sooner seated at the table than Mrs. Patrick placed a cup of tea and a small cake in front of her. She crooned, "Dearie, you look a little weak. I think I remember you take your tea with lemon and honey, no milk, right? Now, you nibble on the little cake Cook sent you, and you'll feel much better in a few."

"Martha, you are a dear. Please tell the cook thank you for me."

Mr. Finch took control of the meeting again. "Now, folks, here is what I propose. I think all of you should take a couple of days to consider all your options. You, Mrs. Patrick and Mr. Bennett, have had your futures secured for you through the generosity of Lady Wellington."

"However, you may not be ready, just yet, to retire to your respective choices. You may want to consider whether or not you would be willing to remain in your positions to assist Mr. Hinton and Mae. All of the employees are also receiving gifts from the dear lady. The cook will get one hundred thousand and each of the remaining staff members will be given fifty thousand.

"Garth, you and Mae will need a few days to absorb the shock of all this, and to consider how you want to proceed. In the meantime, Mrs. Patrick will be preparing rooms for all of you, which if I know her will be ready by this evening. Meanwhile, you are welcome to stay with Mrs. Finch and myself for as long as needed. I suggest we meet back here Wednesday morning and come to some decisions. Mrs. Patrick, if you would be so kind, ask the livery boy to drive round the Wellington car, and we will turn it over to Garth at this time. I believe you and Mr. Bennett can keep the estate going through the day-to-day workings until Wednesday. Now," he said with a smile, "how does that sound to everyone?"

Chapter Seventeen

It was after eight in the evening, and Garth hoped young Patrick was in bed already, because he and Eleanor had much to discuss. He parked the Wellington motorcar in front of the cottage and chuckled to himself as he got out. At some point he would stop referring to things as the Wellington this or that. It would take a while to adjust to all this. He knocked softly on the door and smiled when Eleanor immediately opened it. He didn't think he would ever get used to this feeling in his chest as he gazed at this woman. A man his age should not be feeling like a wet-behind-the-ears schoolboy.

He stepped inside, took Eleanor in his arms, and kissed her long and hard. When he lifted his mouth from hers, he found her eyes twinkling up at him with a smile. "My, my, it is nice to know you missed me."

"You have no idea, woman." He laughed. "Now, could I please have a cup of your wonderful coffee to clear my head, 'cause we have much to talk about?"

When Garth finished his account of the morning's meeting, Eleanor just sat there, looking at him. Her face showed no emotion, and Garth was unsure what she was thinking.

"So, how does this affect our plans?" she asked hesitantly.

"Truth be told, it has no effect at all. It just means instead of trying to run a new business of my own, I will become the overseer of Mae's inheritance. This is the first of November, so we have almost two months before we get married. This cottage is adequate for our needs. Being here in town would keep you closer to your work, but if you would prefer, we can live at the manor. Patrick would have the run of the farm, but then you would have to travel to and from town for your work. The only important matter for me is that you and I will soon be together every night, no matter where we call home." Garth took her hand and waited.

Eleanor took a long time to consider. Then she smiled at Garth. "Well, if Cyrus and Samuel are going to be at the manor, then I know where Patrick will want to be. Will there be much of an added expense, for the burden another family would put on Mae's servants?" she asked hesitantly.

Garth laughed aloud. "I know what you mean. I've never been in the position of not having to worry about how much something would cost. I did have a long afternoon meeting with Mr. Finch, and while he is not privy to every one of the business ventures the Wellington estate is involved in, he did assure me it could support a fair salary for myself, as Mae's overseer. So whatever expense is incurred by our presence, I will be able to cover it. I have another even more important reason for wanting all the people I love close to me. Langford Hardwick was not a happy man. He fully believed he was going to inherit all of Lady Wellington's estate. He as much as threatened to make trouble, and I didn't care for the way he looked at Mae, as if he actually knew her."

****

Mae sat in bed, her arms wrapped round her knees,

staring up at the night sky. Good heavens, this was the first time today her mind had slowed down enough for her to make sense of anything. Who would have believed this turn of events? As her breathing slowed and she could feel herself calming, she lowered her forehead to her knees and began to pray. "Dear Lord, help me to always remember You are my strength and through You I can do all things. Lord, help me keep my feet on the ground. Don't allow me to get caught up in the idea of wealth, but completely in the idea of sharing what You have given me with others less fortunate than I. And thank you, Lord, for my wonderful family, who will stand by me and help me to achieve my dreams through You. In Jesus' name I pray, Amen."

As Mae slipped lower in the bed, the excitement of the day eased from her body, and she fell into a deep and peaceful sleep.

****

Samuel was restless. He hadn't been able to sleep. So here he was, sitting on the back porch of the Finches' home, using the full-moon light to work on a small piece of ivory. He had not been able to put Langford Hardwick out of his mind. There was something about the man that worried him, something about the way he looked at Mae, as if he knew something the rest of them didn't.

Well, Mr. Hardwick might have reason to be upset over losing so much money, but he had no grounds to be threatening Mae. If he knew what was good for him, he would take his money, leave town, and start a life somewhere else, because it didn't sit well with Samuel when someone threatened his family.

****

Across town, in his rented room, Langford Hardwick was halfway through an imported bottle of Walker's Old Highland, a truly fine whiskey. He had gone straight to the bank and determined he had, in fact, been credited with two million dollars.

Then he'd stopped at the first attorney's office he could find. He spilled his story, punctuated with profanity and hate. The attorney listened and then assured him that if all the criteria he named had, in truth, been met, the will was legal and binding. Hardwick had stormed out of the office, still cursing.

As he nursed the glass of imported whiskey, he dreamed of all the painful things he would like to do to the little whore who had his money. He laughed drunkenly. He, of all people, could profess she was not a whore, but all he could think about was what he would have to do to get his money, and how to do it so it could never be traced to him.

****

Mae was amazed at how different the drive to the manor looked today. She was seeing it all through different eyes. It was no longer just a beautiful drive, with fallen leaves scattered along the roadside and fall wildflowers dotting the fields. It was the road to her home.

Papa was going back to Trenton tomorrow to start shutting things down there. He was leaving Samuel with her at the manor. Today they would have the first of many meetings with Mr. Bennett and Mrs. Patrick. They would begin to forge Mae's dream.

At the suggestion of Mr. Finch, she had spent the past couple of days creating an outline for her plans. She'd never expected to be moving so quickly and had not been prepared. That was going to change. She was going to start putting things together. She had almost filled a notebook with ideas already.

Samuel rode along, deep in his own thoughts, none of which had to do with Mae's plans. They all had to do with the conversation he'd had with his pa. He'd still been on the back porch when Pa came in from visiting with Eleanor. The two of them talked for over an hour. Pa explained he'd been considering the sale of the mill for some time. He believed the manor would be a perfect place for Cyrus to learn veterinarian skills. Being closer to the growth of the city would help Samuel's sales. And then they spoke about the most critical business: the business of keeping Mae safe.

It was clear the part of the will about Mae meeting her death before she reached the age of twenty-one placed her in grave danger, but of course that would never occur to Mae. She would never believe someone would hurt her for money. So Samuel would be living at the manor with Mae. When he'd packed his bag this morning, he had included a loaded Colt .45, on loan from Mr. Finch, until Pa could get back with Samuel's own guns.

Garth's mind was going over a list of "things to do" as he drove. First, there was the meeting today with Arthur Bennett and Mrs. Patrick. The two of them had been given sufficient time to decide whether to stay or go. Frankly, Garth was hoping they would stay. They were both hard workers, had tremendous knowledge of the manor and its workings, and would be hard to replace.

The next item on Garth's mental list was the most important. There were to be no new hires until he was back up here to stay. It would make it too difficult to keep Mae safe if they started adding unknown persons to the mix.

He would have this conversation with Mr. Bennett prior to leaving this evening. He and Samuel had discussed it at great length. They were in agreement: Hardwick was not to be trusted. Samuel had told Garth he had a bad feeling about Hardwick.

Ever since Ruth had passed away, Samuel had been given to "feelings." The family had learned to respect them and not question Samuel. In fact, the day of Mae's event, he had come to Garth and said they should go home early. Garth had stopped what he was doing, looked at the boy for a long moment, and finally agreed. Samuel had never put a name to it, but Garth often wondered if it was Ruth's spirit, keeping watch over them all through Samuel.

Mrs. Patrick met them at the door. She turned to Garth. "Sir, Mr. Bennett is in the library. We'll join you as soon as I show these two young ones where their rooms are."

At the top of the stairs, she directed Samuel to a room on the left of the hallway and pointed Mae to the one directly across the hall.

Mae gave a small gasp as she entered the room. It was the loveliest bedroom she had ever been in. First, it was huge. A small sitting room opened off to the left, with a private bath area to the right. There was a large, overstuffed armchair covered in dark rose-colored brocade, with matching cushions lining the window seat. The tall windows opened inward and had been fitted with screens, allowing fresh air to waft through the room without giving entrance to insects. The large, four-poster bed was white, with a coverlet matching the chair and seat cushions. There were vases filled with dark pink roses atop small, white tables around the room. The room reminded her of her mother's roses.

Mae turned to Mrs. Patrick and smiled. "Thank you. This room is perfect, and I'll be very happy here."

"I'm so glad you like it, dear. Lady Wellington had it redesigned right after she first met you, and now I understand why."

Mae had to fight to hold back the tears. She just smiled a watery smile and nodded.

Samuel stepped in the doorway and said, "We ought to get down to the library. Pa has a lot to cover today before he leaves for home."

****

Hardwick had a headache to top all headaches. He'd had good reason to celebrate, though, so it was worth it. He had resolved his problem.

After weeks of hanging out in some scurrilous places, he had found the man for the job. He'd been sitting in the back room of Bailey's Pub when he recognized a familiar face. He waved the man over to his table.

"Well, well, if it ain't the Dandy," the man growled. "Ain't seen you in a 'coon's age."

Hardwick allowed a cold smile to cross his face. "Yes, Frank, isn't it? That's right, your traveling companions called you Frank. It's been what, a couple of years?"

Frank Young didn't like the fact the Dandy knew his name, but it couldn't be helped. Those idiots he'd been running with two years ago didn't know how to keep their mouths shut. He turned a chair around, straddled it, and smiled back at Hardwick.

"So, Dandy, whatcha' been up to? Your old bird finally kick off and leave you flush?"

Hardwick just looked at Frank. He must not have been quite as drunk as he had appeared during their three days of traveling together. "Funny you should mention that. As a matter of fact, she did. However, there was an unforeseen complication."

Frank Young laughed. "Yeah, she wasn't as flush as you figured, huh?"

"No. A friend of yours has come forward to claim a very large part of my money."

Young sat straighter. "What the hell you talkin' about, Dandy? I ain't got any friends."

Hardwick watched Frank's eyes. The man was wary. He might be stupid, but he was wily. He was no doubt already trying to figure out what this conversation might yield him. Hardwick took a long draw from the tankard he was clutching. He set the tankard down and smiled at Young.

"You do remember the young thing we met somewhere near Trenton?" He waited, as Young searched his memory. He could tell the moment remembrance came to the man.

"You mean the little she-cat that almost ruined my manhood?" he growled.

Hardwick nodded. "Yes, the one you laid out with a right hook."

Frank Young raised one eyebrow. "Well, seein' as how we was never properly introduced, I ain't so sure she would consider me a friend, but what the hell does she have to do with your money?"

"Well, it seems she was a friend of the old bird, and

she is now in possession of my money."

Frank looked at him a long moment, then burst out laughing. Hardwick lowered his face until Frank stopped laughing. He didn't want to be remembered as being seen with this man, because already a plan was developing in his mind.

"Well, well." Young chuckled. "It looks like you paid for that little piece after all."

Hardwick raised his face to Young and said, "How would you like to tangle with the little cat again? She has grown more beautiful over the years and thinks she is on top of the world now. It so happens, the old bird did leave me a goodly amount of money, but of course I would like to have all of it. Now, if a man was willing to take care of a certain problem for me, I would be willing to share my newfound wealth, generously, of course."

Frank Young didn't trust the Dandy any farther than he could throw him, but it would be nice to be flush for a while. "So you'd like this little she-cat to disappear?" Young smiled a wicked smile.

Hardwick could have been making a pact with the devil himself, but he could see no other alternative. After all, Young had just strolled in here after all this time as if he were the pre-ordained answer to the problem. "Yes," he answered, "I think we could come to some sort of arrangement."

Hardwick explained how the "deal" would have to go down. He would make a big show of leaving town. Then, after a couple of days, Young would take care of the problem. They would meet in Pensacola for the payment of services. Then they would part forever.

After a few more beers, Hardwick had given him

all the details—where the girl worked, what time the store opened, where all her friends were located, and how she traveled. Of course, it had been necessary to give Young two thousand dollars up front, with the promise of eighteen more after the fact.

Now all Hardwick had to do was rid himself of this headache and make a big show of leaving town. Then wait.

Two hours later, Hardwick stood at the front desk of his hotel. "Yes, I will be out of town for a couple of weeks, leaving on the train this afternoon. I will, however, want you to hold my room for me. I'll be back in a couple of weeks and will want the same room."

"Yes, sir, Mr. Hardwick. We will be happy to hold the room for you. If you will notify us prior to your return, we will have it aired and cleaned for you. And may you have a good trip. I'll have one of the boys place your bags in a taxi for you." The desk clerk smiled as he pocketed the large tip.

Chapter Eighteen

Eleanor dropped her keys. She was juggling her reticule, two new magazines, and a bag of books for Mae. As she stooped to retrieve her keys, she saw a man's reflection in the window. She stood there a moment. *Yes, that is the same man I saw yesterday.* She glanced down to fit the key in the lock, and when she looked up again, the man was gone. She would be so busy today that she would forget she'd ever seen him.

Mae's plate was full to running over. She still had to put the layout for the village on paper. She needed to have this ready for Mr. Bennett by Friday. Papa, Cyrus, and Hansu would be here next week. She also still needed to study for her exams. Oh, yes, she remembered, Eleanor would be getting her books for review today. She had to remind herself: one thing at a time; and with that in mind, Mae hurried to the kitchen.

Mrs. Patrick was speaking with the housemaids about new linens when Mae rushed through the door. "What can I do for you, dear?" The housekeeper smiled. "Did you need a cup of tea?"

"Oh, tea would be nice, but I was wondering if I could borrow one of these dear ladies to run an errand for me? I have so much to get done, and I don't have time to run into town. I need the books Eleanor was getting for me today. I was hoping one of the housemaids might not mind taking the car into town to fetch some things for me." The three young ladies in question all smiled.

Mrs. Patrick looked at them and said, "Well, I'm not sending all three of you off to town, so quit your grinnin'. You, Margaret, you can pick up whatever Miss Mae needs. You can get those new linens we were speaking of at the same time. While you're at it, you can get with Cook to see if we need anything from the market."

Margaret was a tall, dark Irish woman, with the pale skin and blue eyes that accompanied the claim. She had trained in London for a few years and had lost most of her Irish brogue. She smiled now. "Thank you, miss. I would love a ride to town. You can be sure I'll take care of whatever errands you need handled."

Margaret enjoyed the ride to town. It was a mild fall day with bright sunshine, making her glad she had put up her hair and worn her best bonnet.

She'd been to Taylor's and picked up Miss Mae's books. The driver had waited patiently outside Carters Dry Goods Store while she picked up new linens, and now they were headed to the open market on the edge of town. She had a list of things Cook had requested. As she stepped out of the motorcar, Margaret smiled at Henry, the driver. "I'll be a while, Henry, so if you'd like a nap, you might park the car under that old oak."

Henry smiled his thanks, and Margaret took off with her baskets.

Some time later, Margaret stood in the late afternoon sun and looked for the motorcar. She could just see the rear bumper sticking out from behind the huge old oak. She smiled to herself; Henry must have really needed that nap. As Margaret approached the car with her assortment of baskets, she realized the door was standing open, and she could not see Henry. She placed her baskets on the back seat through the open door and stepped to the front of the motorcar—and gasped as her eyes found Henry, sprawled face down on the ground.

She ran and knelt beside the old man. He had a large wound, surrounded with dried blood, on the back of his head. Margaret rolled Henry onto his back and tapped his face. "Henry, can you hear me? Please, Henry, wake up!"

Henry moaned, and his eyelids fluttered. He could hear the fear in Margaret's voice but couldn't quite manage to open his eyes or speak.

Margaret turned to run for help and found herself face to face with a strange man.

Before she could register his rough appearance, he had smashed his fist into her face. He caught her as she collapsed and dragged her away.

Henry was trying so hard to understand what was happening. Just as he was dropping back into a deep, dark hole, a man's voice floated over him. He would later swear the man was talking to a cat.

****

It was late, and Mrs. Patrick didn't want to bother Miss Mae or Samuel, but she was worried. Margaret and Henry were very late. Margaret was not a silly goose. She could be depended on to behave correctly, so it was very unusual for her to be so late. Mrs. Patrick looked out the wide kitchen window one last time and was rewarded with the sight of a motorcar coming down the lane. With a sigh of relief, she stepped out the side door of the kitchen to meet them.

Samuel was just coming in from the barn. He'd been working all day with the two men who lived near the manor. The horses had been moved to a covered paddock, and the barn was being refitted as his work place. They'd made pretty good progress. He was thinking he had better hurry and get cleaned up before supper or Mrs. Patrick would have his hide. He was surprised to see two motorcars pulling into the curved drive in front of the manor. He watched as Mrs. Patrick came out to the drive, and thought maybe she needed help carrying some things inside.

He caught up with her just as the doors to the vehicles opened. Henry was being helped out of the estate car by what appeared to be a deputy. Another constable was climbing out of the second vehicle, which had "Sheriff" in large letters on the side.

"Oh dear, Henry, what's happened? Where's Margaret?" Mrs. Patrick cried, as she looked around for the young woman.

"Ma'am, are you in charge here?" one of the young men asked.

Samuel stepped forward. "My sister is the owner, sir. My name is Samuel Hinton. Can you tell us what has happened?"

"Be glad to, sir, but first we need to take care of this gentleman. He refused to see a doctor in town and said he had to get back to report to the young miss. I'm guessing he meant your sister."

Samuel directed them all through the door and into the kitchen, where they got Henry into a chair. The poor man was as white as one of Mrs. Patrick's sheets hanging on the line.

Shaken to the core, she turned to the kitchen maids

and said, "Run fetch Mr. Bennett, and be quick, child, and you, Alice, run up and get Miss Mae."

As the maids ran to get help, Samuel again asked the question, "Where is Margaret? Can you tell us what happened?"

The young deputy replied, "The owners of the market were closing for the day when they saw Henry's car parked under a tree. They walked over to investigate and found Henry on the ground. All he remembers is getting out of the vehicle to stretch his legs. Someone must have hit him from behind. He says he didn't see the girl again after dropping her off in front of the market. Her baskets of vegetables are on the back seat. The vendors remember her leaving, but she was nowhere near the car when they found Henry. We are searching the woods for her now."

Mr. Bennett and Mae arrived just as the deputy finished speaking. Samuel turned to Mae and said, "Looks like Henry needs taking care of right now. If you ladies can handle this, then we're going to step outside with the deputy."

He motioned toward the door, and Mr. Bennett and the deputy followed him out. Once outside, he repeated for Mr. Bennett everything the deputy had said.

Mr. Bennett turned to the deputy. "Sir, how long do you think it will be before we hear something about Margaret?"

The young man replied, "My name is Deputy Wilkes, sir. I didn't want to alarm the ladies, but it does not look good. The market owners say the woman had been gone for about an hour before they found Henry. Then it took them a while to get word to us. All in all, it was about a three-hour delay. We found several feet of drag marks moving away from the vehicle and heading toward the woods. Further into the woods, we found where a horse had been tied, and that's when we called out the dogs. They will send word to the house as soon as they find the...young lady."

Both Samuel and Mr. Bennett suspected the deputy had been about to say "the body."

While the men were outside, Mae was cleaning Henry's wound. The man had an egg-sized lump that had split and was going to need a couple of stitches. As Mae prepared the silk thread she would use, she kept talking to Henry, afraid he might pass out again.

"Henry, is there anything you can remember? Sometimes we don't realize what we know until we talk it out. While I'm working, you just tell me what you know." Mae had learned from her own horrible event that the more you talked about it, the more you could remember; sometimes more than you wanted.

Henry was telling them, once again, he couldn't remember anything. Mae was on the third stitch when Henry's voice got through to her. Her hands shook. She cut the silk thread, then said, "What did you say, Henry?"

Henry said, "I know it sounds crazy. One minute I thought I heard Margaret's voice, and then the next minute I seemed to hear a man say, "Hello, little she-cat. Long time no see."

Mae was clutching the back of a dining room chair when Samuel walked in.

"Mae, are you okay?"

Mae raised her eyes to Samuel, and he froze. Her eyes were wide with fear, a fear he'd hoped never to see in them again. Even as Samuel crossed the room to her,

Mae reached inside herself and found her strength.

"Well, this is my first real nursing chore, and I guess I wasn't as prepared as I thought I would be." She gave Samuel a weak smile as she wiped her hands on a kitchen towel.

She turned to Mrs. Patrick. "Maybe I could use a sip of brandy after all." Mae took the little glass and drained the golden liquid. She coughed, sputtered, and turned red in the face. Mrs. Patrick and the maids all laughed and relaxed a little.

"Samuel, can you help Henry to his quarters? Mrs. Patrick, if you clean all this up, I'll just go to my room and wash up a little and get to bed. This has been a little more excitement than I'm used to." Mae gave them all a watery smile and headed for the front of the house.

Chapter Nineteen

Margaret couldn't breath. There was something heavy on her chest. She tried to push it off. Her senses were awakening from the sleep she'd been in. She could smell blood, and sweat from an unclean body. Even as she pushed against the weight, she recognized it as a man. Her eyes flew open, and she could see her attacker, and he was raping her.

Margaret was not a young virgin. She knew immediately what was happening, and that she was in terrible danger. Whether she fought or not, this man was probably going to kill her.

She did not want her last moments on this earth to be spent as a helpless victim. She knew when she left this life she would be in the presence of God, and this knowledge gave her strength, as well as peace. Even as she began to scratch and claw his face, she could envision the home she would be going to.

The man looked down at her, brushing her hands away from his already bleeding face, and he was surprised. She was almost smiling, and just before he knocked her out again he thought she had the face of an angel.

****

Frank Young rolled himself a cigarette, lit up, and looked through the open door of the train car. He had just caught the last westbound freight train for the night.

It had been close, and he'd been a little worried. The horse he'd stolen a couple of days ago was not the fastest thing on four legs, that was for damn sure, but he'd made it. He'd had a little fun, made some good money, and all in all, it was a good day's work.

The little she-cat had put up a good fight, just like he'd expected. It was a shame he couldn't have brought her along for the ride, but she screamed like a banshee. It would have been too much trouble trying to keep her quiet.

He lifted his hand to his left ear and it came away bloody. Yep, she had put up a good fight. She had still been unconscious when he mounted her, but boy-howdy, when she woke up it was like riding a wild bronco. He remembered looking down on her face and thinking how innocent and pure it had looked. Then he had knocked her out again and finished the ride. Afterwards he had cut her throat.

He had a good five hours till the train arrived in Pensacola. He knew a place, on the wrong side of the tracks, where a man could do business and no one asked your name. He'd send a message to Hardwick from there.

****

Samuel made sure everyone was tucked in for the night, and then he made the rounds of the house. He checked the windows and doors on the first floor and then let himself out the kitchen door. He walked around the perimeter of the big garage and could see a light on in Mr. Bennett's apartment. The two men who'd been helping him refit the barn had a small cottage on the other side of the lake. They'd been headed for home before the deputies had shown up. They were a couple

143

of steady older men and could take care of themselves, so he mentally took them off the list of people he had to look after.

Mr. Henry had needed a few stitches. Samuel had been real proud of Mae, as she had stepped right in as lady of the house and fixed him up. She'd run the silk thread over the beeswax to help it slide. She made the neatest little stitches you'd ever see. Doc Walters would have been proud of her, too.

She had not fooled Samuel, though. Something had happened while he was outside with the deputy and Mr. Bennett. Samuel knew his sister better than anyone. She'd worn the same haunted look the night of the event. He would question Henry again tomorrow, after the old man had some rest. He didn't want to be pushy, but Henry must have said something to scare Mae so.

Samuel sat down on the edge of a stone planter at the northeast corner of the library, just out of the moonlight, and waited. He had no way of knowing if the deputies would find poor Margaret tonight or not, but he didn't want them banging on the door and wakin' the women, if they did.

Mrs. Patrick had given all the women a little toddy before she sent them to bed. Samuel had thanked her but refused it. It wouldn't be the first time he'd stayed up all night, watchin' over Mae.

He could remember many nights of watching her toss and moan in her sleep. There had been nights when he would have sworn he heard his mother's voice singing softly and Mae would stop tossing and slip into a deep sleep.

Samuel didn't think they had anything to worry about. Whoever had taken Margaret would not be foolish enough to come around here. He would cut a trail to Jacksonville or Pensacola. It sure was strange, though. Mr. Bennett said there had never been a problem like this before, to his recollection. Samuel wasn't one for coincidences.

He'd just laid the pistol down on the planter's edge when a light in the distance caught his attention. It was a vehicle. Samuel stood, still in the shadows, and waited as it stopped in the drive. One of the deputies stepped out and turned toward the front door.

Samuel stepped out of the shadow and spoke. "Don't knock on the door, please."

The deputy almost dropped his gun as he tried to get it out of the holster. "Oh, it's you! You shouldn't sneak up on a person. I could have shot you!"

"I'm sorry, sir. I just didn't want you to wake the women. They were a little upset earlier," Samuel apologized.

"Well, they're not going to feel any better when they hear the news. We found the woman. She was a good mile into the woods. It was not pretty." Deputy Wilkes' voice shook with the anger he was trying to hold in check. This was his first murder of a woman. The brutality of it had shocked him. He shook his head. "What kind of a man can do something like this?" he said, to no one in particular.

Samuel did not respond. He understood all too well just how depraved some men could be.

Mae stood at the window of her darkened room and looked down at Samuel as he spoke with the young deputy. There would be little sleep for her tonight. She was caught up in a revolving circle of bad memories. She could feel the cold steel of the little beauty in her hand. It had been a while since she had needed reassurance, but she was pretty sure she would be sleeping with Doc Walters' gift for some time to come.

****

Hardwick was just coming in from a late game at a local establishment when the desk clerk flagged him down.

"Sir…" The young man handed him a sealed envelope. "This was delivered an hour ago."

Hardwick tossed the young man a coin, then sat on one of the plush sofas while he read the enclosed note. When finished, he turned back toward the front door.

The liveried bellman jumped to his feet. "Can I get you a taxi, sir?"

"No, thank you. I think I'll just walk off a last bit of whiskey before I retire." He didn't need a taxi driver remembering where he took a certain gentleman on this night. His step was light, the step of a very happy man. The deed was done. That damn Finch would be sending him a message in a few days telling him to come and claim what should have been his to begin with.

The slight weight of the derringer in his vest pocket made him feel invincible. The one thing left to do was erase the last possible link between himself and the little cat. He'd been walking almost an hour when he reached his destination. It was a rundown flophouse near the railway.

There was an exterior stairwell, allowing the men who used the place on an hourly basis to come and go without notice. The women paid a weekly rent for the rooms. On a good night, they could pay for the whole week and pocket what was left over. Hardwick opened the door at the top of the stairwell and stepped into a dimly lit, musty-smelling hallway.

Just as he reached number four, the door to number three opened. A small blonde girl, no more than sixteen, draped herself against the doorframe. "Well, it's nice to see a real gent for a change."

The girl must be new to the trade, as she was still reasonably attractive. He was here on business, so he ignored the girl. He knocked once, on number four, then entered and closed the door behind him, in one smooth motion.

The girl wondered what business the gent had with the bastard in room four. She had seen the man in four come in around eleven. He'd been pretty drunk. She'd managed to get into her room and close the door before he spotted her. She was good with faces, and she remembered this one with bitterness. He'd come in a couple of years ago.

He'd been rough, not too clean, and had rushed business before she got her money. Then when she'd asked for her money, he'd knocked her across the room, threw something at her, and stalked out, saying, "The little she-cat I got that from won't be needin' it any more."

The next morning she'd picked the item up from behind a chair. It was a small, intricately carved ivory box, strung on a broken length of rawhide. It must have been a month or so later, as she was stroking the box hanging from her neck, that it popped open. She was amazed and delighted, and then saddened. Inside the small hidden space she found three curls of fine hair. One wrapped in pink ribbon and two wrapped in blue. Then she'd remembered the man's words as he'd thrown the box at her.

Some poor mother had lost her babies' keepsakes, and probably her life. The girl wondered if her mama had cut one of her baby curls to keep. She'd like to think so.

'Course, her mama had died when she was four, and her pa had sold her for twenty-five dollars when she was twelve. There'd not been many keepsakes in her young life.

Hardwick took in the whole room with a quick glance. The one window was open, and the faded curtains moved softly with the night breeze. Frank Young was sitting to the left of the window, finishing off a glass of cheap whiskey. He had some scratches on his face and his shirt was torn, but he was wearing an ear-to-ear grin. The man started to stand, swayed, and dropped back into the chair. Hardwick observed the empty bottle on the nightstand and smiled. Young was very drunk. Good, he thought, this will be easier than I expected.

"Did you take care of the cat?" he asked as he moved to the window.

"Yep, and she was a better fighter this time," Young snarled. "But she won't scratch anymore."

Hardwick placed his left hand on the windowsill, leaned out, and took in a deep draw of cool night air. He slowly removed the derringer from his vest pocket with his right hand. He turned, placed the barrel of the gun against Young's temple, and pulled the trigger before the man even registered what was happening.

The sound of the shot was not overly loud, but the whore in room three had surely heard it; that would merit a visit. Hardwick took one last look around the room. Young had fallen sideways against a dresser.

He'd died before his face could even register surprise.

Hardwick returned the gun to his vest, stepped out into the hallway, and closed the door behind him. A very large man, with the uneven features of a street fighter, was approaching from the outside door.

As Hardwick was reaching for the doorknob of number three, it flew open and the blonde stuck her head out.

"There you are! You almost missed your appointment," the blonde cried, as she grabbed the hand of the big man and pulled him into the room. Her round blue eyes met Hardwick's for one long second as she was closing the door. He measured her fear by her trembling hand.

He stood still for a couple of heartbeats and then headed for the stairwell. It would be too risky to try to take out both of them. He needed to put some distance between himself and the late Frank Young.

He checked his watch as he climbed the steps to the San Carlo Hotel. It was four fifteen in the morning. He would take a long bath, sleep until noon, and wake up a very rich man.

****

Garth stepped out on the porch and took a long look around. It was early morning, and there was just a hint of cool air, like winter was just over a hill somewhere, unseen but close. He'd lived in this house for twenty-two years. It had started as a two-room cabin and then grew to accommodate a large family. He'd added windows with screens in the kitchen for better ventilation. There was a washhouse with a hand pump. He should feel a little sad at leaving, but there was so much life ahead of him he could not, in truth, regret it.

He and Cyrus, with the help of Mrs. Peters, had packed up all the furniture and household items. Mae had wanted it all for her "home." She believed all those homey things would make the women feel more comfortable.

As he gazed at a late blooming rose, he whispered, "Ruth, honey, this will always be our place, but I'm about to move on and build a new place in life, one I'll be better equipped to handle because you made me a better man. If there is one thing I've learned from our time together, it is we should never take life or love for granted. I'll always be grateful for your love and wisdom." The door opened, and he turned to see Cyrus standing in the doorway.

Cyrus looked around, then looked into Garth's eyes and said, "Were you talking to Mama?"

Garth's heart did a little skip, and he was not sure what to say.

Cyrus saved him the trouble. "I talk to her, too. Sometimes I'll have a question about something I know she'd be able to help me with, if she was just here. Then I'll sleep on it, and the next day whatever it was will come to me and I'll know she answered me."

Garth's chest swelled with love for this, his youngest son, who still kept his mama in his heart. He put an arm around Cyrus's shoulder. "Yes," he said, "I was talking to Mama. I was telling her we were only able to move on because she had made us all so strong."

Cyrus smiled at Pa. "She sure was a fighter. You remember the time a panther got into the barn and the cow had just dropped a calf?"

Garth said, "I can laugh now, but the sight of your mama holding that panther at bay with nothing but a pitchfork near did me in! And then, of all things, when I started to shoot it…"

Cyrus broke in laughing. "I know. She started yelling, 'Don't you dare shoot such a beautiful creature.' Then she just stared at it and said, 'I've saved your hide today, but if you ever come after my babies again, I'll just let him have at you.' And then the panther just strolled out of the barn like he knew she meant it."

They laughed together at what was a beautiful memory. Garth said, "Speaking of the barn, have you taken everything from it you want?"

Cyrus nodded. "Yes, sir, I loaded the last of my things in the truck last night. The chickens have all been watered and fed in their crates, and I threw a tarp over them so they won't panic on the drive up. I'll be riding in the train car with the cattle and horses. The last of them were put in Mr. Hiram's holding pens yesterday evening. Hansu is with them now. He didn't want 'em to be nervous, said it could cause 'em to be too high-strung and make 'em sick."

Garth smiled. "That little man has been a Godsend to us. I don't think there is anything he doesn't know a little bit about."

"That's for sure," Cyrus agreed, "and when we get settled in, he's going to teach me about Chinese herbs I can use as medicines for the animals. We're going to start an herb garden first thing, come spring."

"Well, then, I guess the one thing left to do is pick up Mrs. Peters and her things, and get this show on the road."

Mae had sent along a letter to Mrs. Peters, asking her to please move to Tallahassee with the family. The letter said she would need all the help she could get, and that she hadn't had a well-made pie since she left home.

Garth was aware it was an exaggeration, but it had pushed Mrs. Peters' decision-making right over the fence she'd been straddling. If Mae needed her, then she was in for the move.

Garth had finalized the sale of the sawmill to Frank Bell last week. Bell's oldest boy, Matthew, and his brood were going to move into the house next week. Bell had sent Matthew out to spend some time with Hansu as soon as the deal was finalized. Hansu had walked the man through the workings of the mill and finally declared him competent, which was quite a compliment, coming from Hansu. The care of his engine was serious business. If he said Matthew was up to the task...well, then, the boy would be okay.

There had been the business of the cemetery. When Ruth passed away, Garth had picked a beautiful area, about a quarter mile from the house, to lay her to rest. Yesterday he had arranged for three surrounding acres to be cleared, fenced, and deeded to the church to be used as a cemetery. This assured her plot would be given regular care.

Garth took one last, long look around. This place had been his life for many years, but there was a new life waiting for him. A beautiful woman, a great new son, and a chance to help Mae fulfill her dreams awaited him. He asked the Lord to make him worthy of the challenge, to give him wisdom, and to bless his endeavors. Now he was ready to leave.

Chapter Twenty

Samuel figured he might as well catch them all at one time, so he waited until after breakfast to break the bad news. Martha made the sign of the cross and immediately burst into tears. A very pale Mae crossed the breakfast room to console her. Mr. Bennett sat slowly, looking wide-eyed with shock.

"Well," he said, "we've never lost one of our own before. Oh, certainly we've had folks leave for one reason or another, but never anything like this in all the years we've been here."

With one arm around Martha, Mae turned to Mr. Bennett. "Sir, do we know if Margaret had family near?"

"I would have to check my records," he replied.

Martha was shaking her head, as she wiped away a stream of tears. "No, miss, she had an elderly aunt in Dublin, who passed on a couple of years ago. The poor girl was all alone except for us." She hiccupped as a new stream of tears came forth.

"Well, then, we will take care of her now," Mae declared, as she handed Martha a fresh handkerchief. "Samuel, since you spoke with the deputy last night, I'll leave it to you and Mr. Bennett to get with the sheriff's office and make arrangements. Mr. Bennett, does the estate have a cemetery other than where Lady and Lord Wellington were laid to rest?"

"As I said before, Margaret is the first employee we've ever lost to…death."

Arthur Bennett had stopped short of saying "murder" and was thankful he had managed to do so. He didn't think poor Martha could have stood hearing it one more time.

"Well, then, we will decide where we would like to have one, and act accordingly. Martha, I need you to pull yourself together and help me, because I've never planned a funeral before." Wisely, Mae understood the "help me" portion of that statement would give Martha the distraction she needed.

While Bennett had been overwhelmed by the horrible news of Margaret's demise, he was fully aware of, and approved of, the way Mae was handling all this. Obviously the girl had some backbone and could make decisions under pressure. These characteristics showed she was much better equipped than he had first suspected. Grudgingly, he considered how capable she was to handle the project she was about to undertake.

"Martha, can you break the news to the other maids, or do you need me to handle that for you?" Mae asked.

With one last sniff and swipe, Martha shook her head. "No, miss, I'll take care of it meself." With a nod, Martha retreated to the kitchen.

When Mae was sure Martha was out of hearing range, she turned to Mr. Bennett and Samuel. "Now, do either of you think we are in any danger here? I mean, obviously this occurred off our property, but do we need to take some kind of security measures?"

Bennett turned to Samuel. He didn't want to betray any of their previous conversations to Mae. He thought the answer should best come from Samuel, or her father. Samuel inclined his head slightly and turned to Mae.

"Well, before Pa left, he said to be sure to wait until he was back before hiring any new workers to start on your project, so we don't have any strangers on or around the property. I'll speak with the Huebner brothers and see if they've seen anyone around. They're probably wondering where I am right now. We had a lot of work to do in the barn today, but I'll get them started and then take the motorcar into town to talk with the deputy."

Arthur Bennett said to Mae, "I'll just step out to my office to get a map of the twenty acres surrounding the manor. Then we can talk about the cemetery locations later."

The two men did not speak until they reached the barn. Samuel leaned against the doorway and stared at his boots.

"Well, young man, you seem to be thinking hard on something," Bennett said.

Samuel raised his head and looked out across the long, tree-lined drive. "Yes, sir, I was just remembering when I saw Miss Margaret getting into the motorcar. How I was thinking that if I didn't know better, seeing her from behind, I would have taken her for Mae."

Samuel met Mr. Bennett's stare. Bennett was not a man given to suggestion, but a very real shudder passed through him. Margaret was tall. Margaret had dark hair. Margaret was dressed for town. *Oh, my Lord, surely not.* Bennett's horrified face reflected his mind as the man worked his way to the same conclusion.

"Well, sir, I'll just speak with the Huebner brothers

before I head on into town and talk with the deputy in charge."

Samuel thought it best to visit Mr. Finch's office before he went to meet with Deputy Wilkes.

Mr. Finch entered the office with a surprised look on his face. "Well, hello, young man. Good to see you. Come on in and have a seat. What brings you into town?"

Samuel said, "Sir, since my pa's not here, I figured it best to come to you and get some advice before I go to the law."

"Whoa, now, what could you need the law for?" The smile left Mr. Finch's face, and he took on his lawyer air. He became even more lawyerlike as Samuel told his story, and he asked questions here and there. Samuel finished relating the details of the past several hours, then sat back in his chair in silence.

After a long while, Mr. Finch spoke. "So, Samuel, you're saying you think this young woman may have been killed because she was mistaken for Mae. You realize, son, there is only one person who would benefit from Mae's death, right?"

"Yes, sir, that's why I'm here. It would save a lot of time when I tell the law what I believe if you were with me to back up what I'm saying."

Mr. Finch closed his eyes and was still for so long Samuel wondered if he'd fallen asleep. Finally Mr. Finch opened his eyes and spoke.

"Before your father left town, he asked me to keep an eye on Mr. Hardwick. Without a lot of detail, I did just that. I have to tell you, Mr. Hardwick was on a train for Pensacola four days ago. That's not to say he couldn't have come back. The police could easily check all that. He made arrangements to stay at the San Carlos Hotel. It's some sort of new, grand, palace type of thing."

"Well, sir, I reckon you're right, but I'd like to ask some questions about how Margaret was killed. I think they'd be a lot more likely to answer those if you were with me. My pa's gonna want to know some things when he gets here."

Mr. Finch knew Garth well enough by now to know this was true, but only Mr. Finch was aware Garth would be here this evening.

"All right, young man, as Mae's attorney, I believe I'm allowed a few questions. Let's go see what we can find out."

****

Mr. Finch approached the uniformed young man behind the front desk. "Sir," he said, "my name is Myron Finch, and I represent Miss Mae Hinton, who is now owner of the Wellington estate. One of Miss Hinton's servants was murdered yesterday, and we need to speak with the officer in charge of this investigation."

The young officer took Mr. Finch's card and directed them to a row of chairs. "Have a seat, sir, and I'll let the detective know you are here."

After a few minutes, a young woman appeared. She was dressed modestly in a black dress and sensible shoes, and her hair was coiled neatly around her head. There was nothing subdued about the smile on her face, or the twinkle in her large, blue eyes.

"Sir, if you gentlemen will follow me, I will take you to the captain's office. My name is Edith Hampton, and I'm the captain's secretary. If you need anything at all, please let me know." Miss Hampton led them down a long hallway and into a large office with "Captain Lance" stenciled on the door.

The captain stood as they entered. He moved around his imposing desk to shake Mr. Finch's hand. "Good morning, sir. I'm Captain Lance, and I'm sorry to make your acquaintance under such circumstances."

Mr. Finch introduced Samuel. "This is Samuel Hinton, Miss Hinton's brother, and he has been in contact with Deputy Wilkes. Deputy Wilkes was very helpful and represented your agency very well, sir, but I believe the answers we seek should come from someone higher."

Samuel and Mr. Finch sat as the captain moved back to his chair. "All right, you ask, and if I am at liberty to share the information in question, then I will."

"Thank you. Now, we understand the young lady was attacked as she left the produce stand out on Millwood Road. We were told none of the items in the motorcar were taken, and her purse and money were found at the scene. We have reason to believe this may not have been a random thing and that perhaps Miss Margaret was mistaken for Miss Mae Hinton."

They had the captain's complete attention now. "And why would someone want to harm Miss Hinton?"

"Well, sir," said Mr. Finch, "I'll need to give you a little history. The late Lady Wellington had no immediate relatives to inherit her very substantial estate. A Mr. Langford Hardwick, the lady's last living relative, would have been the likely heir. She had been supporting him for some time.

"The lady had paid for his education in England and also arranged for him to receive a quarterly stipend for the past five years. The lady met Miss Hinton several months ago and was very much impressed with the young woman. They became very close friends. The lady looked upon Miss Hinton as the daughter she had lost many years ago. When the lady passed away and the will was read, Mr. Hardwick was not a happy man. He was given a large one-time gift, but this did not seem to be acceptable to him. He made some threats, nothing specific. Unfortunately, the lady did make a stipulation. Should Miss Hinton die before reaching her majority, all would revert to Mr. Hardwick."

After a long pause, Captain Lance turned to Samuel and said, "Well, that certainly lends to motive, but how does this lead to the death of your servant, sir?"

Samuel had been watching the captain as Mr. Finch gave him the facts. The man had listened closely. He seemed genuinely concerned, and he had to be smart to have risen to the rank of captain.

"Well, sir, it didn't click with me until this morning. My sister has been using the estate vehicle to run to and from town for her studies, and to meet with our future stepmother. My sister is tall and slim for a woman. She's always well dressed, but not overly so. She has dark hair that is usually up and under a hat. When Miss Margaret was getting into the estate vehicle the other morning, I would have sworn it was Mae."

Captain Lance pondered this for some time before he responded. "Mr. Hardwick has seen your sister, correct? And at some point he would have known he was dealing with the wrong woman."

Mr. Finch spoke up. "We are not making any accusations, sir, only giving information. In fact, prior to Mr. Garth Hinton returning to Trenton to settle his business there, he asked me to keep a close eye on his family and on Mr. Hardwick. I took the liberty of hiring a private detective. My associate informed me Mr. Hardwick left Tallahassee by train four days prior to the murder. Also, Mr. Hardwick left instructions at the desk, saying he would be in Pensacola for a few weeks and staying at the San Carlo Hotel."

Captain Lance nodded. "Well, all those facts will be easy to confirm."

Samuel had to settle something in his mind. "Sir, was Miss Margaret's death violent?"

The captain's face hid any surprise at this question. "And just how is that pertinent to any of the information you have given me, sir?"

"Well," Samuel drawled, "if Mr. Hardwick had hired someone to do his killin' for him, it would explain how the man may have mistaken Margaret for Mae. If we were lookin' at a hired killer, he'd most likely be the type of man who wouldn't flinch at violence. Mr. Hardwick struck me as the type of man who'd kill quick and clean, and not dawdle over the act."

The captain's face showed none of his thoughts. This young man couldn't be over eighteen or nineteen years, and yet he claimed a knowledge of men some of the captain's officers had yet to develop.

"Have you known many violent men?" The captain tried to keep the sarcasm out of his voice.

Samuel had a good ear and detected the skepticism. He'd spent many years being quiet and letting others do all the talking. He'd learned early on to detect certain emotions in other's speech.

"I've worked in my pa's sawmill since I was ten

years old. A lot of men pass through our neck of the woods. Most all give the feelin' they have something to hide. If they stay for more than a couple of months, you get to know 'em well enough to know that whatever they are hiding is none of your concern. After a while, you get to where you can spot real quick the ones who would hurt a woman. There's a coldness in their eyes and a meanness in the way they treat animals."

Captain Lance had just been reminded of one of the first lessons an officer of the law has to learn. Don't make assumptions about the person you are dealing with.

It was obvious this young man from Trenton was a lot sharper than his demeanor indicated, and he had developed a good way to assess the character of the men he had met in his relatively short life. The captain looked at Mr. Finch, who gave a sympathetic shrug. At first glance, he too had underestimated this quiet young man.

"So, Captain, are you able to answer Samuel's question?" asked Mr. Finch.

Captain Lance replied, "Yes, I can answer the question. And yes, it was a violent murder. She was violated, and then her throat was cut. It will all be public record tomorrow, gentlemen, provided I can keep it under wraps until then." The captain was deliberately blunt. He wanted to observe the reaction. The results were interesting. Mr. Finch gave a small shudder. Samuel, on the other hand, became as still as stone. If the captain had not been watching so intently, he would have missed the tightening of the jaw and the anger that sprang into those dark eyes. This was a young man who had been close to violence.

"What will not be made public coincides with the information you have shared. The young woman gave a good fight. The assailant most likely has some deep scratches on his face. When we found her, she was clutching a piece of torn fabric and a scrap of paper. There was a name of a hotel on the scrap of paper. It was the San Carlos Hotel. Under these circumstances, I think I will be making the trip to Pensacola to personally question your Mr. Hardwick. He may be expecting to hear Miss Hinton has been killed. It will be interesting to see his reaction."

****

They had asked the captain to keep them informed, thanked him for his time, and were now standing outside the sheriff's offices.

Mr. Finch said, "Samuel, how about some lunch? We can go home, visit with Mrs. Finch, and have a good lunch. What do you say?"

"Sir, that would be real nice, but I don't like leaving Mae alone too long. Pa trusts me to take care of her."

Mr. Finch patted Samuel on the back. "Your father has good reason to be proud of you, young man. I didn't want to spoil his surprise, but under the circumstances, I don't think he'll mind. Your father will be rolling into the train station in a few hours. He was going to surprise everyone. He has Mrs. Peters with him, and Cyrus and Hansu are on the train with the animals. Your father wanted to beat the train to arrange for the trucks to take the animals to the manor. We could have a quick lunch and then go take care of the trucks for him. What do you say?"

Samuel broke into a genuine, full-blown grin.

"That, sir, is the best news I've had in a week!"

Mr. Finch laughed out loud. "Well, all right, then, let's get moving."

Chapter Twenty-One

Garth was glad he had a head start on the train. He should get to Tallahassee about an hour ahead of the animals, which would give him time to make the arrangements for all of them to be transported to the manor. He had to stop thinking of the Wellington estate as the manor, but it was going to be a while before he could call it home. Maybe once Eleanor and Patrick were there with him he would relax.

He looked across the picnic basket to Mrs. Peters. She was having a little nap in the corner. The poor woman had been running around like a chicken with its head cut off for days now. She'd not had a lot of personal belongings of her own to pack, but she had taken great care to get all the things she knew Mae would want and need. There were four crates of well-packed canned fruits and vegetables, and the good Lord only knew how many quilts. The woman must have saved every quilt she'd ever made. Of course, Garth could remember how dear all of Ruth's quilts had been to her, especially the ones she and Mae had worked on together.

He was four days ahead of schedule, and the Finches would keep his secret, but he couldn't wait to see the look of surprise on Mae's and Samuel's faces when he arrived this evening with Cyrus, Hansu, and Mrs. Peters in tow. He had missed those two older children of his, even with all the busyness of the move. It was a constant source of amazement to him how they had grown and matured when he wasn't looking. Now, through the generosity of a dear woman, they would all be together and could get back to a normal family life.

Garth turned in to the loading area on the south end of the rail depot. It had been a long drive. Mrs. Peters looked exhausted, but they had beaten the train. He slowed the truck to a stop and stretched his legs. He smiled at Mrs. Peters and said, "Well, welcome to Tallahassee. I know you must be exhausted, but if you'll give me about fifteen more minutes, I'll see if I can get you home."

She smiled back weakly. "I'm fine, dear. You just take your time."

Garth stepped down out of the truck and turned toward the offices.

He was stopped in his tracks by the sight of Samuel and Mr. Finch walking toward him. Samuel threw both arms around his pa and hugged him tightly. Garth couldn't remember the last time Samuel had shown so much open affection. He was surprised but happy.

Samuel stepped back and grinned sheepishly. "Glad to see ya, Pa."

Mr. Finch laughed. "Now, I do believe that's an understatement. How are you, Garth? You'll have to forgive me for spoiling your surprise, but this young man was in town on important business, and I enlisted his help. We have trucks lined up for the animals when the train gets in."

Garth turned to Samuel. "Is everything all right, son?"

Before Samuel could go into his story, Mr. Finch

spoke. "Is that your housekeeper in the truck, Garth? We need to get the poor woman to the house. Samuel, how about you taking her home, and I'll explain everything to your father. Would that be okay, young man?"

Samuel looked at both men. As much as he wanted to stay, he knew Mae would scold him severely if he didn't take proper care of Mrs. Peters. "Yes, sir, it would probably be best. I don't want Mae coming down on my head." Both men laughed.

Samuel helped Mrs. Peters down from the truck and gave her a hug. "My goodness, young man, it's only been three weeks since I've seen you, and I think you've grown!"

Samuel laughed. "Well, I may be taller, but I bet I've lost weight. They don't seem to be able to make a good pie around here."

The little woman stretched up to pat his cheek. "You just let me rest tonight, honey. I've got peaches and blackberries canned, and I'll be able to whip up something for you tomorrow."

Samuel placed Mrs. Peters' small bags in the motorcar hatch and then helped get her seated in the front. He turned to Mr. Finch and shook his hand. "Thank you, sir, for all your help. Please tell Mrs. Finch again how much I enjoyed lunch." He hugged his pa one more time, grinned, and said, "I'll see you at home, sir. Tell Cyrus and Hansu I'll be ready for the animals, and there'll be a good supper waiting for them."

Garth waited until the vehicle was out of sight. He turned to Mr. Finch and gave him a stern look. "My son just hugged me twice in the same day. Am I correct in thinking we have something to talk about?"

Mr. Finch pointed toward the station office and said, "Let's get a cup of coffee, and I'll tell you just how proud you should be of your son."

Mr. Finch finished his tale with very few interruptions for questions. Garth was just sitting there trying to process all the information. He finally turned to Finch. "Do we know if the poor girl has relatives? Is there anything we can do for them?"

"Samuel assures me Mae is handling the arrangements. The detective is supposed to send the body to the undertaker as soon as they release it, and the undertaker will get with Mae. I cannot tell you how amazed I have been with your offspring. Captain Lance was pretty impressed with Samuel, as well. The boy seems to have tremendous insight into the criminal mind."

Garth gave a pained smile of acknowledgment for the compliments. "All of my brood has had to grow up quickly. Cyrus seems to have grown two inches this past month, and he has taken on the raising of all our food for next spring. He and Hansu have big ideas about raising herbs with curative powers for the veterinary business.

"I think it's just as well I'm marrying soon and taking on another family, because this one seems to be leaving me behind. I thank the Lord every night, sir, for watching over my brood. But I give special thanks for my first wife, Ruth. God made that woman about as perfect as a woman could be. She filled those kids with enough love while she was here to get them through the lean times after she was gone. She taught them to do for others before themselves, and how to give thanks to the Man upstairs for every day they're given. Heck, we've been so blessed I'm not so sure she's not up there right now telling the Good Lord how to watch over us."

****

Garth had apologized at least three times to Mrs. Patrick for showing up unannounced and causing such a stir in the household. The dear lady had been glad for the distraction. She'd been so busy preparing rooms for them all that there had actually been moments when she wasn't thinking about Margaret. It was almost ten at night now, and the household had settled down somewhat.

Mrs. Peters had been given a small room on the ground floor behind the kitchen. The poor soul had been exhausted from the trip, but she had made a place for herself in the hearts of all at the manor. She had humbly presented Cook with all her canned goods, and Cook had used several of the items to whip up a light supper for everyone.

The Huebner brothers had helped Cyrus and Hansu get all the animals sorted out and housed for the night. The chickens had been excited and noisy. They would probably not produce eggs for a few days, but they had survived the trip. The two horses, two steers, and three milk cows had all been watered, fed, and brushed down by Cyrus. They were, after all, his children, and he took his care of them very seriously. He and Hansu had needed good baths after their several hours in the train car with the animals. Garth had laughed and asked them to please stay downwind of everyone.

After all the others were either asleep or preparing to retire, Mr. Bennett, Garth, and Samuel were in the library. Samuel had just finished repeating the details of his visit to the sheriff's offices for Mr. Bennett.

"Well, this is just heartbreaking. I hate to think of our young woman dying in such a manner. Do they really think they can trace this to Hardwick?" he asked.

"Mr. Finch seems to think there is a good possibility. Captain Lance will be traveling to Pensacola in a few days. Perhaps then we'll know more. Until they find the animal that did this, we'll use some good common sense. None of the women will go to town without one of us. We'll keep a close eye on things around here, and I'll only enlist known, local workers for the building." Garth patted Samuel on the shoulder. "You've done a good job of keeping watch on everyone here, son. There is no way you could have predicted something like this, and I won't have you thinking you could have. We had all better get some sleep now. The next few days are going to be pretty busy."

Samuel paused outside Mae's door. He could see no light, but he doubted she was asleep. He'd not had an opportunity today to speak with Henry, but he would make time for it tomorrow. Mae could fool the others, but Samuel was sure something Henry had said the other night had upset her.

****

When Samuel's footsteps paused outside Mae's door, she hoped he would not knock. She didn't want to have to lie to her brother, but she would not allow her fear to ruin all the good that was working in their lives right now. Surely Henry's words had nothing to do with her, she thought, as she placed the pistol under her pillow. She lay in bed and listened to the owls outside her window, and she prayed. She asked the Lord to keep all her loved ones safe. She asked for guidance for her project, and she asked the Lord to hold Margaret near to Him and comfort her.

****

It was Friday. They had received word from the undertaker, and he would transport Margaret to them Sunday morning, at ten. Mae and Mr. Bennett had selected a five-acre section for the cemetery. It was about a half mile west of the manor house in a level, open field surrounded by several magnolia trees. The family and servants would have a graveside service for Margaret, followed by a late brunch. All the household servants had Sunday afternoon off and would be given use of the motorcar if they wanted to get away for the day. Mrs. Peters was more than happy to do supper for the family.

Mae carried an armload of books to the back drawing room. It was a little cool this morning, and the girls had not opened the glass doors. Mae stood looking out at the small lake. She remembered the first time she had stood here. It was a lot for her to take in. She deeply regretted not having had time to get to know Lady Wellington better. Mae just prayed she could make the lady proud with the good she intended to do with the inheritance. She smiled to herself. She was sure the lady would approve of educating and uplifting young women. Well, so much for daydreaming. If she was going to pass her exams, she needed to be studying. She spread the books out on the desk and pulled up a chair.

****

Garth and Samuel found Henry in the garage. The old gentleman was polishing the estate motorcar. He still had a bandage secured to the back of his head. Garth smiled at him and said, "Henry, are you feeling up to this? There's no hurry, you know."

Henry's face filled with pain. "Sir, I understand we'll be bringing Miss Margaret home Sunday. I just want the family transportation to look sharp when we lay the girl to rest, sir." Garth could see the man was still a little shaky.

"Well, if you wouldn't mind, could we have a seat and talk for a minute?" Garth indicated a bench against the wall. Once they had the man seated, Garth nodded to Samuel.

"Sir, I hate to ask you to go over the events again, but my pa is trying to get a handle on everything. If you could, just tell us again how it all happened," Samuel said as he knelt by the bench.

Henry stared at the ceiling a moment, took a deep breath, and started at the beginning. "First on the list was Taylor's, to pick up the books the young miss needed. Then we drove to Carters Dry Goods. Miss Margaret went in and shopped for the housekeeper. I helped her load the things in the boot. Then Miss Margaret said we needed to stop at the produce shed on the way out of town. When I let her out there, she said, 'Henry, I'm going to be a while. If you'd like a nap…'" At this point the poor man had to stop.

Garth put a hand on the man's shoulder and said, "Henry, you did nothing wrong. If this man was after Margaret, he would have gotten to her no matter where you were parked."

Henry nodded. "Yes, sir, my head knows it, but my heart doesn't want to hear it."

"That's because you're a good man, Henry. Now, what else can you remember?"

"Well, I drove the motorcar over to the big tree.

The shade was deeper on the backside, so I pulled a little past the tree. I got out to stretch my legs, and that's when he must have hit me. I never heard it coming. Then I think Miss Margaret was calling my name, but I can't be sure. I must have been out of my head, 'cause I coulda swore I heard a man talking to a cat."

Samuel and Garth exchanged looks, and Garth said, "What do you mean, Henry? What did you hear the man say?"

Henry hesitated. "Well, I think he said, 'Hello, little she-cat.'"

Garth stood abruptly, patted Henry on the shoulder again, murmured thanks, and strode away.

Samuel thanked Henry, told him to rest awhile, and took off after his pa.

Garth walked to the paddock rail and leaned his head against it.

Samuel waited for Pa to calm himself. Finally, Garth raised his head and looked at his son. The hair on the back of Samuel's neck stood. He wasn't sure he wanted to hear what Pa was about to say.

"What are the chances this man would call Margaret the same thing one of Mae's attackers called her? And then he would kill Margaret?"

****

Sunday arrived with the first cold morning of the season, not quite cold enough for frost, but cold enough to see your breath on the air. The household had an early breakfast, in near silence. It would be a hard day for all of them, but for many different reasons.

The household servants had all known and loved Margaret for the smiling, always cheerful, sometimes teasing young woman she was. They'd had a few years to develop friendships and maybe share secrets with her.

Mae had only known Margaret marginally, but there would always be a place deep inside her that wept for her. She'd known the fear Margaret must have felt, and that knowledge would forever connect their souls.

Garth had only met the girl once, but if there was the slimmest chance he could bring her killer to justice, he wanted the chance. His stomach knotted, just thinking of what the girl must have endured.

Samuel had seen the woman at work and admired her ability to be comfortable with anyone. She always had a smile and a helping hand and would have been a great friend to Mae. Now a man had cut her life short, thinking he was killing Mae. That alone was reason enough for Samuel to find him and stop him.

The Huebner brothers dug the grave for Margaret. The casket was plain, but Mae had arranged to have several bouquets of beautiful flowers placed atop it. The priest from the small Catholic chapel on Beacon Street would give the service. Mae had contacted him after Martha mentioned Margaret occasionally attended services there. The service was short but beautiful. Three young choirboys, who sang "Ave Maria" at the closing, accompanied the priest. Their music was so beautifully haunting you could imagine the angels in heaven singing.

Everyone returned to the manor for coffee, tea, and hot chocolate. Cook and Mrs. Peters had baked cookies and pies. After everyone had their fill, the leftovers were wrapped for the priest to take back to the rectory. He thanked the ladies heartily and advised them of the baking contests held annually at his parish. By his account, they had every chance of winning.

After the priest departed, Garth gathered everyone into the kitchen. "I want all of you to know we will be doing everything we can to find Margaret's killer. In the meantime, just as a precaution, I don't want any of you to go into town alone. If you ladies need to run errands, or just spend some time away from the manor, ask one of us men to accompany you. It will not be a bother, I promise you.

"Now, we are all going to take some time this coming week to rest, get settled in, and then celebrate Thanksgiving on Thursday. Mae and I want to have the Finches here, since they have been so good to us. Eleanor Taylor, my fiancée, and her son, Patrick, will be here also.

"The following Monday, work will begin. I'll be going into town to hire some carpenters to start work on Mae's 'village.' I expect to hire about ten to fifteen men. Mrs. Patrick, do you think we could provide lunch for so many on a regular basis? If you need to hire a couple more girls to help, please do so, as long as they are local people you know and trust."

She looked at Cook, who nodded and said, "Yes, sir, I will probably need two more girls to do the heavy lifting, but I believe we can handle it."

"Wonderful. You'll have Cyrus and Hansu to carry and distribute it to the men. All you ladies have to do is just keep that wonderful stuff coming."

Garth thanked them all again, and then they were free to spend the rest of the day at their leisure.

Chapter Twenty-Two

Mae woke to beautiful sunshine streaming through her bedroom windows. She had actually slept all night, no tossing or turning, just a deep sleep. She ran her hand under her pillow, pulled out the pistol, and placed it in the box at the bottom of her wardrobe. She always worried one of the girls would find it and be alarmed. As far as they knew, they were all safe, but Mae had lived in a state of unease since the night they'd found Margaret's body. She had a feeling of something yet to come. She refused to allow herself to worry today. Today was Thanksgiving. She had all of her family around her, and the Finches were yet to arrive. She would not let anything interrupt this beautiful day. After a quick wash, she pulled her hair back into a bun and dressed for cooking.

Garth opened the front door as Mae was bouncing down the stairs. "You look like you had a good night's rest." He smiled.

She skipped the rest of the way down, kissed Papa on the cheek, and smiled back. "Can't stay to talk. I have cooking to do."

Garth watched her parade off toward the kitchen and said a prayer of thanks. Thanks for his wonderful family, that they were all safe with him, and that Mae seemed to be coming out of her recent quiet spell. Yes, he had much for which to thank the Lord, including

Eleanor and Patrick. Garth took off up the stairs at a run. The time for him to pick them up was getting close, and he needed to get washed up and changed.

****

Mae was just finishing her hair for the second time that day when Cyrus knocked on the door. "Come in."

Cyrus opened the door and stopped abruptly. "Good golly Moses!" He inhaled sharply. "You startled me."

"I startled you?" Mae laughed.

"Yes, you look just like Mama."

Mae took a deep breath. "Oh, sweetie, I'm so sorry. I didn't mean to alarm you. I could never be as beautiful as Mama."

She looked at herself in the mirror. She was wearing a maroon silk gown with an underskirt of pale pink and a fitted waist that emphasized her bosom. She had pulled her hair straight back, then piled all the curls loosely on top of her head, with a pale pink ribbon woven through them. Her face was a glowing pink from her time in the kitchen, and her eyes were shining with the excitement of the day. Yes, maybe she did look a little like Mama, but never as beautiful. She walked over and kissed her not-so-little brother on the cheek.

"Well, it's only right." She smiled. "You look just like Papa." She hooked her arm through his and said, "You can escort me downstairs, sir."

"Oh, I forgot to tell you I saw the cars coming up the lane. The Finches and Eleanor are here."

"Oh!" She dropped his arm and took the stairs two at a time. Cyrus laughed all the way down behind her.

Mae bounded out the front door just as Eleanor stepped out of the first motorcar. Eleanor was beautiful, as always, and Patrick was hopping from foot to foot, as usual. She had hugged Eleanor, patted Patrick on the head, and turned to greet the Finches when she ran smack into a solid chest.

Mae stumbled and was immediately caught up in a pair of strong arms. She raised her head and found herself looking into the bluest eyes she'd ever seen. The man gazing down at her had dark blond hair, and smile lines around his mouth. He relaxed his hands but did not let go of her. They both smiled slowly.

"Hello."

"Hello to you, sir," she replied just above a whisper.

"Are you the incomparable Mae I've been hearing so much about?"

Mae gazed at his mouth as he spoke. Without any awareness of her actions, she reached up and touched the side of his face. "I am Mae, and you would be?"

"Very glad to meet you," he responded. They suddenly became aware of the people watching them. Mae stepped back as the gentleman dropped his hands to his sides.

A grinning Doc Walters stepped forward. "All right, young man, let's do this the right way. Miss Mae Hinton, may I introduce my nephew, Dr. Edward Finch? Edward wanted to surprise his mother with an unannounced visit for Thanksgiving. We didn't think you'd mind one more guest for dinner."

Mae laughed as she threw both arms around Doc Walters. "Oh! I am so glad you could make it. I have missed you, Doc." She turned to the handsome Dr. Finch. "And of course, sir, there is always room for one more at our table. Please, everyone, let's go inside. Our cooks have outdone themselves. We don't want to keep them waiting."

Later, as the delicious meal was winding down, Garth looked around the table. He'd never been so proud of Mae. While his heart swelled with pride, he was also filled with a sense of loss. Gone was his little girl. She had been replaced by this elegant young woman, who was obviously charming the socks off Dr. Edward Finch.

As if reading her father's thoughts, Mae stood and addressed them all. "If everyone would find their way to the back parlor, we could all rest for a few minutes. Martha will bring us a dessert cart later." Everyone moaned and spoke of how wonderful all the food had been, and how they might not be able to eat again for at least a week.

Hansu took Mae's hand. "You very grown lady today, Missy. Mama would be proud. Thank you for big dinner. I go see to animals now."

Mae kissed the little man's cheek. "Thank you, Hansu. I'll save you some pumpkin pie."

Mae led her guests to the back parlor. The girls had opened the drapes to a beautiful view of the lake. The water was dotted with birds resting from their winter trip south.

There was a small fire in the fireplace, filling the room with peaceful warmth. Patrick grabbed a checkerboard from the sideboard and placed it on the small bench in front of the fire. "Okay, who wants to be beat at checkers?" He grinned.

"Well!" Dr. Finch laughed. "I cannot pass up a challenge like that." The tall man pulled a chair over to the bench, and the game was on. Mae stared from across the room. There was something very endearing about a man who would meet a child on his level. Mae was aware that she was inexperienced where men were concerned. This was the first time she had cared about impressing any man other than her papa.

She wanted this man to see her as a woman. A new and exciting feeling had run through her when she'd been in his arms. When those blue eyes met hers, it was as if they could see into her soul.

Ruth had told Mae the story of how Grandma Rebecca had met Grandpa Harding. She'd been a spinster helping her pa run his farm. She'd gone to take food and healing herbs to a sick neighbor one day, and as she was loosening the basket from the horse, a deep, melodious voice said, "Here let me take that." When she'd turned, she was looking up into the bluest eyes she'd ever seen. She had known this was the gift the Lord had sent her for being patient. But had Grandma experienced a sweet burn when Grandpa touched her hand? Had she been excited but also a little frightened?

When Doctor Finch met her gaze over Patrick's head, Mae was embarrassed to realize she had been caught staring. Her face burned, as she turned to gaze out the French doors.

She heard the doctor say, "That's it for me, young man; I'm not up to your skill. You're going to have to find another pigeon." As Patrick was trying to rope Samuel into a game, the doctor walked over to Mae.

"I remember visiting here once before I left for England, but I don't think I've seen the grounds. Perhaps we could get some air and you could show me around, Miss Mae?"

Mae stood, and stuttered, "I...I would have to get a

wrap…I…"

Eleanor saved her from further embarrassment. "Here, dear, take my shawl."

The doctor took the extended wrap and placed it around Mae's shoulders. She looked into those eyes again, and a peaceful calm washed over her. There was nothing frightening about this man.

This feeling was right, meant to be, and blessed from above. She looked up at him, and her heart told her she would always be comfortable with this man.

With a smile, she told him, "Yes, I would love to show you around."

He opened the French door and placed his hand in the small of her back, and they moved outside.

There was a moment of silence in the parlor as Patrick reset the board, but everyone else was watching the couple standing on the lawn.

Each of them experienced different feelings as the handsome couple strolled toward the lake.

Garth's mind turned to Ruth and how she would have loved seeing Mae blossom.

Eleanor worried over Mae's past and wondered how she would find the courage to tell a young man her story.

Mrs. Finch was giddy with happiness. She had dreamed Edward would find some nice young woman here, not in England, and settle down.

Mr. Finch was thinking, "Well, son, if you have to fall for a young woman, you couldn't find a better one."

Doc Walters was filled with pride. He had seen the potential in Mae years ago. And now here she was, grown, beautiful, and accomplished, and impressing the heck out of his young nephew.

Samuel only wanted what was best for Mae; if this was the man who would give her all the love and care she deserved, then Samuel would be his strongest supporter. If not, then he'd better watch his step.

****

"So, Miss Mae, my uncle tells me you are a progressive woman who wants to help fix the world."

Mae stopped walking and turned, about to defend herself, when she caught the teasing look in his eyes. He laughed out loud. "I was afraid for my life. There for a moment, you looked like you were about to strangle me."

Mae blushed and smiled. "I'm not so foolish as to think I could fix the whole world, sir, but there are women who could use a hand up in the world."

"I apologize, Mae, if I sounded condescending. My experience as a doctor has shown me that the least of us, the women and children, are often treated the worst. Anyone who works toward correcting such is a hero, as far as I am concerned. I have to ask, though, what set you on this path?"

Mae stared out across the lake for several long heartbeats. At last she met his gaze. Her eyes were shining, not quite tear-filled.

He understood his question had caused her pain. He couldn't imagine why, but he would not question her further.

"Doctor Finch, one day I will tell you what set me on this path, but not today, sir."

He took her hand and pulled her arm through his. "Please, call me Edward. And someday, when you are ready, I will be humbled to have you confide in me."

Mae gave him a grateful smile. "Now, please,

Edward, tell me all about your work in England."

They spent the next half hour strolling around the property while Edward filled her mind with descriptions of the people he worked with day to day. He told her about the baker in London who bought a newfangled machine to slice his bread and promptly lost a finger, and the boy who lived on the streets and developed pneumonia. He had allowed the lad to sleep in his offices until he healed. He then found the boy had robbed him blind. There was also the tavern wench who gave birth to triplets. Mae believed she could listen to his voice forever; however, she was neglecting her other guests.

"Edward, much as I love listening to these accounts, I am afraid I'm being a rude hostess by allowing one guest to monopolize my time. I believe we should return to the others."

Edward was still holding her hand in his. He smiled down at her in such a way her heart swelled, and she caught her breath.

"You are right, of course. I have been selfish. I will share you with the others, but only on one condition. You have to promise that tomorrow you will allow me to monopolize you again, and the next day, and…" They were nearing the house now, and the folks inside could hear Mae's laughter. It was a beautiful sound to all of them.

Chapter Twenty-Three

They were going riding today. Yesterday, they had attended an afternoon tea at the Finches' home. Mae had been somewhat overwhelmed at all the attention. The guests had all been school friends of Edward's, and while it had been a last-minute invitation, there had been at least twenty people in attendance. The guests had all been older than Mae. The men were successful businessmen and local leaders. Their wives had either their charity work or small children to talk about. When questioned, Mae had talked about her plans. Some of the women had asked polite questions, while others had looked at her askance, as if she had no idea what she was undertaking. While Mae had been, understandably, a little intimidated, Edward had been at her side most of the afternoon. He'd been a tower of support.

Mae had taken great care with her appearance. She wore a lovely rust-colored suit. The pattern was the latest out of Paris, and several of the women had commented on the style. The jacket had wide lapels, shoulder pads, and was nipped at the waist, with a peplum, which gave Mae a deceptively willowy appearance, as if she might break if someone bumped her. She had chosen to go with the suit a very simple saucer-style hat, with one silk rose, in the same peach shade as her blouse. While the other ladies may have been more sophisticated, with more social experience than Mae, none were lovelier. Edward told her so on the ride home.

It was late evening when they headed to the manor. Edward stopped the motorcar as he left the main road. He turned to Mae and said, "I cannot thank you enough for sharing today with me. I know my friends can be a bit stuffy, and perhaps a little condescending, but social standing is very important to my mother. She always tries to keep me in the circle when I am home. She doesn't realize how little knowledge some of them have of the real world. She likes to pretend I only treat English aristocrats." Edward shook his head. "I have learned more medicine from the 'street doctors' of London than I ever did from my professors, but Mother wouldn't want to know this. And you, well, you just fit right in, as if you'd visited with each of them before. I must say, I was very proud."

Mae blushed. "Thank you, sir, for staying close and guiding me through it all."

Edward smoothed a stray curl back into place. "Staying close to you is becoming easier each time we're together, Mae. I'm not a young schoolboy, and I would be lying if I said I'd had no previous interest in women, but I can say, with all honesty, you intrigue me. This feeling is new to me, and I very much want to explore it with you."

Mae could feel her heart pounding. "Edward, these feelings are new to me, and it is a little frightening. I want to know everything about you and your life, and…" She stopped as Edward took her hand and placed a kiss in the palm. Mae closed her eyes and tried to steady her breathing.

Edward closed her hand over the kiss. "It is enough

for now, to know that you do not find me completely boring and unacceptable."

With her eyes still closed, Mae gave a shaky laugh. "Oh, Edward, I find you very acceptable."

"Good. Then you won't run right out and look for someone else to keep you entertained when I leave for England." He gave a short laugh.

Her eyes flew open and widened with shock. "You are leaving? So soon?" she whispered, tightening her hold on his hand.

"Oh, Mae, don't look at me that way. It makes me want to sweep you up in my arms and never let you go. Let me get you home before I lose my sense of decency. I will come out tomorrow, and we can go riding. Maybe your wonderful cook can pack us a lunch, and we can discuss my return to England, all right?"

****

Mae was unable to sleep for quite some time. She sat in the dark on the window seat, gazing at the stars. Finally, she prayed. "Lord, thank you for this wonderful gift, this man who makes my heart swell with what must be love. Thank you, Lord, for the opportunity to share all the blessings you've given me. Lord, I just ask you to guide me, to direct my steps and behavior, so I would do nothing to displease you, or dishonor what I have been given. Amen." At last she slept.

****

Mae checked the mirror one last time. If she'd been going riding with Samuel, she would have just slipped on a pair of trousers and been off, but this was Edward, so she had donned a split riding skirt with matching vest, both in a forest green, and a pristine white, long-sleeved blouse with a high, ruffled collar. Her boots and

185

gloves were black. She had twisted her hair into a secure bun at the nape of her neck, leaving one or two stray curls teasing her face. She pinned a small, black, silk riding hat on top of her head, with just a little tilt to the left. She looked at the mantel clock. *Another half hour before he gets here. All right, good.* She had time to calm down and make sure the horses and picnic were ready.

Mae met her papa and Mr. Bennett in the library. They were going over the layout for the village. Garth looked up and smiled. "Guessing from your riding outfit, I'd say you are not going to be joining us, right?"

"Don't tease, Papa. I told you last night Edward would be here at ten this morning and we were going riding."

The smile left Garth's face. "Has Edward been advised of what happened to Margaret? He should be told so he can be alert."

Mae looked into her Papa's face. She could see the worry in his eyes. While keeping eye contact with him, she reached into the pocket of her skirt and removed the little beauty.

With a slow, sad acknowledgment, Garth nodded. "All right, baby girl, just don't become so wrapped up in Edward you forget to keep an eye on your surroundings."

Mr. Bennett was startled when Mae pulled the small pistol out of a pocket in her skirt. The longer his association with this family, the more he was amazed. They were the epitome of the pioneer spirit, with young men who could carve and assemble beautiful pieces of furniture, or nurture and heal small animals. Then here was this young woman who carried her own pistol.

Garth had certainly raised a diverse brood.

Mae put the pistol back in her pocket, kissed her papa's cheek, and thanked Mr. Bennett for being so diligent and helping Papa. Then she took off for the kitchen. She had asked Mrs. Peters to put together a light lunch for two.

Mae blushed when the woman teased. "Is this for the doctor gentleman who was here the other day? So, the winds are blowing in his direction, eh? I caught the young man eyeing you across the dinner table on Thanksgiving. He had the look of a man who'd just won a great prize. But you make sure he has to work hard for the prize, young lady. Don't be makin' the winning too easy for him. Now, that's all I'll say on the matter. There is some sliced ham, cheese, a small loaf of bread, and some of my bread-and-butter pickles in this basket. Cook added some cookies for good measure."

Mae took the basket. "Thank you for the lunch and the good advice. I shall keep it in mind." She grinned as she headed out the side door.

She was almost to the barn when she heard the sound of an engine. She looked back over her shoulder and smiled as the Finches' motorcar pulled up to the paddock rail. Edward climbed out, stretching to his full six foot four inches. The sun was shining behind him, turning his hair a golden hue.

Mae had never paid much notice to how men looked. Her Papa was a very handsome man, and Samuel and Cyrus already had his looks, but she'd never given much thought to men outside her family until now. Edward was tall and lean. He walked with a long graceful stride. His teeth were very white and even. Today he was wearing black riding britches and a tan shirt, with the sleeves rolled up to reveal muscular arms.

He smiled as he moved toward Mae. She could see approval in his eyes, which caused a warm flush to spread throughout her body. To Mae's mind, he was the most handsome man she'd ever seen.

They were securing the basket behind Edward's saddle when one of the Huebner brothers spoke from behind them. "Beggin' your pardon, miss, but if you're lookin' for a nice place to picnic, you'll find a small creek a few hundred yards past the cemetery. There's some good shade there, and cool water."

Mae thanked the man, and they were off.

Edward said it was Mae's turn to talk, so she spent the next half hour telling him about their home in Trenton, how she had helped raise her brothers, and how she had met Lady Wellington. She of course did not mention what had made their connection so strong. That telling would come later.

They had just passed through the cemetery and had fallen into a comfortable silence, so that Mae thought she could hear the trickle of running water, when Edward's horse snorted and reared. Edward, caught off guard, was thrown off to the side. Before he had completely hit the ground, Mae had pulled the pistol and turned her horse toward him.

"Don't move! Edward, please, do not move!"

By then Edward could hear the rattlesnake. He very carefully turned his head toward the sound, and there was the snake, coiled between himself and Mae. Mae slid slowly off her horse, and he saw that, of all things, she was holding a pistol. "Edward, be very still, and I'll take care of this." Mae turned her body sideways, slowly raised her arm, and shot the head off the offending snake.

Edward exhaled in a burst and only then realized he had been holding his breath. He wasn't sure which had startled him more, the sudden appearance of the large snake or the speed with which a pistol had appeared in Mae's hand. Where in the world had she been hiding it?

Mae stepped around the snake and ran to Edward. "Are you all right? Did he get you?"

Her obvious concern was a small balm to his ego. He stood, dusted sand off himself, and was about to speak, when Mae threw herself at him. She had both arms around his chest.

"I was so afraid you'd been bitten, or broken something in the fall. Thank the good Lord you are okay," she sobbed.

Edward was undone by her tears. He pressed her to his chest, rubbing her back and speaking softly. "I'm all right, darling, just a little embarrassed I had to be saved by you. Now stop crying and let me look at you."

Mae turned her face up to Edward, and he was lost. Her brown eyes were luminous with tears, and her mouth gave an invitation he could not ignore. He lowered his lips to hers. He could taste her tears as their mouths melted together. It was a slow, sensual kiss, fueled by Mae's fears for his safety and his desire for her.

Edward raised his head and whispered, "The snake did me no harm, but I may never recover from that kiss."

Mae laid her head against his chest and tried to

compose herself. She was embarrassed. She had literally thrown herself at this man. So much for "making him work for the prize."

She pushed herself away from him and raised her chin. "Well, if you are okay, then we should check the poor horse."

She started to turn away, but Edward caught her arm. She looked back at him, and he lifted one eyebrow at her.

"So. We're simply going to pretend the kiss never happened, are we?"

She gave him a hesitant look. "Well, I think we should at least try, don't you?"

He looked at her for a moment before he burst out laughing. "Oh, woman, you have no idea what you've done to me, do you?"

Mae looked confused, and Edward laughed harder. "Never mind, love, let's just catch the poor horse and find some water. I desperately need to cool off."

By the time they had calmed the horse and checked him out, Mae needed cool water, too. They found the creek and opened the basket. On top of the food was a neatly folded blanket, which Edward spread out under a tree.

He dug in the basket until he found a cup, which he handed to Mae, saying, "You get us some water, and I'll lay out the food."

Mae moved to a flat limestone rock at the edge of the creek and knelt. The water was clear and cool as she dragged the cup through it. She sipped from the cup, then topped it off and stood. Edward had laid out linen napkins, slices of ham, cheese, and bread, and was popping the seal on the canned pickles when Mae gracefully lowered herself to the blanket.

She handed the cup to Edward. "Here, drink some, and it will help cool you off."

It took all of Edward's self-control not to laugh again. This beautiful creature had no idea what a woman could do to a man with just a look. He was never so grateful for anything in his life. He had found the perfect, pure treasure. There was no doubt she would belong to him. He accepted the cup from her hands and took a deep swallow. Setting the cup down, he smiled across the blanket. "Now, my lovely, you will tell me all about the pistol."

Chapter Twenty-Four

Garth and Mr. Bennett spent at least an hour going over all the plans. "Well, sir, I think maybe fifteen good men. I can drive the truck out in the morning, pick them up and transport them to the work site, then take them back to town each evening, so none of them will have much contact with the manor or the ladies."

"It sounds like a good plan, Garth. I believe I can start getting the supplies, lumber and such, delivered by the middle of next week. We should be able to start work the following Monday, which will give Samuel and the Huebner brothers time to finish the apartments over the garage. We had never anticipated anyone else living there, so we never expanded beyond my apartment."

Garth smiled. "Samuel always liked the idea of his own space, and Hansu has always lived separate from the family. I'm just glad we have enough room there to accommodate both of them."

Mrs. Patrick stuck her head around the door. "Mr. Hinton, there was an officer at the front door. He said he would like to speak with you, so I have put him in the back parlor, sir." Both men stood.

"Come along with me, Arthur. This is probably something to do with Margaret."

As they entered the parlor, the tall, broad-shouldered man standing at the French doors, looking out across the lake, turned and came to meet them. "Good morning, sir. I am Captain Lance, with the Leon County sheriff's office. I believe I have met your son, Samuel," he said as he shook Garth's hand.

"Yes, sir, you did. This is Arthur Bennett, my daughter's business manager. Have a seat, Captain, and tell us why you are here."

"Is Samuel around, sir? I would like to speak with him, as well."

Arthur stood. "Keep your seat, Garth. I'll get Samuel."

"You have a pretty impressive place here, Mr. Hinton."

"Truth be told, Captain, this all belongs to my daughter, Mae. I'm just keeping an eye on things until Mae reaches her majority. She inherited all this, and a great deal more, from the late Lady Wellington, which is one of the reasons we are concerned about what happened to Margaret. A young lady is always prey for those who would take advantage of her, but in Mae's case even more so. Mr. Hardwick has everything to gain if something should happen to Mae."

"Well, Mr. Hinton, after personally meeting with Hardwick, I can say your distrust of the man is totally rational."

"I told you, sir, the man is cold," Samuel said as he entered the parlor.

Captain Lance stood and reached to shake Samuel's hand. "Son, after meeting with Hardwick, I remembered a lot of things you said." To Garth, the captain said, "Your son has an insight into human nature that cannot be taught, sir, but is a gift from inside. When he is old enough, I'll probably offer him a job."

Garth nodded. "Captain, you have no idea just how insightful Samuel can be. Now, tell us about your meeting with Hardwick."

"Well, I took the train over to Pensacola last Monday. I went first to the local police precinct and spoke with a detective there. When I told him what we were working on, he was more than happy to accompany me to the San Carlo. We got there around eleven in the morning, and Hardwick was having a late breakfast, which we were happy to be able to interrupt. We introduced ourselves, and I told him that a young woman in Tallahassee had been murdered, and I needed to ask a few questions about his relationship to her."

The captain turned to look at Samuel. "You were right, Samuel, the man is cold. Only someone watching very closely would have seen the greed light up his eyes. He said he would be glad to help in any way. I told him we were talking to everyone who had any connection to the manor belonging to the late Lady Wellington. He said certainly, the lady had been a distant relative of his, and he was familiar with the new owner, Mae Hinton."

"Then I said we were investigating the murder of one of her female servants."

"He was shocked, but only a trained eye would have seen it. The only hint he gave was a lowering of his eyes. He said, 'A servant, you say?' Then we established he had come straight to the San Carlo upon leaving Tallahassee and had been residing there since.

"As we were about to leave, he said, 'Captain, why would you come all the way to Pensacola to question me about a servant's death?' I turned to face him and said that because the killer left a trail to the San Carlo, and since he had recently traveled to the hotel, perhaps he might know something. He never blinked. Just a long, cold stare from those blank eyes, and then, 'Very well, I certainly hope you find the killer. We can't have someone like that running around loose, now, can we?' I thanked him for his time, and we left.

"But there was more, gentlemen. As we were walking out the front door of the San Carlo, Detective Harris asked me, 'What day was your murder?' I told him, 'Wednesday the twentieth.' He said to come back to the station, because he had a report to show me. We returned, and he handed me a folder.

"It was the report of a shooting death in a flophouse near the railway. He said women rented rooms by the week and had customers who paid by the hour. On the morning of the twenty-first, one of the cleaning ladies found the body of a man in room three. He had been shot once in the temple. The man had numerous scratches around his face and neck. His shirt was torn, with a piece of a pocket missing. Upon questioning everyone at the business, they determined the young lady who rented room four was missing. The general consensus was that she had, in fact, killed the man and left town. I continued to read and found the dead man had over fifteen hundred dollars on his person."

"I asked if anyone had taken photos of the dead man, and they gave me the photos from the postmortem. I can say conclusively that the scrap of fabric Margaret held in her hand was torn from Frank Young's shirt. Does his name mean anything to either of you?"

****

Mae had never learned deceit. She did not know how to lie convincingly. She looked at Edward with pain-filled eyes and tried to smile. "Well, in truth, your uncle, Doc Walters, gave me this pistol over two years ago. He said a young woman living in a remote area, quite often alone, needed to be able to protect herself. I agreed with him. So I practiced every day until I was very comfortable with it. When I feel the need, I keep it close."

Mae picked up the cup and took a long swallow of water. All without making eye contact with Edward.

Edward was an intelligent man. There were so many things about Mae that screamed innocence; like the way she had touched his face the first day they met, or the way she was open and honest about everything, and how she had thrown herself at him a few minutes ago. Innocence in everything, that is, except this. She looked like she would burst into tears if he pressed her. So...he would wait.

There would come a time when she would know him well enough to share with him the thing that frightened her so much; whatever it was had robbed her of her innocence and made her a very bad liar.

"Well, I am certainly grateful for all those hours of practice." He smiled. "The picnic would have been completely ruined if I had been bitten. Now, eat, woman." He laughed. "Even heroines need their strength!" They ate in silence, each with their own thoughts.

Edward was trying to picture Mae in England, mingling with the London aristocracy he dealt with every day. They would think she was beautiful but of no importance. They would look down their aristocratic noses and find her unpolished and unworthy of their time.

Oh, how wrong they would be. Edward had seen enough of humanity to recognize a true gem when he was in the presence of one. Mae was a rare find these days. She was a woman who didn't think about herself but did for others first. Edward gave an inward smile. She was the kind of woman who would make a great wife for a doctor.

Mae was not hungry. She was trembling inside. She hated not telling Edward the truth. They were not bound to each other, and yet she believed she had somehow violated his trust by keeping something from him. She nibbled on a piece of bread. He seemed genuinely interested in her plans for her village. Being a doctor, he seemed to understand her desire to help others. Was it such a great stretch of the imagination to think he would understand about her past? Perhaps she should leave this in God's hands.

Mae turned to Edward. She had to know. "Edward, do you believe in God? Do you believe He made each of us for another?"

Edward was taken aback. He'd seen miracles occur in medicine, where there was no logical explanation. He looked into Mae's beautiful eyes and understood his answer was very important to her. He did not want to tell her he had stopped believing when his sisters died. "I feel when a person believes in something, I mean truly believes, the something becomes very strong and powerful. I know I see things in my practice that have no earthly explanation. I've seen people pray until their knees were bruised, and their prayers go unanswered, and others who have seen a miracle, and believed it was a gift from heaven. Have I, personally, ever had reason to believe in a God? No."

Mae's eyes shone with unshed tears. She reached out her hand and stroked Edward's face. "Then I shall have to have enough faith for both of us for a while. Now, tell me how long I have to enjoy your company? How long will you be staying here with your family?"

Edward moved closer and pulled Mae into his arms. Her head rested on his shoulder, and he could not see her face. "I have commitments in England, Mae. I have promised the man who has been so gracious in training me that I would give him another nine months before I strike out on my own." He could not see the tears that pooled and then ran from Mae's eyes.

They held each other for long moments. Mae closed her eyes, concentrating on the sound of Edward's heartbeat.

Finally he spoke. "I will be leaving Wednesday, Mae." Edward felt the shudder pass through her. "But the important thing to remember is that I will be back. I had not given a lot of consideration to where I would begin my practice once my commitment was filled, but now I know. I will be coming home. The question is...what will I be coming home to?"

Mae lifted her head from his shoulder and smiled through the tears. Edward tenderly wiped them from her cheeks.

"To me," Mae breathed, as she moved her mouth to his, "to me."

This kiss was different. It burned straight to Mae's insides. She never wanted it to end. The longer it continued, the more it burned. She wanted Edward to hold her closer and tighter, and while this wanting embarrassed her, she could not control it.

Edward finally raised his head. He was breathing as if he'd run a mile. There was a slight shake in his hand, as he stroked Mae's face. "Sweetheart, I am a man with some self-control, but I find you are testing me to the verge of breaking. I need some water, and we need to start home."

Mae's face flamed, while Edward walked to the creek and splashed water on his own. He must think she was some kind of loose woman. She had never suspected she had the kind of passion in her that would make her cling to a man. She straightened her blouse and her loosened hair.

When Edward turned to her, he smiled and shook his head. "Woman, you have no idea how tempting you look, standing there like a goddess and still managing to look innocent."

Mae returned a weak smile. "And you, sir, should know no man's touch has ever made me feel so helpless and so strong, all at the same moment."

The passion blazed in Edward's eyes again for a brief moment, and then he burst out laughing. "Mae, you had better prepare yourself for my return, because when I get back there will be no stopping me."

Mae stood a little straighter and exhaled slowly. "Edward, please don't be gone any longer than absolutely necessary." They laughed together as they packed up and headed for home.

Chapter Twenty-Five

It had been a few days since the law had come to visit. Hardwick wasn't sure how many, because he had been drunk during most of them. There was unfinished business to handle now, and unfortunately he would have to do this himself. After Frank Young's fiasco, he couldn't trust anyone. He needed to make sure the little girl in room number four had a poor memory. He'd have a late supper and then pay her a visit.

Tonight he used the front door of the flophouse instead of the back stairs. He was surprised to see there was actually someone at a front desk. This woman had seen better days, but she hid it well. She managed a smile. "Good evenin', sir, is there something I can do for you?"

"I was here a while back. There was a nice little bird in room four. Is she busy tonight?" he asked.

The woman had been in the business all her life. She had an inner alarm system, and it was screaming at her now. "You mean the little blond, about sixteen?"

"Yes," Hardwick replied, "that sounds about right."

"Well, honey, you're a little too late. That one lit out for Texas. Found a cowboy type that wanted all her time." She searched the gentleman's face for any sign he might not believe her. He gave away nothing. "I've got another girl in number seven, not quite as young…" She let the invitation hang there.

"I'll pass," he snapped as he turned and left.

Well, well, the woman thought to herself. Roxanne had been right. There was something scary about this one. Maybe the girl should have lit out for Texas, instead of Tallahassee.

Hardwick stood in the cool night air, inhaling and exhaling deeply. Well, the little bird has taken care of itself and flown west. Good. One less thing to worry about.

He reasoned he had at least eleven months to take care of the bigger problem. He would need to be a little more frugal and find a more affordable place to hole up for a while. If he handled it right, he would soon fade from everyone's memory.

Hardwick was picking up the morning papers at the newsstand in the lobby of the San Carlo. He looked at the clock above the front desk. From the corner of his eye, he observed the boy running through the front doors and waving an envelope. Ten o'clock, right on time. He had turned toward the stairs when the bellboy pointed him out to the runner.

The young boy approached and said loudly, "Important telegram for you, sir."

Hardwick turned to the boy. The boy handed over the envelope and then stood with his hand out. Hardwick raised one eyebrow. The little snit had been paid the night before. The boy continued to stand there grinning, his hand still out. Hardwick reached into his coat pocket and pulled out a wallet. He peeled off one dollar and placed it in the little thief's hand. The boy grabbed the dollar, saluted sharply, and then ran out the front doors.

Hardwick made a show of sitting on the main sofa

and slowly ripping open the envelope. After some moments, he stood and approached the desk. "I will need a taxi to the train station in an hour. I have received news and must leave for London. If you could have a car brought round, I'll ring for the bellboy when I'm ready."

An hour and a half later, Hardwick had purchased a ticket for the two o'clock train to Jacksonville. He then exited through the rear of the station and walked a mile. After taking a second car to the docks, he got passage on a steamer to Miami. He was on the water, and on his way to a good hangover, by three in the afternoon.

It was almost six in the evening before Captain Lance received a telegram.

Hardwick was gone.

****

Eleanor had just received Mae's test scores from the college. Mae had passed all her business courses and her one English class with flying colors. Eleanor was running around like a madwoman, and as selfish as it sounded, she was glad to see the classes over until after Christmas. She was trying to get her orders out before the holiday, not to mention preparing for the small matter of a wedding.

Mrs. Finch wanted to host the wedding at her home. She insisted on handling all the arrangements, which was a blessing from above. Garth would be coming for her at eleven to go to the manor and choose a suite for them. Eleanor's life was about to change in ways she would never have anticipated. She was thrilled to be marrying a wonderful man whose children were a testament to his faith and his wisdom. The fact that the mere touch of his hand was like electricity to her was an unexpected but greatly appreciated bonus.

Eleanor was sure most widows her age tried to put romance and physical love out of their minds. It was less painful to ignore it altogether than to acknowledge how much you missed it. She had forgotten what it was like to walk into a room, meet the eyes of the man you love, and feel an instant fire spark to life. She thanked the Lord every night for sending this man to her.

The bell above the front door alerted Eleanor. She walked into the showroom expecting to see Garth but found instead a small, pretty, blonde girl.

"Hello," she greeted the newcomer with a smile. "Welcome to Taylor's. Is there something I can help you with?"

The girl smiled back. "To tell the truth, ma'am, I was walking by and saw all the beautiful hats in the window and just had to look closer. I hope you don't mind. I mean, I can't afford to buy anything, but they just looked so beautiful."

Eleanor could see the appreciation in the girl's eyes. She remembered a time when she had loved the sight of beautiful fabrics and believed she could never afford such things. "Do you sew?"

"Well, yes, ma'am, I do. I made this dress by hand, but never anything like these beautiful things," replied the girl as she touched one finger to a feather.

Eleanor took a long look at the girl. She was small, appeared to be about fifteen years old, and had a tight grip on an old, faded carpetbag. Her dress was a dove gray, cut from a simple pattern.

The fit was good, and it did not have the appearance of a handmade garment. "Your dress is very well made, dear. Someone must have taken great care to teach you to sew. Your mother, perhaps?"

The girl was stroking a piece of peacock blue silk. "No, ma'am. My ma passed on when I was four. My nana taught me to sew. We never got much past the basics, though. She passed on when I was twelve."

Eleanor smiled. "I'm sure your family has been grateful for your talent, then."

The girl withdrew her hand, smiled a bitter smile, and reddened as she said, "My pa and I had a partin' of the ways as to which talent I should be usin' to support him. So...I have been on my own ever since. Thank you, ma'am, for lettin' me look." The girl nodded to Eleanor and turned toward the door.

"Wait, dear. Are you telling me you've been supporting yourself with your sewing?"

The girl stiffened, turned to Eleanor, and snapped, "No, ma'am, ladies seldom want to have it known that a whore sewed their dresses. So I just make my own when I can."

Eleanor was stunned. This was a child, a talented one, but a child nonetheless. As the girl neared the door, Eleanor reached out to her. "Wait. Just wait a minute."

The girl paused. Eleanor pointed to a chair. "Sit a moment. I have some questions for you."

The girl raised one eyebrow and said, "Beggin' your pardon, ma'am, but my life ain't nobody's business. I don't need any of your Christian 'holier than thou' charity, either."

"Well, then, how about a job? Could you use one of those?" Eleanor snapped back.

The girl gave Eleanor a long, unreadable stare. "I'm listenin'."

Eleanor let out a long sigh. "I apologize, dear, I

wasn't very diplomatic. I have no right to question you, but I do have a possible solution to your...needs."

She'd been about to say problem, but did not want to offend the girl any further. "Please, have a seat and let's talk business."

The girl perched on the edge of a silk-covered chair, her back rigid and her eyes dark with anger.

"All right, let's start again. My name is Eleanor Taylor. I own this business. Before the business, I was a schoolteacher. I suddenly became a widow, with a young son to care for. I could not make ends meet on a teacher's salary, but I did know how to sew. So I took a chance and some very dear ladies propped me up for a while, until the word got around. Now I have more business than I can handle alone. I have a young assistant, but she is about to embark on a new business of her own. I am going to need some help. I would, of course, need to see some samples of your work, but I think we could help each other." Eleanor just sat back and waited.

The girl looked at Eleanor for several long moments, as if she was coming to some momentous decision. "My name is...well, everyone just calls me Roxanne. Like I said, I don't have nobody besides me to care for. I do know how to sew. I reckon there's a bunch I don't know about it, from the looks of the beautiful bits here, but I'm a fast learner. I just got into town a few days ago, and I ain't found a...proper place to stay yet. How much do you think you could pay me?"

Before Eleanor could answer, the door opened and Garth stepped in, smiling. "Good morning, ladies. Beautiful day, isn't it?"

Eleanor stood, returning his smile. "Good morning, Mr. Hinton. I was just interviewing a possible replacement for Mae. I think she may be a perfect fit for Mae's village."

Garth turned to the girl. "Well, we're headed out there, so if she needs a ride…" He let the invitation speak for itself.

Roxanne's demeanor lit up like the morning sun had just risen. "Why, thank you, sir, if it wouldn't be too much trouble."

Eleanor almost laughed out loud. She'd never seen such a quick transformation. It was time to nip this in the bud.

She smiled at Roxanne. "Mr. Hinton is my assistant's father, and my fiancé. We'll be getting married Christmas Eve."

Roxanne looked into Eleanor's eyes and recognized the humorous warning. She smiled her acceptance and said, "How wonderful."

It didn't take Eleanor long to close up the shop, and then they were on their way.

Chapter Twenty-Six

Roxanne sat in the back seat of the motorcar. She had never seen the inside of one before. The seats were covered in leather, and the interior was lined with polished wood. She only half listened to the conversation in the front seat. She wondered what in the heck she had walked into.

They seemed like nice folks, but it had been her experience that "nice" folks had agendas of their own when they extended help to her kind. She'd give them what-for in a hurry if they tried to put something over on her.

She became aware the vehicle had left the main road and was traveling down a tree-lined lane. There were cleared and fenced fields as far as the eye could see. Then she saw the…house? You couldn't call that huge thing a house. Roxanne sat forward and peered through the glass as the vehicle made the circle in front. The front door opened, and a beautiful, smiling young woman stepped out. She had on a blouse so white it almost hurt Roxanne's eyes. Her skirt was dark blue serge and split like a riding outfit, but it completely covered her black boots. Her dark hair was pulled back and tied with a white ribbon. When she turned, you could see waves all the way to her waist.

Roxanne realized she was staring and felt like a complete fool. She opened the door and stepped out.

The beauty was speaking to the man. Even her voice was attractive.

"Papa, you missed the first load of lumber! I'm so excited. It is really happening. Samuel took the trucks down to the site, to unload them under the temporary shelters... Oh, we have company," she sputtered as Roxanne walked around the back of the motorcar and into view. "Hello, my name is Mae. Welcome to our home." Mae extended her hand, and Roxanne took it.

She was still standing there in awe when Eleanor spoke. "Mae, this is Roxanne. She made the dress she is wearing, and I think we just might have found your replacement."

"Oh, how wonderful! Well, come in, and we can have some tea, and you can tell me all about it."

The next few minutes were just a blur. Before Roxanne could protest, she was sitting in a beautiful room, holding a plate with a heavenly roast beef sandwich, and sipping lemonade.

Mae apologized. "Please excuse my poor manners, but I was starving. I missed lunch because the trucks arrived, and I was too excited to eat. Martha makes the best sandwiches in the world, and Mrs. Peters made cobbler this morning, so we have to have some or her feelings will be hurt." Mae smiled as she picked up her sandwich.

Roxanne looked around as she ate. She guessed this was the parlor. The room was bigger than most houses she'd ever been in. The furnishings were soft and covered in fabrics she had never seen before. She could see a small lake through the glass doors.

There were pots of roses, all pinks and reds, surrounding a porch. Roxanne finished her sandwich and then carefully set the plate down on the table next to her. It was the most she had eaten in three days. She'd been saving her money for a room.

Mae took one last swallow of lemonade, wiped her mouth, and smiled at Roxanne. "Roxanne, I am so happy you have come to us. I am working on a project to help young women like you. Women who find themselves in less than satisfactory circumstances— ones who, through no fault of their own, are unable to care for themselves."

Roxanne had started to burn from the moment the word "project" spewed from Mae's mouth, and the anger just grew. What in the world did this pampered, beautiful woman know about "less than satisfactory" circumstances? Yep, she was another do-gooder who had no real knowledge of the world. Probably born into all this money and never had to get her hands dirty in her life. Mae had stopped speaking, and she and Eleanor were looking at Roxanne.

Roxanne realized she had missed the last of the speech, but it didn't matter.

She stood, grabbed her carpetbag, and snapped, "Well, ma'am, the sandwich was real good, and it was a pretty good speech. But as I told her"—she gestured toward Eleanor—"I'm not some charity case for you to squander time on. I can take care of meself, and I'll just be off now." Roxanne had taken about three steps toward the door before Mae understood what was happening.

Eleanor had recognized the look on the girl's face even before she'd opened her mouth. Mae was about to be faced with the reality of her dream. It was a wonderful dream, but sometimes people just would not accept help.

Eleanor snapped, "All right, young lady, just stop right there." Roxanne and Mae both froze. "This is not my problem. Mae, I can always find someone to help me sew. But, if you intend to move forward, this is going to be your first step. I'm going to find your father now, so you're on your own." She turned to Roxanne. "And you, little miss, had better not be foolish enough to lose the best chance at a decent life you've come across in years, just because of an overabundance of pride." And with a hard look at both girls, she left the parlor, closing the door firmly behind her.

Mae understood perfectly what had just happened. Eleanor had left so Mae could step into the role of leader and find out if she was really cut out for this project she had taken on. Mae closed her eyes, took a deep breath, asked the Lord for guidance, and exhaled slowly.

"Why don't we start over? Would you please have a seat, and let's take a few moments to get to know one another? If you still want to leave, then my papa will take you back into town."

Roxanne stared out the French doors for several moments. She looked back at Mae and with a slight smile said, "Well, I'd hate to offend that lady, 'cause I didn't try the cobbler."

Mae burst out laughing and answered, "I promise we will try the cobbler later. Now, let me try again to explain what I have in mind. I'm going to build a village. There will be a few houses built around a central community building. In this building we will educate and train women—young women, old women, any woman who wants to learn how to take care of herself. Some of these women may have children. We will educate the children, too. I want to teach the women crafts they can sell in a store I will build for them. They'll have a communal garden. It will be a place where they can learn to build up themselves and support each other." Mae stopped. She flushed a light pink. "I hope I don't sound like a pompous blowhard. This is the first time I've told my plans to anyone outside of my immediate family and circle of friends."

Roxanne wasn't sure what to say. It sounded like a good plan. She certainly didn't look forward to another back room in another shabby hotel. She never let herself wallow in some make-believe dream, where some man would take her away from all this. Hell, it was a man who'd sold her into this life. If anyone was ever going to get her out of it, it was going to be herself.

She looked at Mae now and said the first thing that came to mind. "Why? Why would you do all this? Why would you care about what happens to a bunch of prostitutes?"

Mae spoke softly. "If it would not be too painful, tell me a little about yourself, and then I'll try to explain my reasoning."

Roxanne had never had a friend. She had never talked about her life with anyone.

She wasn't sure why she could talk to this woman. She didn't feel like Mae would judge her, but for some reason she didn't want this woman to pity her, either. For so long, in her mind, she had kept herself separate from the reality of it all. She wasn't sure she wanted to knock the dust off it now. She looked at Mae. There was real interest. Not ugly curiosity, not pious disdain, just an interest in another human being. And so she spoke.

"I was born in a little town in Kentucky, just across the river from Williamson, West Virginia. You know, coal country. Everything is black from the dust. Maybe not at first, but the older anything gets, the darker it becomes from the coal dust. Maybe even people's hearts, and certainly their lungs. My mama died when I was four. I don't even have a faded memory of her. Then there was my nana. I don't remember a lot about my pa in the early years, just my nana. She taught me to sew. And she told me the things a girl is supposed to know. She sensed I was gonna sprout early, as she called it. That happened when I was eleven."

"About that time, my pa started staying around more. He worked in the mines most all his life, but he got the black lung and wasn't doin' so well. And then one mornin' my nana just died. Just keeled over in the kitchen. And then it was just Pa and me. Pa took to buying me dresses. Not little-girl dresses. He would dress me up and take me to town on a Saturday night. And all the men would look at me like I was a piece of candy. I hated it. Pa started talking about how if I played my cards right, we could both have an easy life. All I had to do was be friendly with some of the men at the hall.

"I wasn't sure exactly how that was supposed to get us an easy life. And then one Saturday night Pa was real drunk. When we got home, he said seein' as how I was gonna give it to somebody sooner or later, I might as well give it to him. I fought him like a wild animal. I managed to get away from him and hide in the woods the rest of the night, till he sobered up the next morning. And when he did, he reckoned he'd almost broke the one thing he had to sell. Me."

Mae was very still. She sensed this was something Roxanne had never talked about before. Quite possibly she'd never even remembered it until this moment. She knew the girl was unaware of the tears, spilling from those blue eyes.

"So before he could get drunk again and ruin things, he dragged me to an old rundown house at the head of the holler. When the door opened and an old man stepped out, I tried to run. But Pa was tired, so he just knocked me out cold. And when I woke up I was chained to an old iron bedstead." Roxanne turned to Mae and saw her own pain reflected in those dark eyes. She took a shuddering breath and managed a weak smile. "It was a year before I escaped."

Mae took Roxanne's hand. "And yet you lived. You took responsibility for your own life, and you did what you had to do. God gave you this life that you have fought so hard to keep, and no one but Him has the right to take it." Mae stood and said, "And now it is my turn. I was born in Trenton, Florida. My mama died when I was ten. My papa is a wonderful man, and he did everything he could to make our lives good. He owned a sawmill. I would take care of Cyrus, my youngest brother, while Papa took Samuel, the oldest boy, to work with him.

"My mama had taught us all to read as soon as we could hold a book. Papa would work with us at night on our mathematics and history and such. We all worked hard, but we had each other, and all the loving memories of our mama, to keep us going. We were getting on with our lives. Then the event happened."

Mae stopped speaking, let out a long sigh, and resumed. "I was almost seventeen. The boys were at the mill with Papa. There was a roaming band of men, and I was caught outside with no gun. It was a dark time for all of us, but at least we had each other. I had my faith in God, and the love of my family, to keep me strong. And then I moved to Tallahassee to further my education. I had been here a few months when I met Lady Wellington. She lived here in this beautiful home.

"That dear lady had a sad story of her own. Her only child was attacked a few months before she was to be married. The girl had no foundation to lean on, and lost all hope. In the end, she took her own life.

"Lady Wellington and I became close friends, and when she passed on, she left me this property and a very large amount of money. I intend to put all the money to good use. So, what do you think?"

Roxanne was humbled. Grandma used to say you shouldn't ought to pass judgment on someone till you'd carried their load a while. She would never have guessed Mae's secret. The woman had so much compassion and kindness you'd think she'd never known any pain or sadness. Maybe it was the God thing she talked about. Whatever it was, Roxanne found she wanted it, too. She wanted to walk away from all the black in her life and be filled with light. She looked up at Mae and said, "I've always wanted to know how to make cobbler."

After much discussion, it was settled. Roxanne would go home with Eleanor, and tomorrow they would establish how much she would need to learn to be beneficial to Taylor's. Mae was sure Roxanne would be a fast learner.

It was late evening, and Garth had taken Eleanor home. Mae was in the parlor with Samuel and Cyrus, watching as each pursued his favorite pastime. Cyrus was reading *Plant Relations, A First Book of Botany* by John Coulter. It was a new book Doc Walters had sent him. The boy was considering classes in horticulture and agriculture at the university. Mae thought about how their mama had instilled a love for all growing things in this boy.

Samuel had several small pieces of wood spread out on a linen cloth on the table. Mae had seen him do this many times. He would just sit and look at them until one of them spoke to his heart, and then he would lovingly transform it into a beautiful piece of art. Lately, though, he had been working so hard on the apartments over the barn and on managing the supply site for the village that he had not had a lot of spare time for the work that brought him peace.

Mae smiled a private little smile. She had to stop thinking of Samuel as a boy. He was eighteen. Anyone outside the family would look at him and see a grown man, and a handsome one, at that. He was well over six feet tall, with broad shoulders and strong arms. His dark hair and eyes, coupled with the fact he was seldom seen smiling, gave folks the idea he was unapproachable. He was slow to speak, and someone who didn't know him might think this was a reflection of his intelligence level. But they would be so wrong. He was slow to speak because he was always observing. He had a natural eye for detail, and his memory held everything his eyes took in.

He finally held out one finger and touched a piece of corkwood. He stroked it gently, then picked it up and set it aside. He stood and wrapped the others in the linen. *Ah.* Mae smiled. *He has chosen.*

Mae stood also and said, "Cyrus, I'm off to bed. Don't leave the lamp on, and don't be up all night."

Cyrus mumbled, "Uh-huh," as he turned a page.

Samuel just shook his head and smiled.

Mae stood on tiptoe to kiss his cheek. "Goodnight, dear one. Thank you for all you are doing for the village."

Samuel looked down at his sister for a long moment. "If it makes you happy, then it's worth doin'," he drawled. "Good night, sis. Lock this door behind me."

Mae followed him to the French doors and turned the big key as he walked toward the barn. She tousled Cyrus' hair as she left the parlor.

Garth was just coming in the front door when she entered the foyer. She waited as her father made sure the doors were secured.

"Did you get Eleanor and Roxanne home safely?" she enquired.

"Yes, little missy, I did. Patrick was still up, and we had a game of checkers. He assured me Samuel was a better player than me." Garth grinned. "He is so excited to be moving to the 'farm,' as he calls it. He has big plans for Cyrus, and he can't wait for Hansu to teach him to break boards with his feet. His poor mama almost fainted at the thought."

Mae was laughing. "Yes, he is going to have a great time wearing us all out." She put her arm around her papa and smiled up at him. "It fills my heart to overflowing to see you so happy."

Garth looked down at his beautiful daughter and

said, "How strange. I was thinking the same thing about you. I couldn't help but notice the way Dr. Finch was looking at you after the picnic yesterday. Do I need to be havin' a talk with the gentleman about his intentions, young lady?"

Mae's eyes shone as she reddened. "I can assure you his intentions are honorable, Papa. And besides, he is leaving Wednesday at noontime." She raised her face, and her smile was gone. "And I'm going to miss him something terrible," she whispered.

Garth wrapped both arms around her and drew her close. "Oh, baby girl. So that's how it is. Well, he seems to be a fine young man. I guess it's a good thing you are about to be a very busy young woman. Why, here you are with your very first resident for your village, and you've got all sorts of things to keep you occupied until he returns."

"Thank you, Papa. You always know how to smooth out the wrinkles in life."

Garth's gaze followed her as she climbed the stairs. Good Lord, he thought, his baby girl was in love. His heart seemed to swell in his chest. He was glad Eleanor would be here to help him through this event in Mae's life.

He had struggled through the last one on his own...well, not on his own. The Lord had propped him up every day. But it would be good to have Eleanor to share this. Heck, it would just be good to have Eleanor. He grinned to himself as he headed to the kitchen.

Mae sat in her window seat with the lights out so she could better see the stars. She liked to say her prayers as she looked to the heavens. "Lord, I have so much to thank you for. Thank you for my wonderful family. A girl could not ask for a more loving and supporting family. And thank you for bringing Eleanor and Patrick into our lives. Thank you for Roxanne, Lord. Please give me the wisdom to help her regain her life and realize she has You to thank. And now, Lord, thank you for Edward. Lord, I have nothing to compare these feelings to, so I don't know if I should call this love. I just know he takes my breath away with his kindness, his intelligence, and yes, Lord, with his touch. And I know I will feel like part of me is lost until he returns. If this is love, then so be it. Just please keep him safe, and return him to me quickly. Amen."

Chapter Twenty-Seven

It was a cold, gray morning. Rain had swept through during the night, bringing the chill of the coming winter. Mae woke early. How could she sleep on this, her last day with Edward? He was coming to pick her up, and they were going to spend the entire day together. Edward wanted to show her some of his favorite places.

She just wanted to be near him, to drink in his voice, to thrill to his touch, and to make enough warm memories to hold her for nine long months. She looked at herself in the mirror. Mae was not a vain woman. Others might find her pretty, but this morning she wanted to be beautiful. She wanted Edward's heart to skip a beat when he looked at her. She wanted…well, she just wanted. She didn't even know how to put this feeling into words. She just wanted.

She chose a dark red suit with black trim. The sleeves belled out below the elbow, with insets of black lace draping over the backs of her hands. The bodice was cut in a heart shape. Her bosom was concealed behind a fan-shaped gathering of black lace. The skirt was full and stopped just at her ankles, allowing her boots to show beneath. She was aware her hair was her shining glory, with a red ribbon woven into the braid atop her head and the back portion allowed to hang to her waist. She picked up her black gloves and dark red muff. She was ready. She would smile and be witty, and do her best to charm Edward—so thoroughly, in fact, that he would miss her as much as she missed him. She deliberately waited to go downstairs until he arrived. She smiled wickedly to herself. She intended to make an entrance. And she did.

Edward was standing in the foyer with Garth when Mae stepped to the edge of the staircase. Both men looked up at her. It only took a moment for Garth to realize his little girl was, indeed, all grown up. He glanced over at Edward and had to hold back a grin. The poor man never knew what hit him. You could see the surrender wash all over him. Yep, Garth thought, it's love.

Edward watched Mae float down the staircase. Good Lord, was there ever a more sensual woman? How was he going to be able to leave her?

He could feel the need growing, and he had to take a deep breath and exhale slowly. It seemed like it took her ten minutes to work her way to the bottom; ten minutes of watching those hips sway from side to side, as her skirt swished around her ankles. Just the way her hand stroked the banister was enough to make him sweat.

Mae never broke eye contact with Edward. She moved slowly and gracefully down the stairs, trailing her right hand over the banister as if it were a lover's arm. She would be embarrassed if she gave herself a moment to consider her actions. So she didn't.

When she reached the bottom, she turned to her papa. He was smiling broadly. She kissed him on the cheek, whispered goodbye, and then turned to Edward. She could see the fire in his eyes and suspected her performance had been worth the effort. Edward tore his eyes away and turned to Garth. "I'll take good care of her, sir, and have her home by ten this evening."

It took all Garth's concentration not to laugh out loud. "You do that, young man." He grinned. "You do that."

It was a day they would both remember. Edward had planned every moment. He seated Mae in the motorcar and leaned in to place a warm blanket across her lap. She turned to thank him, and he stole a kiss, then grinned like a twelve-year-old boy, causing Mae to laugh like a girl of the same age. It was as if there were an unspoken agreement between them. They would ignore the reality of it being their last day together for almost a year.

They drove to Mr. Finch's offices. Edward pointed out a building across the street. It had an empty suite of rooms on the second floor. He told Mae if they were still empty when he returned, he would consider setting up his practice there.

Then they drove to the Mallard Farm on the east side of the county. A client of his father owned this property. The Mallard Gardens were known throughout the South for their roses. The sun had finally reached full strength and taken the chill from the air. They strolled through the gardens holding hands, telling each other of their childhood dreams. When they reached the rear of the gardens, Mae was almost moved to tears.

Edward had arranged to have a small lunch served. A silk-draped table had been set near a carved bench under a spreading oak. There was a sweet pink-and-white quilt covering the table's contents. Edward seated Mae on the bench and then proceeded to serve lunch, removing the quilt to reveal a tureen of warm potato soup, crusty bread to spread with fresh churned butter, and glasses of cold milk to go with warm, cinnamon-flavored bread pudding.

There was little conversation as they ate their fill, but their eyes spoke volumes. When they had finished, Edward placed the quilt back over the table before sitting next to Mae and pulling her gently back against his chest.

She rested her head on his shoulder while his arms circled her possessively. Mae closed her eyes, allowing all her other senses to take over. She could feel the beat of Edward's heart against her shoulder. She could hear the soft in-and-out movement of his breath. She could smell the faint perfume of roses in the air. She had no concept of time. The world just floated around them.

Finally, Edward spoke gently. "Have I told you how beautiful you are? How I sometimes lose my breath at the sight of you? How much I want to hold you in my arms and feel you tremble with anticipation?"

Mae opened her eyes and tilted her head to look at him. "You mean like now?" she whispered.

He cradled her face in both his hands and kissed her. As the kiss deepened, Mae pressed her body to his. He could feel her need and sensed that, if he led her, she would surrender to him. This knowledge carried such a weight of responsibility that he was able to break the kiss.

Breathless and a little shaky, Mae felt tears rising up. She raised her face and gazed at him with eyes filled with longing.

"I'm so sorry, sweetheart. One of us has to keep

our wits about us, and if I don't put a stop to this right now... I've never wanted anything more than I want you right now, but I have no right to take what you offer so sweetly. The man who takes your innocence should be your husband, and I cannot be that man today."

It was as if he had thrown a glass of cold water in her face. *The man who takes your innocence. Oh, Lord, how can I tell him I have no innocence to take?* The tears spilled over, and Edward took his handkerchief and patted her face.

"Please, sweetheart, don't cry. It breaks my heart to think I've caused you any pain."

Mae laughed between broken sobs. "I have to put out this fire you started somehow!" Edward smiled, then chuckled, and soon they were holding onto each other and laughing helplessly together.

The afternoon was spent storefront shopping. Edward bought her lily of the valley perfume in a beautiful cut-glass atomizer.

She bought him a pair of fine leather gloves for the winter in England. They had a quiet supper with his parents. It was homey, and Mrs. Finch had told the cook to prepare his favorite foods. They laughed and talked gaily over coffee, and suddenly it was over. It was time to get Mae home. She kissed the Finches good night and promised to get together with Mrs. Finch about the wedding plans for Eleanor and Garth on Friday.

And then they were in the motorcar and on the way home. There was little to say, so they savored the silence, each filled with their favorite memories of the day. As they pulled up to the front door, Edward made a decision. When they entered the foyer, Garth was strolling down the hall from the library.

"Oh, good, sir, you're still up. If you have a moment, I would like to speak with you," Edward said formally.

Garth looked from one to the other, and decided he might need a drink for this conversation. He looked at Edward and said, "I'll be in the library," and turned and headed back down the hall.

When he was out of sight, Edward took Mae into his arms and kissed her, almost roughly, then set her aside. "Try to sleep, my love, and I'll see you at the station in the morning. My train leaves at eleven, and I want your face to be the last thing I see when it leaves." As Mae climbed the stairs, he went down the hall with a purposeful stride.

Garth had poured two small glasses of brandy and set them on the table between the great chairs in front of the fireplace. The fire had burned low and was now just red embers.

Edward marched through the door, and Garth started to stand. "Please, keep your seat, sir. I have something to ask you." And suddenly Edward was mute. He didn't know where to start. After all, this had to be done properly.

Garth knew full well what was coming. He could see from the panic on Edward's face the boy didn't know how to begin, and he would have laughed if his heart were not in his own throat.

Finally, he said, "Son, sit down, take a drink, and let's talk about this."

Edward blinked, nodded, and sat down in the empty chair. To his credit, his hand only shook a little as he reached for the glass. Garth drained the remainder of his, then sat back and waited.

Edward took a large sip, swallowed sharply, and blurted out, "I'm in love with your daughter."

Garth did laugh then. "Young man, tell me something I don't know."

"Well, sir, I want to marry her. When I get home from England in nine months, I will have completed my training and be ready to set up my own offices, and I will be able to provide nicely for her, and I swear I will do everything in my power to make her happy." The brandy had kicked in, and Edward had found his voice.

Garth raised a hand to silence Edward. "Son, the beauty of Mae is, if she loves you, you won't have to do anything but love her back. That is what will make her happy. Not your status in this world, not the things you can give her, but the love the two of you will share. Mae is not a complicated woman. She has a heart made for love."

Edward sighed deeply and sat back in the chair. "Sir, can I ask you a question?"

Garth smiled. "Son, I'm not an expert on relationships, but I'll give it a try. Go ahead."

"How did this happen so quickly? I mean, I've known women before..." Edward immediately turned bright red and started stuttering. "I don't mean...well, you know, I've been involved in romances before, but this—this has hit me like a ton of bricks. Oh, don't misunderstand; I'm the happiest man in the world. I just don't know how this happened so fast, you know?"

Garth let the poor boy squirm for a moment before he took pity on him and answered, "I know exactly what you mean, son. It's how it was for Ruth and me. She had never been involved with a man. I had been interested in a few women, but I had never known the kind of magic she created. I've always believed, and Ruth always said, it was God who directed our love, and He knew us better than we knew ourselves." Garth could tell from the look on Edward's face that this answer was not satisfactory.

"Son, do you believe in God?"

"Mae asked me the very same question. I don't disbelieve. In my line of work, we see things that cannot be explained. And simple folks usually attribute these things to Him."

Garth smiled sadly. "Well, son, simple folks have no trouble believing in God, because it's usually about all they have to rely on."

Edward had the grace to be embarrassed. "I meant no disrespect, sir."

"It's all right, none taken. If there's one thing I've learned in this life, it's that we all come to the Lord in our own time. And if you build a life with Mae, your time will come, son, because she is as close to the Lord as cane is to sugar. Now, you say you want to marry my daughter, but have you spoken with her about this?"

"Well, I have not actually spoken the words, but I did tell her I loved her and I want her waiting for me when I get back."

Garth grinned. "Word to the wise, son, ask her before you leave. Her anticipation will make the homecoming all the sweeter." Garth stood and stuck out his hand.

Edward stood also, and the two men looked into each other's eyes. Garth took Edward's hand in both of his with a smile. "Welcome to the family, son."

****

The day broke clear and cold. Mae stood at her

226

window and looked out across the meadow. Her papa was going to drive her to the station to say goodbye to Edward. She was glad Papa would be there. She was aware she needed to be strong and not put a burden on poor Edward. She must not let him know how painful it would be to see him leave. It was only for nine months, she told herself. Why, it was a drop in a bucket compared to the years they would have together. That thought helped...a little.

She hadn't been able to sleep last night or eat a thing this morning, and she was afraid she did not look her best. This morning, of all mornings, she needed to be beautiful. Mae stared at herself in the mirror. She wanted to be so beautiful that Edward would hold her image in his mind the whole time he was gone. She chose a forest green suit and a white blouse with a fountain of lace ruffles at the neck. She kept her hair simple, with a small braid around the crown and the rest hanging in ringlets down her back. She took one last look in the mirror. It was the best she could do.

Garth stood at the bottom of the staircase, watching his baby girl glide down the stairs. The wonderful thing about Mae was that she had no idea how the world saw her. Her mother had been the same way. These strong-willed, intelligent, beautiful women moved through life handling whatever calamity was put in their path. They couldn't see themselves as being any stronger or more resilient than anyone else. They couldn't see how they inspired others, and their blindness to their own worth was most endearing.

Mae moved to her papa's side and took his hand in hers. "Thank you, Papa, for going with me." He squeezed her hand and opened the front door.

227

****

Garth leaned against the motorcar and watched the couple on the platform. The Finches had already made their goodbyes and were standing with Garth.

Mrs. Finch was dabbing at her eyes with a small handkerchief. "They make such a beautiful couple," she whimpered.

"All right, Mother, I'm taking you home for some hot chocolate and a good cry. The boy will be back before you know it. And it looks like you have found a good anchor to keep him here, once he gets back." Mr. Finch put his arm around her and directed her to the carriage. He nodded at Garth as they passed, and Garth gave a sympathetic smile in return.

Meanwhile, Edward was saying, "Sweetheart, I had a long talk with your father last night, and he gave me a piece of advice I think was very sound."

Mae smiled up at him, eyes shining with unshed tears. "Yes, dear, did he tell you to wear extra socks this winter? Or use camphor if you developed a cough?" she teased.

Edward threw back his head and laughed out loud. "Mae, stop that. I'm trying to be serious here. Now, I've never done this before, but I believe there is a standard formula involved. So...Mae Hinton, will you marry me? Will you make me the happiest and luckiest man on this earth? Will you let me spend the rest of my life being this happy?"

Mae took his face in both her gloved hands and pulled his mouth down to hers. She kissed him as she had never kissed a man before, with all the passion she could put into one meeting of their lips. After several long seconds their mouths parted.

Edward was trying to catch his breath when Mae said, "The sooner you get home, the sooner we'll continue to explore just how many ways there are to say I love you. And, yes, I'll marry you."

Edward lifted her and swung her in a circle, yelling, "Yes," at the top of his lungs.

Garth smiled and said, to no one in particular, "I'm guessin' that was a yes."

Chapter Twenty-Eight

Mae woke to the sound of birds. Their singing and chirping put a smile on her face. Christmas Eve and a wedding, all in one day—what more could a body ask for? Her smile saddened just a little. If only Edward were here, then the day would be perfect. Well, she was not going to mope and ruin Papa and Eleanor's day. She laughed out loud, thinking she had better get moving, as she had a full day ahead of her.

A quick wash and some comfortable clothes later, she was bouncing down the stairs, following the smell of bacon to the kitchen. Mrs. Patrick and Cook turned to the door as Mae practically skipped into the kitchen. Mrs. Patrick smiled as she said, "You're up and about early, missy. Could it be you're just a wee bit excited?"

Mae grinned and popped an orange slice into her mouth. "That and I have a dozen things to see to before this afternoon."

Samuel entered through the back door and stopped as all three women turned to him. "Somethin' sure smells good. It called to me, clear out to the barn." He grinned.

Garth burst through the door right behind him and stopped short to avoid a collision. There was a long silence, all of them looking at him and grinning like he had grown a second nose.

"What?" he asked. "What are you all looking at?"

Mae took pity on him and crossed the kitchen to give him a kiss on the cheek. "Why, just the most handsome soon-to-be groom we've ever seen." She laughed.

Garth reddened, then grinned. "I don't know about the handsome part, but surely the happiest," he replied. "May I suggest we all sit down together and have a nice, peaceful breakfast, because tomorrow Patrick will be here, and it will be Christmas morning, and there will be nothing peaceful around here for some time to come."

Once their peaceful breakfast was done, Mae stood and advised them all they had better be clean, dressed, and ready to go at four o'clock this afternoon, or heads would roll. The men all laughed as she left the room, then looked at each other and decided they'd better get moving. No one wanted to be the reason this day would be less than perfect.

****

Mae sat in her bedroom, looking out over the property. It was still hard to believe sometimes. She had much to be grateful for. Here she was about to have a second mother and another little brother. Those would be enough, but to have her papa so happy again was just more than she had ever expected. For this, she was truly thankful to the Lord.

She had spent the day making sure all was in readiness, including that the rooms Eleanor and Papa had chosen were in the best of order. The suite was at the end of the west hallway, separated from the other bedrooms by an open sitting room. The large bedroom had a good-sized dressing room and private bath.

Mae made sure the newest sheets were ironed and

the bed coverlet freshly aired. Every surface was dusted, and there were bouquets of fresh flowers on all the tables. There was a fireplace on the outer wall of the bedroom, directly above the one in the library, and she made certain the wood basket was full. The bride and groom were spending their first night together in the bridal suite of the Leon Hotel, but Mae wanted everything ready for their return home tomorrow. Cyrus would be sharing his room with Patrick until the apartments in the carriage house were complete.

She stood and looked in the mirror one last time. Eleanor would be wearing a powder-blue lace dress, so she had chosen a royal blue one. The long sleeves had lace overlays, but the rest of the dress was unadorned. Only the bride should be beautifully dressed today. She would have all eyes on her, as it should be. Mae braided her hair loosely and wound the braid around her crown with only one small blue silk flower to dress it. With a nod to herself, Mae picked up her reticule and headed for the foyer, to make sure everyone was on time.

As Mae observed Samuel and Cyrus sitting there, she thought how handsome they must appear to the world.

But it was not just their outward appearance that made them so. She looked into their faces as she came down the staircase. Samuel was steadfast and honorable, possessed of a fierce sense of responsibility to safeguard his family; it was almost as if someone had put him in charge of the wellbeing of all of them. And Cyrus, well, Cyrus had the most loving, joyful heart of them all. Because of his young age, he had been the closest to Mama before she passed. It was almost as if she had never left him. He would often say things that led you to believe he had just spoken with her.

Mae loved them both with all her heart, and at this moment was very proud of them. They were both wearing the black serge suits she herself had made for them. Of course, they were both still growing, and next year those suits would go to the church for distribution. For today, they were a perfect fit. Cyrus had cut a small camellia blossom for each of their lapels, and was holding one for Papa. Mae was about to speak when both boys stood and looked to the top of the stairs. Mae turned and saw her papa start down.

****

Three faces smiled as Garth stepped closer. Garth looked at those upturned faces and his heart swelled with love. No man could ask for a finer family than the one he was blessed with. His sons were growing strong and honorable, and his daughter was blessed with an incomparable inner beauty.

Now he was about to give them another brother and a woman who would love them as if they were her own. Cyrus solemnly handed the flower to Mae, who then pinned it to Garth's suit. Her eyes were shining.

He was afraid if she cried now they would all be undone, so he said, "No long faces, you three. Today is Christmas Eve, and we're all being given a couple of beautiful presents, so let's get this show on the road." Samuel got the door, and Garth shooed them all out to the motorcar.

****

Mrs. Finch had outdone herself. The large front parlor was decked with greenery and shining in the light of dozens of candles. It was fragrant with the scents of pine and vanilla. They were all assembled and

233

waiting for Mr. Finch and Eleanor to enter. They turned at the sound of footsteps. There stood Patrick. His freckled face was split with a toothy grin. He was holding a powder-blue satin pillow. Tied to the pillow were two plain gold circles.

Patrick walked forward, his head held high. He had been given a very important job, and he was determined to complete it with all the grownup dignity he could muster. He stopped when he got to Garth and looked up at his soon-to-be father.

Mae's eyes filled as Garth placed his hand on Patrick's shoulder, signaling a job well done. And then the doorway was filled with Eleanor and Mr. Finch.

Mae looked at Eleanor and then turned her attention to Papa. She gave a deep sigh. If Edward looked at her one day with half the love she could see in her papa's eyes, she would die a happy woman. She turned back to Eleanor. No wonder Garth's eyes were shining. The woman was always beautiful, but today, well, she was angelic. Her red hair was softened by the candlelight, and her complexion took on a peachy glow. The dress was designed to be demure and enticing at the same time, which was no mean trick. It accentuated Eleanor's full bosom, clung to her neat waist, and then belled gently over her hips to swish against the floor when she moved. The top of her bosom was covered in an opaque, chiffon ruffle, with similar ruffles at the ends of her sleeves. While all this was beautiful, nothing compared with the look of love on her face.

They stopped in front of the minister; Mr. Finch placed a kiss on her right hand, which he then gave to Garth. When their hands met, Eleanor began to melt. She had resigned herself to her widowhood. Then the

Lord had given her a totally unexpected gift. He had wrapped it up in this handsome, virile man, this man who made her feel young and special and womanly. This man who made her want things she'd long forgotten.

The service was simple and short. In no time, the minister was saying, "You may kiss the bride." As their lips met, Eleanor could hear the clapping, but when his mouth took hers she lost all sense of others. They were suspended in time.

Garth became aware the room had gone silent. He lifted his head and took a deep breath, then turned to face the room. "Thank you, all of you, for sharing this celebration with us."

Eleanor knew he was giving her time to collect herself. She now turned to face this group of wonderful people she held so dear.

She smiled at them as she turned a becoming shade of pink. "My thanks, as well. Having you all here to share this moment means so much to us."

****

Mrs. Finch had champagne for the adults and apple cider for the young ones.

Toasts were made amid much laughter. Mrs. Finch was very proud of her cook, Louise, especially tonight, and with just cause. The wedding party and guests dined on delicious roast pork with candied yams, followed by a beautiful three-tiered cake with sugared violets sprinkled over it.

They gathered in the parlor later, for the gift giving. Hansu presented Eleanor with a bolt of purple silk from China. Cyrus gave her a bottle of lavender water he had infused himself. And then there was

Samuel's gift. He presented her with an eight-inch by eight-inch square box. It was made of cherry wood and intricately carved. Each side showed a pair of clasped hands displaying a wedding ring on each.

"Oh, Samuel, this is beautiful, and I will treasure it always," Eleanor said with tears in her eyes.

There was much hugging, and good wishes given, as they prepared to leave for the hotel. Finally, there was the tossing of the flower petals.

Mr. Finch had made arrangements for a driver to take them to the Leon, and Samuel would pick them up tomorrow after lunch.

Mae thanked the Finches again for helping to make the ceremony a wonderful memory for all of them. Samuel rounded up the boys, and soon they were on the way home. Patrick and Cyrus kept up a constant stream of chatter, allowing Mae's mind to wander. How would she feel when it was her time to be a bride? But, before that time arrived, there would be a huge hurdle to cross. She would need to tell Edward about the event. She would need to know, in her heart, that he had no misgivings. She would need to hear him say the words, tell her he loved her no matter what her past held. She would not dwell on that now, though. Today was the beginning of a new family. Next week was the beginning of her project. It would be a new year, and she would not mar it with old memories.

****

Garth was aware of the soft pace of Eleanor's breath as she drifted off to sleep. Her head was on his shoulder, and she was wrapped in his arms. He could feel the beat of her heart against his chest. It was slower now, but a short time ago, it had pounded with the strength of their passion. Each of them had been surprised by their response to one another. Surprised, but very happy. The instant ignition had climbed to a blinding blaze before they had surrendered to the heat. As they lay there looking into each other's eyes, Garth had kissed her softly and said, "I am truly a blessed man."

She had stroked his face and smiled. "No more blessed than I, sweetheart, for you have helped me remember what it feels like to be a well-loved woman."

Now, as he lay listening to the slow in and out of her breath, his mind was filled with the abundance of good in his life. He knew he'd done nothing to deserve the many blessings he'd been given, and so he vowed he would try to live his life in a manner of thanks to his Lord.

Chapter Twenty-Nine

Hardwick woke with a start. His heart was pounding, and he found his legs damn near tied to the bed by the twisted sheets. Awareness seeped in slowly. He'd been dreaming. The dream was hanging on to the edge of his awareness like a spider refusing to let go of his web even as it gets torn down. Ah, there it was. He'd been dreaming about the old bird. She was giving him the same lecture she had given him in life. He was smart. He was educated. He was even charming. He should try to find a legitimate occupation to which he could dedicate his life.

Hardwick stretched, jerked his legs free of the sheets, and stood. The smell of coffee finally worked its way into his mind. The old Cuban housekeeper must have brought it in. He poured a cup and moved to the window. It had to be near noon. The sun was blazing in a cloudless sky. It was the end of March, with the temperature staying a balmy eighty degrees, cooled only by the sea breeze sweeping in off the Atlantic. He tried to clear his head as he sipped the strong brew, but the old bird would not leave him alone.

He remembered clearly the first time they'd met. He had been a defiant sixteen-year-old orphan. She had been a shrewd, rich, old widow. Hardwick had been forced to stand by while his father squandered the family fortune and then took the cowardly way out,

A Heart Made for Love

with a pistol. His mother had written him a letter of introduction on her deathbed. Alone and angry, he'd made his way from England. The letter had been sealed, so he'd never known exactly what pleas for help were enclosed. He'd practically dared the old bird to have sympathy for him. He'd had all the pity he could stand from those looking to collect on his father's debts. They had descended like buzzards, when his mother finally succumbed to her own weakness.

His father had been a mean, abusive drunk who beat him whenever he was down on his luck, which near the end was daily. His mother had been a weak, whining, sickly thing who had no spine. He could have forgiven the old man the beatings, but not the theft of his birthright.

A man who had no property could have no standing in society. If you were not born of noble blood and you had no land, you were nobody. He had vowed, at an early age, to become someone to be reckoned with and respected. And be damned if the old bird hadn't turned on him just like his pitiful excuse for a family.

She'd obviously gone weak in the head, to leave so much money and property to a backwoods female. It was his money, and was to have been his salvation, his means of becoming someone. He would be damned if he would lose everything again.

He sipped the coffee and found it cold. Cold like the years he'd spent in English schools. Oh, the old bird had been generous with his education, his wardrobe, and his vacations. Because of her generosity, and the appearance of old money, his schoolmates had accepted him. He had taken advantage of their acceptance at every opportunity. He'd visited the homes of many old-money families. He'd learned the habits and ideologies of the rich. He had used his charm on many women. All had known the extent of the old bird's holdings, so he had always been welcome. They, like he, had assumed it would all be his. It would still be his, one day soon.

He looked at himself in the dresser mirror. The new beard was longer than was fashionable, but it hid his countenance well. Put on some old clothes and throw in a tired old horse, and he would never be recognized. The time was nearing when he would have to move. When he would reclaim what was his.

****

Mae was excited. At breakfast this morning, Papa had advised they were putting the finishing touches on the first two houses in her village. She had been so busy trying to explain her project to local ministers that she had not actually visited the village in a couple of weeks.

She was glad to have good news from the construction site, as she had run into some brick walls with the public in general.

Mae could not understand why anyone would be opposed to her helping women in need, but several of the ministers she had spoken with had warned her, saying she was naïve and really didn't understand what she was undertaking. One had even said "no decent young woman should be putting herself in such a compromising position. Does your father know you want to fraternize with harlots?"

She had been near to angry tears when she related this to Eleanor and Roxanne. Eleanor had tried to soothe her disappointment, but Roxanne had given her an angry "I told you so" look. She was now on her way to a meeting with the Methodist Ladies Society. They held a meeting the first Wednesday of the month to assemble quilts for the needy, and Mae was optimistic. Surely if they were concerned with keeping poor folks warm, they would understand her desire to help young women.

As Mae entered the church hall at the rear of the sanctuary, she was happy to see such a good turnout. There were at least thirty women gathered around quilt frames, chatting and sewing happily.

Mrs. MacGruder, the head deacon's wife, came toward her smiling. "Miss Hinton, thank you for joining us. We are always grateful for another pair of hands."

Mae took her outstretched hand and smiled in return. "I truly appreciate you allowing me to come speak to your group, ma'am."

Mrs. MacGruder turned to the room and raised her voice. "Ladies, may I have your attention, please?" When the chattering had stopped and all heads were turned her way, she said, "Miss Mae Hinton has come to speak with us today about some sort of project she has in mind for helping the needy. Now, we all know Miss Hinton was the beneficiary of the late Lady Wellington's estate, and we all know how generous she was when it came to helping others, so I'm sure we'll all be excited about this project. Miss Hinton, go ahead."

During Mrs. MacGruder's introduction, Mae realized these women had no idea why she was here. Well, they were about to be enlightened.

"Good morning to you all. Let me say thank you for allowing me to speak with you here today. Some of you may be aware I have been working on a project, specifically a project for women."

"I have been very fortunate in my life to have a loving family. They would support me, no matter what the circumstances might be. However, I have seen enough of the world to know this is not always the case. For some women, circumstances arise that place them in very vulnerable positions. They find they have nowhere to turn. I intend to remedy this for as many as possible."

"My father is constructing a small village on our property. It will house women who have no home or who need a safe haven to rest in while they try to piece their lives together."

Mae could see some of the women turning to each other with questioning looks.

She said, "Perhaps I can take some questions from you?"

A tall thin woman stood. "What do you mean when you say 'vulnerable positions'?"

"Often young women find themselves expecting children. Women who had no say in creating the child. Sometimes their families choose to disown them. Or a married woman may find she has made a bad choice and her husband beats her, but she has no way to support herself and her children, so she stays, and the beatings continue."

There was muttering among the group now. Some of the women still looked confused, and some of them looked incredulous, while some of them looked outraged. One stood and said, "Are you saying you want women to leave their husbands and come live at your 'village'? Just up and leave their husbands?"

Before Mae could respond, another said, "A decent young woman would not find herself in such a predicament!" The women were beginning to speak aloud their thoughts and feelings. As the chatter grew in volume, Mae held up a hand and tried to calm them.

A white-haired matron stood, cleared her throat, and immediately the chatter began to subside. The woman looked around the room, making eye contact with several of the women, some of whom had the grace to blush. Then she turned to Mae and spoke.

"My dear, I am the Widow Harrison. I've known most of these women since they were in diapers. It is easier for them to pretend these things just don't happen in polite society than to decide how they can help. When you get to be my age, you have the privilege of speaking your mind and not caring what others think about it. Let me say I think it is a good idea, but I'd like to hear more."

Mae gave Mrs. Harrison a grateful smile. "Ma'am, I thank you for your interest. I'm not asking you ladies to do anything you might feel is contrary to your beliefs. I only ask that if you know of a woman in need of assistance, please send her to me. We are building houses and a communal learning center for the women and their children. I intend to educate them and teach them a marketable skill so they can care for themselves and their families."

One brave soul glared at Mrs. Harrison and said, "Do you have any idea what kind of women you are going to be inviting into our town? Do we want these loose women around our families?" She looked around the room for support.

Mae smiled sweetly. "Yes, ma'am, I do know what kind of women I will be inviting—the kind who need support financially, emotionally, and spiritually." Some ladies looked sheepish, but others were still glaring at Mae as if she were about to open a leper colony.

Mae turned to Mrs. MacGruder. "Thank you, all of you, for your time and consideration. I am grateful for any interest you may have in assisting in this project. If you ever need to contact me, you can leave word with my stepmother, Eleanor Hinton, at Taylor's."

There would be lots of lively conversation for the rest of the meeting, Mae thought. She smiled at Henry as she climbed into the motorcar.

Chapter Thirty

It was a beautiful spring morning. It was moving day, and Mae could not be happier. Samuel had driven into town to pick up Roxanne. She was moving into the first completed village home this morning. Papa had loaded all of Mrs. Peters' things and brought them down. She and Roxanne would be sharing the house, and both of them were excited. Roxanne had learned to use the treadle sewing machine and was going to teach Mrs. Peters. Mrs. Peters was going to teach Roxanne to make cobbler. To Mae, it was a perfect exchange.

Mae had just gathered an armload of linens from Papa's truck when Samuel and Roxanne drove in. Mae looked at Roxanne and silently thanked the Lord. The change in her was nothing short of a miracle. Gone were the circles under her eyes. She had gained fifteen pounds and no longer looked as if a strong wind would blow her away. Her hair had begun to shine, and her complexion was now clear and rosy. While she had been beautiful before, now she looked healthy, as well. She was dragging the old carpetbag with her and grinning at Mae.

"Welcome to your new home, dear. Mrs. Peters has already staked out her room, but you have two left to choose from." Roxanne chose the room nearest the kitchen. It had been painted a soft yellow, with gleaming white window frames. Mae had asked Samuel to make a chest of drawers and a night table for each room. He had painted each white to match the trim.

Roxanne laid the carpetbag on the bed and stood at the foot, trying to believe the idea of this house belonging to her for as long as she needed to be here. She could sleep in peace at night.

Mae laid the armload of linens on the bed. "I'm going to the truck to get some flowers while you start loading those drawers."

Roxanne, who had placed her meager wardrobe in the chest of drawers and was making the bed when Mae returned, heard a sharply indrawn breath, a low moan, and then the breaking of glass. She turned from the bed just in time to see Mae hit the floor. Mae had fallen on the broken vase, and there was blood pooling on the floor. Roxanne screamed for help and tried to roll Mae off the broken glass. She was holding Mae in her arms when Samuel and Garth came running in.

"What happened?" Garth snapped.

"I don't know, sir. She dropped the vase, and then she collapsed and fell on the broken glass."

Garth gently took Mae in his arms and laid her on the bed. Eleanor and Mrs. Peters ran for towels to stop the bleeding.

Samuel stood rooted to the floor at the foot of the bed. Garth looked up at him and froze.

"What's the matter, son?"

Samuel was staring at the chest of drawers. He walked over and picked up something as he grabbed Roxanne by the arm and jerked her to his side.

"Where the hell did this come from?" he barked.

It wasn't the first time she'd been manhandled, and by men a lot meaner than this one, but it was the first time she was really frightened since coming to Tallahassee. When Samuel opened his hand, she saw the little ivory box.

She tried to calm herself. She stood a little straighter and took a deep breath. "What are you asking me? Where was it made, how did I get it, or what?"

"I know who made the damn thing, girl. What I want to know is where you got your hands on it," he growled.

She met Garth's stare and swallowed hard.

She turned back to Samuel and lifted her chin. "I'm not going anywhere, so can you please let go of my arm?"

Samuel let out a slow, deep breath, closed his eyes, and dropped her arm.

Eleanor came back with a burned feather and a bowl of water and towels. She ran the feather under Mae's nose until she began to stir. Eleanor was aware of the tension in the room but was more concerned about Mae at the moment.

As Mae's eyes began to flutter open, Eleanor whispered to her, "It's okay, sweetie. Don't move around. Just be still and let me check you for glass." It appeared all the blood was coming from one wound, high up on Mae's right arm. The sleeve was already sliced, so Garth ripped the pieces apart to reveal a two-inch cut. He pulled one long shard of glass from Mae's arm, causing her to moan in pain.

"Hold on, baby girl. We're done. It's okay now."

Eleanor finished ripping the sleeve away and washed the blood from the arm, then wrapped it snugly with a strip of towel to stop the bleeding. Mae was awake now, white as a sheet, and very frightened.

Her eyes met Samuel's, and she began to cry. He moved to the bed and, taking her hand, asked, "Do you trust me, sister?"

She nodded, tears running down her cheeks.

"Then know you are safe. Do you understand, Mae? You are safe."

Even as Roxanne rubbed her already bruised arm, she envied Mae. No man had ever stood over her and declared her to be safe.

Garth turned to Mrs. Peters. "Ma'am, could you make us some tea?" The little lady nodded briskly and left, closing the door quietly behind her.

"Now, young lady, sit down. You look a little shaky yourself," Garth said to Roxanne. "Samuel, take a deep breath, son, and just think a minute."

Samuel exhaled slowly and ran his hand through his dark hair. He was still clutching the ivory box. He looked at the box with so much love in his eyes Roxanne immediately understood.

"Oh, good Lord," she whispered. They all looked at her. "The curls, they belong to all of you, don't they? You, and Mae, and Cyrus, those are your baby curls inside."

Samuel looked like he had reached the end of his patience. "Just tell us where you got the box."

It was one thing for people to assume she was a whore, but it was another thing entirely to have to talk about it to people. Roxanne pulled herself to her full height and said, "A man threw it at me one night. He owed me money, and when I asked for it, he threw this thing at me and said the woman who had it before didn't have any need for it now."

Mae whimpered and closed her eyes tightly, trying

to stem the flow of tears.

"Does this man have a name? Do you know where to find him?" Garth asked.

Roxanne shook her head regretfully. "No sir, I don't know his name. But if it's any consolation, someone killed him around Thanksgiving last year, in Pensacola."

Upon hearing this, the two men exchanged a knowing look.

Garth turned to Mae. "Honey, I'm going to take you to the truck, and we're going home. Eleanor's going to get you fixed up, and then we're all going to sit down and have a little chat, all right?"

Mrs. Peters assured them she would clean everything up and have Roxanne's room all ready when they brought her home later.

Two hours later, Mae had been stitched, washed, and sedated, with a glass of brandy. The others had eaten a light lunch and were now seated in the library. Garth looked at Roxanne. The girl wasn't as big as a minute, but she had stood up to Samuel and had the bruises to show for it.

Samuel saw his father's gaze and turned to look at Roxanne. His stomach clenched at the sight of the marks on her arm. Samuel had never hurt a woman in his life. Well, he couldn't say that any more. He was ashamed he had let his temper get the best of him.

Roxanne couldn't stand the quiet a minute longer. "All right, can someone please tell me what's going on? Am I in some kind of trouble?"

Garth sat back in the chair and stretched his long legs out toward the fire. "No, no." He sighed. "You haven't done anything, missy. We just need to get some facts straight. Suppose you tell us everything you know about this man."

Roxanne stood and walked to the window seat. She looked out across the lawn at the tree-lined lane. It was peaceful, and she tried to use the peacefulness to calm herself. She sat in the window, pulled her knees up, and hugged them tightly to her ample chest.

Finally she spoke. "I first met the man about two years ago in Pensacola. Afterwards, when he tried to leave, I asked for my money. He knocked me around a little, and then just before he left he threw something at me and said, 'The one that had this won't be needin' it anymore.' I found it the next morning, and I'd never seen anything like it. It was beautiful."

Samuel's chest tightened. He was ashamed of the thoughts he'd had about this girl.

Roxanne continued, "So I kept it. And sometimes when I needed cheerin' up, I'd take it out and stroke it. And one day whilst I was holdin' it, it just popped open. That's when I found the little curls inside, tied in ribbons. And I figured he had killed someone's mama. It made me sad 'cause it was clear she must have loved her babies, to save their little curls."

The tightness in Samuel's chest deepened, and he realized it was his heart.

"When I saw the man again, it was just around Thanksgiving last year. He was drunk, real drunk, and I got to my room and locked the door before he spotted me. He went into the room next to mine, and I didn't hear anymore, so I figured he passed out. Then, much later, I heard someone in the hallway, and I opened my door. There was a gentleman, a real looker, coming down the hall. I said hello, and he looked at me but just walked straight to the room next door and went in. I could hear them talk for a couple minutes but never really heard what was said. There was one shot, then nothing.

"I'm not stupid. He looked right in my face. And he had to know I heard the shot. I figured I'd better run, so I jerked open the door, and sure enough, he was coming out. The bartender, from the next block over, was coming down the hall, and he was a really big guy, so I grabbed his hand and dragged him into my room. But the gentleman looked right into my eyes as the door closed." Roxanne gripped her knees even tighter.

"I figured he'd be back. So…I left. I waited an hour or so, then gathered my stuff and lit out to the depot and hopped the first train out. It was going to Tallahassee, so here I am." She turned and looked at Garth and then Samuel. "Will someone please tell me why Mae fainted at the sight of the little box?"

Garth said, "The box belonged to Mae's mother. When she passed away, I gave it to Mae. She always wore it on its leather thong round her neck. The day Mae was attacked, the box disappeared. We always suspected one of the men must have taken it."

"Well, then, he got just what he deserved," Roxanne snapped.

Samuel walked over to the window seat and sat next to Roxanne. "It's not that simple. We had a maid who was murdered just before Thanksgiving. We think she may have been killed because she was mistaken for Mae."

Roxanne gasped. "No! You mean someone may have tried to kill Mae? But who would…" She stopped as she answered her own question in her mind.

Samuel looked at Roxanne. "Ma'am, you're gonna have to go with me Monday and talk with Captain Lance. He's gonna need to know all this, and he may have some questions for you."

She looked up at Samuel with a question in her eyes. "I'm not real comfortable talkin' to the law."

"It'll be okay," he assured her. "I'll be with you."

She looked at him for several long seconds, and then turned to Garth. "Sir, I'm about run out of steam. Would it be okay if I go home now?"

Samuel drove Roxanne home in silence. It was near dusk, and they passed a small group of deer. "Oh, they are so beautiful. I used to feed some in the woods out behind our shack when I was a kid. If I sat real still, they'd come right up and eat from the corn pile, and I could almost touch them. They had the most beautiful, sad eyes. Kinda like they were born knowing that, eventually, someone would shoot 'em."

Samuel didn't speak.

"I know. You think I'm stupid, don't you?"

He turned to look at her. She was really a beautiful girl. "No. Anyone who appreciates the beauty of a wild animal must be pretty smart."

When the motorcar stopped in front of Roxanne's new home, she turned to the door, and Samuel reached out and caught her hand in his. She turned and looked up at him. He looked into her eyes for a long time. "I'm sorry," he said.

"For what?"

He reached out and lightly ran his fingertip over the bruises on her arm. Roxanne was mesmerized, as his finger traced the marks on her arm.

"For this," he whispered. "I would never hurt a

woman on purpose. God made women to be loved and respected. I'm sorry."

Roxanne sensed this man was gentle to the bone, until you threatened someone he loved.

She put her hand on his. "It's okay. I know you didn't mean to hurt me." She slid out the door and almost ran to the house. Roxanne was already older in her heart than this man would ever be. And she didn't like the way her heart turned over at his touch.

Chapter Thirty-One

It was Monday morning, and Roxanne sat stiffly in the front seat of the motorcar.

She had visited Mae Sunday afternoon, just to make sure she didn't blame her somehow. Mae had actually thanked her for taking good care of the little locket. It was now hanging from a gold chain and nestled against Mae's heart. She had been pale, with a look in her eyes that Roxanne knew well, the look of a terrified woman aware of her own vulnerability.

Mae was surrounded by people who loved her. Which was more than Roxanne could ever claim. Roxanne remembered when she had been afraid, and vulnerable, and chained to an iron bedstead. It had been three years ago, and she'd never looked back, until now. She doubted the old man who'd bought her was going to go to the law and complain about the beating she'd given him. He had still been breathing when she left, not that she cared one little bit.

However, now she was going to have to talk to the law, and it made her skittish.

She looked over at Samuel. He was always a little standoffish, but this morning he really seemed to be in another world. He looked as if he was working on a serious problem and couldn't be bothered with anything else.

Roxanne had deliberately worn her long-sleeved

white blouse with her brown serge skirt. The bruising on her arm, a sickly yellow-green this morning, covered a large area. She hadn't wanted to explain it to anyone, so she'd just covered it.

Samuel spoke, and it startled her. "How is your arm this morning? I hope it's not painin' you any."

That he asked about her arm at the same moment she was thinking about it startled her even more.

"No. It's not pretty, but it don't hurt any."

"Good, and I'm real sorry."

Roxanne nodded her acceptance. "Once your pa told me what was going on, I could see as how you'd be a right bit touchy about the little box. Who did you say made the box?"

"Hansu, the little Chinaman you see around the house sometimes. He's been working for my family since before I was born. He taught me how to carve, make furniture, and a lot of things I would never have known about if he hadn't showed up."

It was one of the longest speeches Roxanne had ever heard come out of him. The little Chinaman must mean a lot to him. The only person Roxanne had ever had feelings for was her nana. So much had happened, in the almost four years since her death, she'd never had time to grieve the loss.

They coasted to a stop in front of a big building. The sign over the front doors announced it: Leon County Sheriff Office. Roxanne just sat, still as a statue.

"I promise you this will not be hard. The man we're going to talk with is a good man. He won't pressure you. And I'll be right there with you."

Roxanne gave a deep sigh. "All right. Let's just get this over with."

Miss Edith Hampton gave Samuel a bright smile. "Is the captain expecting you, Mr. Hinton?"

Samuel colored slightly. "No, ma'am, but we really need to speak with him."

The young secretary gave Roxanne a long look and then entered the captain's office.

"Well, now…" Roxanne smirked. "That one would like to get to know you better."

Samuel gave her an alarmed look. "What?"

"Didn't you see the look she was givin' you? She wouldn't scream if she ran up on you in a dark alley."

Samuel had turned a deep red. "That's enough foolishness." He was saved from any further response by the captain's arrival.

"Good morning, Samuel. I hope this is a social visit?" Captain Lance took a moment to assess Roxanne and then nodded. "Ma'am."

Samuel stood and shook the captain's hand. "Good mornin', sir. I wish it was a social visit. This is Miss Roxanne…" Samuel realized he did not know her last name. He turned to Roxanne and waited for her to speak. She stubbornly refused, standing mute.

Samuel continued, after the captain had seated them in his office. "Roxanne arrived in Tallahassee sometime around Thanksgiving. She was in Pensacola prior to coming here." The captain sensed the tension between the two. He was totally familiar with the stubborn look on the young woman's face.

"She is working for Taylor's now, and just moved to one of my sister's houses. While she was moving in, some important information came out. Pa and I figured you should know about it."

Both men waited for Roxanne to provide further

information. And waited. Samuel, usually very patient, snapped. "Roxanne, just tell the man what you know."

She looked at the captain and could see the hint of a smile. "Oh, all right. I don't know anything for sure, but I can tell you what I saw that night. A couple of years ago I met this man. He was mean. We…had business."

The captain made an assumption about what kind of business, based on Samuel's discomfort.

"And when I asked for my money, he knocked me across the room. And then he threw something at me and said, 'The woman who had this won't be needin' it anymore.' The next morning I found it. It was a pretty little carved box, so I kept it. A few months ago, I came across this same man. He was very drunk, and I managed to get into my room and lock the door before he spotted me."

Roxanne was unaware she was wringing her hands. "I heard him go into the room next to mine, and I didn't hear anything else, so I figured he had passed out. About three hours later, I heard someone in the hall, so I opened the door. There was this gentleman, you know, dressed like a dandy, and real high-toned."

Samuel made a choking sound. Roxanne shot him an impatient look, then continued. "I spoke to him, but he pretty much ignored me and walked into the room next door. I could hear them talking but couldn't make out the words. A short time later, there was a shot, just one, from that room. I knew the gent had seen my face, so I jerked open the door to run. The gent was coming out of the room, so when I saw the bartender from around the corner coming down the hall, I grabbed his hand and pulled him into my room."

She looked at the captain but could tell nothing of his thoughts from his expression. "But as I was closing the door, the gent looked me right in the eye, and he knew that I knew. I'm no fool. I packed my stuff, waited a couple of hours, then headed to the train depot and took the first one out, which was to Tallahassee." She folded her hands in her lap, and met the captain's stare head on.

"Now, that's an interesting story. It would seem, Miss..." The captain just waited, with a polite smile hovering around his mouth. After what seemed like forever, Roxanne gave in. "Gibson. It's Roxanne Gibson."

"It would seem, Miss Gibson, you are a very fortunate young lady, to be here telling this story. Did you ever know this man's name?"

"Men don't usually talk a lot while we're doing business. I don't get a lot of names."

Samuel had a pained look when he spoke to the captain. "Sir, the thing the man threw at Roxanne belonged to my sister. It was taken from her almost three years ago, during an attack. Mae never saw the faces of her attackers, so we were never able to hunt them down."

Captain Lance shook his head. "That's way too many connections to be coincidental. Miss Gibson, if you saw the gentleman again, could you identify him?"

"Oh, yes. He had some of the coldest blue eyes I've ever seen."

"Could you describe him well enough for a police artist to draw a likeness?"

"Well, I guess it depends on how good your artist is."

The captain smiled. He stood, went to the door, and leaned out to speak. "Miss Hampton, I have a job for you."

Samuel had sat quietly for most of an hour now, just watching Miss Hampton draw. Roxanne had been very persistent about the man's features.

Finally, Miss Hampton laid down her charcoal and looked at the finished drawing. She looked up as she turned the drawing around for Roxanne to inspect. Neither woman was prepared for Samuel's reaction.

"Damn!" Samuel immediately reddened. "Beggin' your pardon, but I know him."

The captain looked at the drawing and smiled a very cold smile. "Well, it appears I will be needing to speak with one Langford Hardwick again."

****

Mae sat in the back garden, holding the latest of Edward's letters. She could almost feel his lips on hers when he wrote of missing her. Remembering how well she fit in his embrace started her imagination running wild.

What would it be like to have him make love to her? She almost laughed aloud at her own foolishness. He was coming home soon. One more month and she would have everything a woman could ask for.

She had filled three houses with women and children. The newest "family" member was a fourteen-year-old girl by the name of Louise. She was five months pregnant and had been disowned by her parents. The father was the drunken son of a neighbor. She told her parents he attacked her in the barn one evening. Somehow all the blame had been placed squarely on Louise. She'd heard about Mae's village from the sister of her Sunday school teacher.

Mae gave a contented sigh and smiled to herself. The Methodist ladies were spreading the word. Maybe not intentionally, but then, gossip did spread like wildfire. It was not important how they heard of her, as long as they arrived for help. Mae was thinking about how well these displaced women had melded together when she heard a step behind her.

"I'm not disturbing you, am I, dear?" asked Eleanor.

Mae laughed. "No. I have a new letter from Edward, and nothing could ruffle my feathers right now." Eleanor joined Mae on the bench.

"When will he be home, dear?"

"He says early September, no specific date, just when he can tie things up."

"Mae, I don't mean to pry, but have you spoken with Edward about your event?"

The smile slowly faded from Mae's face. She had worried over this matter for some time. "No, I haven't told Edward, but I have accepted the fact I will have to, at some point. I tried a few times, but the time just never seemed right. It's a difficult conversation to begin."

"Mae, I know you were very young when your mother passed away. I don't know how much you know or have learned over the years about what goes on between a husband and wife. If you have questions, dear, I would be glad to answer them for you."

"Eleanor, you are my dearest friend, and I know you would help me with any problem I might come against. A few weeks after the event, Doc Walters visited to check up on me. He wanted to make sure I was not with child, and that my menses had stabilized. He said that, from all he could see, I was going to be fine. I should still be able to have children when the time comes."

Eleanor was certainly glad to hear all this, but it still did not address the facts. Mae was going to have to tell Edward she was not a virgin, and why.

"Mae, Edward seems like an honorable man. And the Lord knows a doctor should be able to understand what you have been through. But I suggest you tell Edward everything, at the earliest possible opportunity. He may need some time to adjust to the idea. You want to know in your heart that he has absolutely no reservations when the two of you marry. You want no secrets between you when you begin your life together."

"Thank you, Eleanor, for being such a wonderful friend. You are a wise woman, and I will do as you say. Edward says we have much to talk about, but he has no idea how much."

Chapter Thirty-Two

It was late, and the sun was orange and low in the western sky. Mae had better pick up her pace or she would be late for supper. She had been busy with Emma while time had slipped away.

Mrs. Harrison had sent Emma and Jimmie to Mae. She was the cousin of Mrs. Harrison's cook. Mae had worked with Emma on the sewing machine today, and Emma was making good progress. She had been a little hesitant, as she had a natural fear of all things mechanical. Her years of living in the backwoods had kept her isolated from such things. It had also kept her in bondage to a man who had brutalized her and her young son.

She'd been with Mae for three weeks now, and it showed. The bruises had faded on both of them, and little Jimmie no longer had the dark circles under his beautiful blue eyes. He seldom spoke, but Mae did see an "almost" smile yesterday, when Samuel gave the child a small horse he'd carved for him.

Mae had just cinched the saddle on her horse when a scream rent the evening air. She ran around the house to see a very large dark-skinned man dragging Emma by her braids. Little Jimmie was frozen in place, with a look of resigned terror on his face as if this was a scene he had witnessed many times.

Mae found herself suddenly back in time, in a

place she had hoped she would never have to visit again. She could smell whiskey and feel rough hands. Her vision began to blur. She might have fainted if Emma hadn't screamed again.

Mae sucked in a deep breath and yelled at the man, "You let go of her, right now!" The man paused, looked at Mae, and then continued to drag Emma toward a horse and wagon.

Even as her eyes were seeing this, her mind was saying, "This is what Papa feared; this is why he was worried about this project."

This was the moment Mae would have to prove herself. Instinctively, she found the little beauty and fired a round into the air. The man froze and then turned slowly toward Mae. The look on his face would have urged most men to full retreat.

"I said let her go, and I meant it. I don't want to have to shoot you, mister."

The man let out a bark of laughter. "You think you can hit me, little lady, before I can take your gun away from you?"

Mae stood her ground. Her heart was racing and her insides quivering, but her voice was firm. "You can try, but I warn you, I will not hesitate."

The man had let go of Emma and now turned fully to face Mae. "You're the reason I'm here, ain't ya? You're the one who put some crazy notion in her head, like she can just up and leave and get away with it. She's got a home, and I'm takin' her back to it."

As the man reached out to grab Emma again, Mae fired. The man's arm jerked in reaction to the white-hot pain. He wheeled sharply and took a step toward Mae, then stopped. He could see she had gone pale, but her grip on the pistol was firm, and her arm was rock steady.

"Emma, get up off the ground and come here. Jimmie, you come to me, too. Now."

Jimmie's eyes were round, admiration shining through them. He kept one eye on the angry man and began to walk slowly toward Mae. Emma was scrambling away from the man, but she didn't have to worry. He was busy stanching the blood flow from the flesh wound in his upper right arm.

When both Emma and Jimmy were standing behind her, Mae lowered the pistol.

"Sir, I suggest you get in your wagon and leave. My papa has heard the shots, and by now he's about two minutes away. I don't mind telling you he feels even more strongly about men who abuse women and children than I do."

Emma whispered something in Mae's ear. The man had not moved and still looked as if he would gladly kill her. Mae spoke again.

"You just stand right there and don't move." Mae walked to the wagon, keeping a close eye on the man. She reached in under the seat and took out a rifle. Keeping one eye on him, she unloaded the rifle, placing the bullets in her pocket, and then shoved it back under the seat. Mae stepped back from the wagon.

"All right, you can go now."

The man stood there, staring at Mae. "I'll be back. And I'll take what's mine. And you..." Before he could finish his threat, they all heard the truck tearing up the road.

Samuel jumped out before Garth came to a complete stop. He had a rifle in his hand and had it pointed at the man, moving toward Mae as he asked, "Is everyone okay? Did he hurt anyone?"

Mae shook her head. "No, we're all right. And he was just leaving."

Garth looked at Mae. She was pale. He could see the man had a wound in his upper arm. He turned back to Mae. "Did you do this?"

She nodded. "Yes, sir. I did warn him not to touch Emma again, but I guess he doesn't hear well."

Garth turned to the man. "Sir, I'm going to give you a piece of sound advice. You need to leave now, and don't even think about coming back. There is nothing here for you."

The man's face was red with rage. "That woman belongs to me. You can keep the brat, 'cause he's a useless, sickly thing, but the woman belongs to me and you ain't got no right to her."

Garth wanted nothing more than to walk over and loosen some of the big man's teeth, but that would not change anything. Instead, he turned to Emma.

"Ma'am, is this man your husband?" She shook her head no.

"Sir, this is not your wife. She is a human being and does not belong to anyone but the good Lord who made her. And if she were your wife, she would still stay here, where she would be safe from your abuse. Now, before you leave, I want to make sure you understand the situation here. There is nothing belonging to you. You are not welcome here. If you are found on this property again, you will be shot. Are we clear? And if you're under any illusion the wound in your arm was a bad shot, let me assure you my daughter could have taken out one of your eyes if she had so desired. She is a crack shot. So consider yourself lucky, and leave. Now."

The man gave Mae one more hate-filled look, then climbed into the wagon and drove away.

There was a collective sigh from everyone. Samuel looked down and found Jimmie wrapped around his leg, pale and shaking. He reached down and picked the boy up. Jimmie immediately wrapped both arms around his neck. When Samuel looked back up, there were Roxanne and Mrs. Peters standing in the doorway of their home. He was glad to see Mrs. Peters had her rifle in her hand.

He said to Jimmie, "I don't know about you, little buddy, but it's my supper time, and I'm hungry. Let's go see if Mrs. Peters has something cooked up, okay?" Jimmie just nodded as Samuel strode toward the house.

Emma was trying to tidy up her hair and knock the dust off her dress. Mae asked, "Emma, are you hurt anywhere?"

"No, ma'am, and I am real sorry for all the trouble. I'm surprised it took him this long to find me."

"Well, he's gone now, and I don't think he'll be back."

Garth looked at his daughter. "You did good, baby girl. I'm thankful you didn't have to kill him. He's been warned now. First thing in the morning, Samuel will be coming to start working with all the ladies. They all need to learn how to handle a gun. There may come a time when you're not here and they have to take care of themselves."

The next night the lumber stockpile burned to the ground.

****

It was late summer, and the heat had been intolerable for two days, and now the southwestern sky looked like a giant bruise, all black and blue. Mae observed a flock of birds flying north as she walked to the barn. She found Samuel sanding a small desk.

"Brother, do you think we should shelter all the women at the manor, in case this storm turns out to be a bad one?"

Samuel walked to the barometer hanging on the barn's center pole. The pressure had been twenty-eight point nine when he milked this morning. It was now hovering around twenty-eight point two. He shouted, "Hansu!"

The little man entered through the rear door of the barn. "Good day, Missy." He turned to Samuel. "What you need, Sammy?"

Samuel smiled to himself. He had a good foot and a half on Hansu, and the old man still called him Sammy. "What do you think about the storm? Is it going to be a bad one?" They had relied on Hansu's weather reading skills for as far back as Samuel could remember. The old man had never failed them.

Hansu tilted his head back to look up at Samuel and smiled. "Hansu already lock chickens up and send young Cyrus to herd in cows."

"Well, that answers that question." Samuel turned to Mae. "Let me check on Cyrus, and see if he needs help, and then I'll drive the truck over to get the women."

Mae said, "I'm going to saddle Zeus and cut across the fields. I'll have them ready when you get there with the truck."

As Mae was crossing the fields, she tried to

remember when she'd last seen such an angry sky. The wind had picked up, and her horse was nervous, telling her the storm might be closer than they had anticipated. Roxanne was grabbing clothes off the line when Mae rode into the yard. She tied her horse securely and ran to help.

"Thanks. I was afraid the wind would take 'em before I could get 'em in." Roxanne laughed. They carried the basket into the school building. Mae was glad to see all her extended family was gathered there.

"Hello, all," she called. "I'm going to ask all of you to grab whatever you might need for the rest of the day. When Samuel gets here with the truck, we're all going to ride up to the manor and sit out this storm. Samuel and Hansu seem to think it may be more than just a good rain. We'll make a party out of it, so grab your sewing kits and maybe we'll do a little sewing for Louise's little one. Hurry, ladies. Samuel will be here in a few minutes."

Within fifteen minutes they could hear continuous rolling thunder in the distance, and the wind had gotten stronger. Mae had everyone assembled back in the school area when Samuel pulled in with the truck. It took a few minutes to get them all seated in the back, except for Louise, who was eight months along. Samuel gently helped her into the front seat. Mae headed for her horse. When the truck started moving, Roxanne stood, and yelled, "Mae, make sure I moved the bean pot off the stove in the kitchen before you leave."

Mae waved and nodded and turned toward the little house shared by Roxanne and Mrs. Peters. Mae shook her head as she spotted the pot still on the stove. She had to find a towel and then look for a "spider" to set the pot on. She took a moment to make sure the damper on the stove was closed and would smother the fire. Closing the door firmly, she headed for her horse again.

The wind was blowing fiercely now, and the lightning was getting closer. Zeus pawed the ground. She was glad she'd secured him well or she would be walking home. She leaned in close, patting his neck and telling him it would be okay. She loosened the reins just as a bolt of lightning struck a tree on the far side of the compound. Zeus reared, catching Mae by surprise. She stumbled, and by the time she righted herself, Zeus was fifty yards away.

She was yelling at him to stop, when a movement caught her eye. Mae turned toward the tree line and could see a man moving toward her. He was dusty, tall and lean, with a full dark beard.

Over his shoulder, she could see a horse tied to a slender oak. By the time Mae considered her own safety, the man was only ten feet away.

Chapter Thirty-Three

Samuel was unloading the last woman from the back of the truck when he saw a motorcar coming down the lane. When it rolled to a stop, he was surprised to see Edward's long frame climb out.

Edward was smiling. "I'm impressed, Samuel. Not many men can say they have a truckload of women."

Samuel reddened slightly and grinned. "If you're looking for one woman in particular, she'll be here any minute. And she'll be happy to see you. She wasn't expectin' you till next week. She's coming through the fields, from the village, on Zeus. In the meantime, you can help me unload these ladies and their things into the back parlor."

When they had everyone settled in and Martha was brewing tea to go with the cakes Cook had made that morning, Samuel turned to Edward. "Mae should be here by now. Come with me." When they got to the courtyard, they could see the lightning continually flashing, back toward the village. Samuel was about to speak when he stiffened, then shuddered.

Edward placed a hand on his shoulder, and asked, "Are you okay?"

"No. Something's wrong."

Edward looked around, but could see nothing. "What's wrong?"

"It's Mae. Something's wrong."

Samuel looked pale, and Edward felt goose bumps rise on his arms. Samuel was running for the truck before Edward could question him again. It was all Edward could do to make it to the truck and get in before it was moving.

****

Mae stood her ground. The storm was very close now, and the black clouds smothered the daylight. She yelled above the wind, "What do you want, mister?"

The man looked vaguely familiar, but Mae could not place him. He never spoke, just continued walking toward her. Mae slipped her hand in her pocket, and was feeling for the little beauty, when lightning struck again. It was so close it sizzled, and the hair on Mae's arms lifted as she flinched at the brightness. By the time the roar of the thunder rolled over them, the man had grabbed Mae's arm, jerking her hand with the little beauty out of her pocket. The gun flew several feet away. His face was close enough for recognition now.

Mae gasped, "You! What are you doing here?"

The man snarled, "Why, I've come to claim what's mine, dear."

Mae drew in her breath sharply as Hardwick twisted her arm behind her back. Mae could feel the first big drops of rain hit her face. She could smell the earth in the air as the wind whipped around them. Hardwick jerked her back against his chest, and with his free hand grabbed her breast. Mae jerked and could feel her arm separate from her shoulder as he yanked it upward. She had been angry before, but now Mae was afraid. Something was dancing frantically in the back of her mind. Something in her subconscious was screaming at her. She swayed as her eyes closed. She could smell it now. Not the rain, or the moist earth, but lemongrass. She could smell lemongrass. Oh, Lord, she could feel the shirt over her face, the buttons pressing down, the hands holding her, and the voice saying... Mae screamed.

A scream from the depths of every nightmare she had lived through over the past three years.

The scream covered the sound of the approaching truck. The man was not aware of the truck until a door slammed nearby.

Mae believed she heard her brother yelling. She opened her eyes and imagined Edward, her beloved, running toward her. Even as she told herself this could not be, the hair on her arms stood, and the brightest light her eyes had ever beheld blinded her.

Samuel had the rifle in his hand and was out of the truck before Edward could register what he was seeing. There was Mae, standing in the rain, being held up by some bearded man who had his arm around her throat. Samuel was pointing a gun at them both. Edward was about to yell at Samuel to lower the gun when a white-hot bolt blinded them all. When Edward could see again, his mouth erupted in a scream.

"NO!" There was Mae lying on the ground. The bearded man was lying several feet away, and Edward could see smoke rising from his clothing.

Edward ran to Mae and began to search her body for injuries. Her right arm was dislocated, and she had a small burn on her throat. As he touched the burn, he became aware she had no pulse. He froze for several seconds of panic, and then he slammed his fist on her chest; still nothing. He raised his arm again, and Samuel grabbed his fist.

"What the hell are you doing?" he roared over the thunder.

Edward jerked his arm free. "Her heart has stopped." He slammed his fist down again.

He touched her neck, tears mingling with the rain on his cheeks. "There," he yelled, "There it is."

Samuel could feel his own heart start beating again.

Edward raised his head. "What about him?" he asked.

"Dead, and if he hadn't been, he would be now." Edward could see the truth of this in Samuel's eyes. He became aware of hail slamming into his back as he scooped Mae into his arms and ran for the truck.

It took about ten seconds for the whole house to be in an uproar as Edward ran inside carrying Mae's limp body. Garth was shouting, and most of the women were crying.

Samuel had had enough. He shouted, "Shut up! Everyone just shut up! Edward, what do you need?"

"I need my bag from the motorcar, I need brandy, and right this minute I need to put her into her bed."

Eleanor jumped to life. "Garth, get the bag. Edward, follow me." And as they started up the stairs, over her shoulder she yelled, "Martha, fetch the brandy."

Eleanor grabbed the covers and cleared the bed. Edward placed Mae down gently and immediately checked for a pulse. "All right, my love," he whispered. "You are alive, and you damn well better stay that way."

He began undressing Mae, and Eleanor said, "Perhaps I should do that?"

Edward snorted. "It wouldn't matter who took the

clothes off. I'm still the one who is going to examine her body." Eleanor conceded the wisdom of this with a nod of her head.

Garth ran in with the black bag and stopped abruptly at the sight of Edward undressing Mae. At the look on his face, Eleanor spoke quickly. "Today he's her doctor, not her fiancé, dear, so just give him the bag."

"All right, but can someone tell me what the hell happened?"

Samuel spoke from the doorway. "Pa, if you step out here, I'll tell you what I know." Garth stepped into the hallway and pulled the door partially closed behind him.

"All right, Samuel, let's have it."

Samuel took a deep breath and exhaled slowly. "Well, Mae found me around two and said she was worried about the storm. She rode over to the village while I checked to see if Cyrus needed help in getting the animals in to safety. Then I drove over. We gathered up the women, and Mae was going to ride back. I was unloading the women when Edward pulled up. We got the women settled, and then…" Samuel looked away from his father. He wasn't sure how to describe what his mind had not yet absorbed.

"What, son? Just say it."

Samuel looked in his father's eyes and said, "Mama spoke to me. She said Mae was in trouble." Garth could see the pain on Samuel's face. "I'm not crazy, Pa. She really spoke to me. For just a moment I could see her, and then she was gone."

Garth wrapped his son in his arms and simply held him for a few seconds. "It's okay, son. I believe you.

Then what happened?"

Samuel wiped his eyes and continued, "Me and Edward pulled into the yard, and there he was, holding onto Mae."

Garth looked confused. "He who, son?"

"Hardwick. That damn Hardwick had Mae in a bear hug in front of him, and I couldn't get a shot. But then the Lord took care of it. Lightning struck, right there in front of us. When I could see again, there was Hardwick, dead and smoking, and Mae was on the ground. I thought she was dead. Well, she was, sort of. Edward had to pound her chest to start her heart again."

Garth fought the sudden urge to vomit. He had to brace himself on the doorframe. "All right, son, go down and try to reassure the women while I see how Mae's doing."

****

Mae was so tired. Her body ached with heaviness. She could hear soft voices but couldn't care enough to listen. She wanted to sleep for a long, long time.

Edward searched her body over. The only wound he could find was the burn on the side of her throat. Eleanor had shuddered when Edward put Mae's arm back in the socket. He had forcefully placed his thumb against the ball at the top of the arm and applied constant pressure as he rotated the arm over Mae's head. Eleanor flinched when she heard the *pop* of the ball returning to the socket.

Eleanor spoke quietly. "Edward, what caused this huge bruise on Mae's chest?"

Edward lowered his head, and Eleanor thought he might not have heard her. He finally raised his head to meet her eyes. "I'm afraid I did. The lightning strike did something to the rhythm of her heart, and it stopped beating. I had to shock it back into some kind of rhythm, and I used my fist to beat her chest." He paused, remembering the fear washing over him in that moment. "I've never been so frightened in my life. I didn't know if it would work, and if it hadn't, she would have been dead in a few moments." His eyes filled with tears as he reached out to stroke Mae's hair.

Garth had entered the room in time to hear this last. As soon as he could speak around the lump in his throat, he said, "Thank you, son, for saving my baby girl."

Edward turned to Garth. "Don't thank me yet, sir. You should know—she has dropped into a deep sleep, possibly a coma. Her pupils are still somewhat responsive, so there is hope she will wake soon, but there is little we can do except wait."

Garth took Eleanor's hand and smiled. "Of course there is something we can do. We can pray, and we will. The Lord did not bring this girl through all she has suffered to take her from the life He has led her to."

"What do you mean, sir? If Mae has experienced some sort of illness, I need to know. I need to know her medical history to help me understand how to help her."

"Oh, she's never been sick a day in her life. I meant…" Garth broke off as Eleanor squeezed his hand. He looked down at her, and she gave a barely perceptible shake of her head.

He was confused and started to finish his sentence, but she interrupted. "Edward, what do you need right now to make Mae more comfortable? Maybe another blanket, or some water to sip on?"

Edward had seen the exchange between Garth and

Eleanor. Normally Edward was a calm, understanding physician, but there was nothing normal about this day or this patient. This was the woman he loved, and obviously these people did not understand the seriousness of the situation.

"Is there something else I need to know?" he asked. "Has Mae had some medical issues I need to be aware of?"

Again, Garth turned to Eleanor.

That was it. Edward was beyond being rational. He jumped to his feet and shouted, "Listen to me! I am the doctor here. It is for me to decide what is best for Mae at this moment. If you two know something that might help me understand why she is not waking, then you need to tell me, and I mean now."

Garth was about to take exception to Edward's attitude when Eleanor spoke. "Edward, this was to have been Mae's story. She had prepared herself to share it with you, no matter how difficult it might have been for you to accept."

Edward let out a deep sigh. "Look," he said, as he wiped a hand over his face, "now is not the time for secrets. If there is anything you can tell me that might shed some light on her condition, then I beg you to do so now. I have never loved a woman before. Not the deep, to-the-bone love I have for this woman. Nor have I ever felt so helpless before. I am a damn good doctor, but I have to know what I'm working against here. So, please, if there is something you need to tell me, just do it. We'll worry about ethics and apologies later."

"All right, son, sit down, and I will tell you about the only medical issue Mae has ever experienced." Garth and Eleanor sat in the window seat, and Edward resumed his seat by the bed.

"When Mae was seventeen, she was attacked by a group of men. She never saw their faces because they threw something over her head. We don't know how many there were, but we know she was violated. Your uncle, Doc Walters, treated Mae. She had been beaten. She was knocked unconscious before the rape and had very little memory of the entire event." Garth paused and looked directly at Edward. The poor man was as white as the sheets on Mae's bed and had gripped his hands together to stop the trembling.

"Doc Walters said he believed Mae would heal, physically. After several weeks, we knew there would be no child involved. But it was months before the screams in the middle of the night stopped. I don't believe the trauma of the event has ever completely left her, and what just happened may have brought too much of it back to her. Her mind may not want to wake up and face it. But this time it could have been worse. Recently, one of the maids was attacked and murdered, and we found out it was probably because she was mistaken for Mae, and Hardwick was probably responsible."

Edward's eyes burned with unshed tears. "No wonder the poor girl carried a pistol all the time."

"She wanted to tell you about what had happened to her, Edward, but she did not want to risk losing you. She was afraid you might be repulsed by the idea that not only was she not a virgin but there had been an act of violence involved." Eleanor laid her head against Garth's shoulder and pitied Edward. The man looked absolutely broken.

"You mean she was ashamed to tell me, because

she believed I might blame her, don't you? Good Lord, what kind of man does she think I am?" he cried.

"No, Edward, she does not think you are the type of man who would blame her. A young woman wants so desperately to be perfect for the man she loves, and Mae could not come to you as a whole woman, but she does have a whole heart, and she has given it all to you, Edward. She wants nothing more than to spend the rest of her life making you happy and proud that you chose her for your wife."

Edward dropped his head into both his hands. He had to save Mae from this deep sleep. He had to have the opportunity to tell her how little the event meant to him or to their future. He had to be able to tell her how much he loved her.

It was midnight. Samuel had gone to town and informed the law, bringing some of the sheriff's men back with him. Deputy Wilkes had taken charge, and Hardwick's body and horse had been removed.

Samuel had stopped at the Finches' home and told them what had happened and that Edward would be staying until he felt he could leave Mae. Mae's extended family had all been moved back to their respective homes, since the storm had blown itself out, and they had been assured if there were any changes in her condition they would be notified immediately.

Martha handed Edward a small bowl of stew and stood over him until he ate every bite. "You'll need your strength to help the little missy." She choked back a sob and took the now empty bowl from Edward. "If you be needing anythin' at all, you just call me, young man."

Edward smiled weakly. He listened to her sniffle as

she moved down the staircase. There was no doubt; Mae was truly loved. He tenderly touched her cheek. It was a gray, almost waxen color, cool to the touch. Her pupils were still responsive, and her heart rhythm had been steady for hours now. He would just have to be patient.

Eleanor offered to sit with Mae, but Edward asked them all to just go on to bed and leave her to him. He was aware Samuel was bedded down in the hallway, and he was not about to argue with him.

Edward turned off the light and left only a large candle burning near the window. He stretched out on the bed beside Mae and laid his left hand gently on her chest to monitor her breathing. The household had finally gone quiet.

Chapter Thirty-Four

As Edward lay there, he wondered if Mae had any idea how important she was to so many people. Did she comprehend how many lives she had touched in her short time here on earth? Did she know how much he loved and admired her? If she came through this, he would spend the rest of his life making sure she did.

Edward became aware of a subtle change in Mae's breathing and realized he must have dozed off. His eyes were drawn to the window seat, where Mae was sitting. Wait! His hand was on Mae's chest, here, on the bed with him. He rose up on one elbow, blinked his eyes, and realized the image was an older version of Mae. Even as he was telling himself he must be dreaming, the older Mae spoke.

"You must speak to your heavenly Father if you wish to keep her with you. You must accept it is He, and not you, who has the power to save her." Even as the voice grew softer, the vision faded away.

Edward jumped up from the bed and rubbed his face. No, there was no one on the window seat. He was about to laugh at himself, when he became aware of Samuel, standing beside him. Samuel was staring at the window seat. He turned to Edward and said, "You'd better do what she said, or we'll lose Mae."

As Samuel turned to leave, Edward grabbed him by the arm. "Wait, are you saying you heard someone speak?"

Samuel gave Edward a sad smile. "That wasn't someone. That was our mother. And if she says you need to pray, then you'd better pray. You remember earlier when I told you something was wrong with Mae? Well, Mama appeared to me just then and told me Mae was in danger. Now is not the time to ask a lot of questions. I don't know if I would have any answers that would make sense to you anyway. I began to feel Mama's presence a few months after she passed on. It was odd, but not frightening. I never told anyone because I was just a kid and didn't know how to explain it. I just walked around knowing she was never far away. The day Mae was attacked was the first time Mama actually spoke to me. She didn't say why, only saying we needed to go home to help Mae."

"We found her bloody clothes on the porch and her broken body in the bed. For now, all you need to know is that Mae needs you to pray. I don't know what your problem is with the Lord, but now is the time to get it straightened out. I'll leave now, so you can pray." Samuel turned and left, closing the door quietly behind him.

Edward was left speechless and a little weak in the knees. He lowered himself slowly to the floor and leaned back against the bed. He remembered his previous conversations with Mae about God. Obviously she was a believer, and her God was important to her. The night he had asked Garth for Mae's hand, Garth had told him that, in time, he would have to come to terms with God because He was such an important part of Mae's life.

Edward stood and returned to the chair by the bed.

He reached out and touched Mae's face. Oh, no! She was warm to the touch, developing a fever. He was even more afraid. There was no outward sign of injury to her body. If she was developing a fever, he had no idea what the root cause might be. He was filled with despair, and he hated himself for giving in to it. Tears burned his tired eyes, and he angrily wiped them away.

He dropped to his knees beside the bed and looked out the window at the beginnings of dawn in the late summer sky. The night's blackness had given way to a dark gray. The day would be in full swing in another hour or so. Edward accepted the fact he was just filling his head with trivia to keep from addressing the all-important issue here. Hell, he hadn't prayed since the day his sisters died, and he didn't know where to begin. *Do I clasp my hands? Do I speak out loud? Just exactly what am I supposed to say? What good will it do anyway?* Hadn't they all prayed for days when his sisters became ill? Where had God been then?

He laid his head down on the bed. He was exhausted. He was probably delirious. He raised his head, and there, through the window, he could see the morning star. He began to speak. "Good morning, God. It's me, Edward Finch. Well, I guess you know who I am, right? It's been a very long time since we've spoken, hasn't it? I remember as a young boy saying my prayers with my sisters. They never missed their nightly prayers. In fact, I guess I haven't prayed since you took them. Oh, how angry I was when they died. In fact, I remember telling you I hated you for taking them to heaven. It was such a hate it made me decide to become a doctor. So I could save people and keep them from you."

Edward shook his head at his own foolishness. He looked again at the star, which was starting to fade with the oncoming daylight. "But I never really saved anyone, did I? You still always had the last word. I just patched folks up, and you made the decision to take them or leave them, right? Well, I'm asking you, God— hell, I'm begging you—please don't take this woman! This woman has so much love for you and for the world in general. She has made her life a mission for you, God. She has set out to fix the lives of as many women as she can. And it's working, God. Look at all she has accomplished. And she could do so much more, if you would just let her stay. If you'll let her stay, I will try to help her do your work. She and I could be such a good team, God. I'm begging you to let me try. Lord, please help me." Edward wiped tears from his face. "Lord, help me to believe in you again, to have the childlike faith which gave me such joy. Please, Lord. Amen."

He rested his forehead on the coverlet. He dropped into a light sleep and was still groggy when wakened by the crowing of a rooster. But he became instantly alert when a soft, sweet voice whispered, "Edward, what are you doing on the floor?"

Epilogue

She was marrying her love today. Life with Edward would be every wonderful thing she could imagine.

Edward had been so strong; he had proven himself as a doctor, a caring man, and the lover every woman dreams of. He had not left her side for two days. He'd finally carried her out to the gardens and held her in his arms while they talked.

"Mae, I love you. There is nothing I would not do for you. But from this moment on, you must always tell me what is on your mind. There can be no secrets between us. There is nothing in your past that could hinder our future together. If there were some way I could go back and change your past, so that you never had to remember bad things, I would do it. I can't. But what I can do is promise you that you will never have to face anything alone, for the rest of your life. I will always be there for you. I will be your friend when you need to talk. I will be your strength if you feel weak. I will be the lover who gives you children. I will be the helpmeet for your dreams. If the Lord will allow it, I will be the man you deserve. I will spend the rest of my life by your side."

What do you say when a man opens his heart to you in such a way? She smiled through her tears and promised to try to be worthy of the love he was offering. There, in the garden, they prayed together and forged a bond that would last a lifetime.

But today they would take those vows in front of family and friends.

She had so much to be grateful for. All her ghosts had been laid. Her past was just that, over and done.

She had a wonderful, exciting life ahead of her, and a truly great man to share it with. If God chose to bless them with children, she would have all a woman could ask for in this life.

There was a soft knock on the door. "Come in."

It opened, and Garth stepped in. "Lord, child, you take my breath away."

Mae reached up and touched her papa's face.

"Thank you, Papa, for so many things. But mostly for being the man you are."

Garth took her hand and kissed it. "You know, Mae, I could not be giving you away today if I were not absolutely sure Edward was going to love you the way you deserve to be loved, right?"

"I know, Papa. My heart feels full to overflowing."

"Baby girl, it's because the Lord gave you a heart made for love."

If you enjoyed meeting the Hinton family, you won't
want to miss…

A Man with a Pure Heart

by Linda Tillis

Sequel to A Heart Made for Love

Chapter One

There were three men in the room. That is, three men and a dead woman.

Two of the men stood stiffly in the corner, just inside the open doorway. The door itself hung askew, held only by the rusted lower hinge. The two men in the corner had been cautioned by their commanding officer not to move, speak, or otherwise disturb the third man. One was there to photograph at the direction of the tall man, and the youngest of the three had been told to be quiet, and to learn.

The third, a very tall man, knelt by the woman. She was small and completely naked. Long, thick hanks of copper-colored hair covered her face.

The two in the corner turned questioningly to each other. *Was he actually speaking to the woman?* It was so soft that neither of the two could make out his words.

"Tell me where to look, and I'll find the animal who did this. Give me somewhere to start. Then you can be at peace with the angels," the man whispered softly, as he gently uncovered her face.

The photographer didn't flinch, but the younger man was unable to hold in a shocked gasp. The only recognizable part of the woman's face was at the corner of her left eye, where two moles were evident. The face had been punched, and punched again and again.

Samuel Hinton rose to his full six foot five inches

and looked slowly around the room. His eyes took in the four walls of the old, abandoned cabin deep in the woods. The broken chair and three-legged table were covered in what was, probably, years of dust. Vines had welcomed themselves in through the long-broken windows, and some had even entered through the rotten flooring.

Only the dust in the corner where the woman lay had been disturbed. Samuel was careful not to step on the already present prints. The killer would be a large man, he thought to himself. The foot that made those marks would be about the size of his. But it wasn't really a boot...or shoe, he thought. He could plainly see the outline of his own boot. The killer's was more of a scuff, or a...moccasin! Ah, a moccasin. He looked at the bruises on the woman's upper arms. They were larger than even his hands would have made. Yep, he was a big one.

Samuel stood and spoke to the photographer. "Be sure to get the bruises on her arms."

Samuel leaned against the doorframe and stared out through the trees as the photographer set up his equipment. He could hear the tap-tap-tap of a woodpecker somewhere close by. Samuel suddenly pushed off and crossed the clearing. He stopped near the edge of the forest and knelt slowly. The youngest man watched from the doorway as Samuel reached into his pocket and pulled out a handkerchief-sized square of linen. He picked up something from the ground and held it close to his face. Then he placed it in the linen and carefully put it in his pocket. He walked back inside and knelt by the woman; with the thumb of his right hand, he gently raised her upper lip. He lowered the lip, raised her right hand, and looked at the long fingers for a while.

The younger man cleared his throat, and the photographer shot him a warning look. Samuel turned to him. "Yes, you have a question?"

"Y-yes, sir," he stuttered. "Why did you look in her mouth?"

"Well," Samuel drawled, "I found a cigarette butt on the ground. It looks like somebody's been smoking. Her teeth are very white, and her hands have no nicotine stains. If she smoked that cigarette, then it was probably the first one she ever smoked." As Samuel stood and turned to the door, the young man spoke again.

"But why did you take the cigarette, sir?"

Samuel let out a long sigh. It wasn't that he minded the questions. He didn't. He just didn't feel qualified to be training these boys. Shoot fire, he'd only graduated from Tallahassee's Police Academy two years ago himself. He felt Captain Lance should have named an older, more experienced man to train these green ones. Two years on the job did not make him an expert. Besides, what Samuel had to share could not be spoken of, or written in a manual. There was no way he could tell them about the feelings that came over him, or the visits from his mama, who had died when he was eight. No one outside his family would understand.

He turned to the young man again. "If the cigarette is not hers, then it probably belongs to the killer. The tobacco has an unusual aroma, and it might help us locate the man."

Samuel could tell when the young man made the mental connection. His eyes widened in surprise, then focused on Samuel in awe.

Now that, Samuel did mind. Most of what he did was common sense, paying attention to detail and just looking at things with open eyes. He was no one special, just a man who hated violence, especially violence to women.

A word about the author...

Linda was born in Goody, Kentucky, in the heart of coal mining country. Her mother moved her to Cleveland, Ohio, when she was a small child. In the summer she ran barefoot on her grandparents' farm, and during the school year she attended concerts and visited museums. She was able to experience the best of both worlds.

Her careers have been just as varied. She spent eighteen years in the manufacturing end of the fashion industry, which fed her love of color and style. From there she went on to spend twenty years as a Crime Scene Investigator. This gave her an insider's perspective on the abuse of women and children.

You will find her stories are of strong women who have overcome adversity to find the love and stability they deserve, and there will usually be a milliner involved.

http://lindatillisauthor.com

92877991R00165

Made in the USA
Columbia, SC
01 April 2018